INSPECTOR FRENCH:
A LOSING GAME

Freeman Wills Crofts (1879–1957), the son of an army doctor who died before he was born, was raised in Northern Ireland and became a civil engineer on the railways. His first book, *The Cask*, written in 1919 during a long illness, was published in the summer of 1920, immediately establishing him as a new master of detective fiction. Regularly outselling Agatha Christie, it was with his fifth book that Crofts introduced his iconic Scotland Yard detective, Inspector Joseph French, who would feature in no less than thirty books over the next three decades. He was a founder member of the Detection Club and was elected a Fellow of the Royal Society of Arts in 1939. Continually praised for his ingenious plotting and meticulous attention to detail—including the intricacies of railway time-tables—Crofts was once dubbed 'The King of Detective Story Writers' and described by Raymond Chandler as 'the soundest builder of them all'.

Also in this series

By the same author

*with other Detection Club authors

FREEMAN WILLS CROFTS

Inspector French:
A Losing Game

COLLINS
CRIME
CLUB

COLLINS CRIME CLUB

An imprint of HarperCollins*Publishers*
1 London Bridge Street
London SE1 9GF
www.harpercollins.co.uk

HarperCollins*Publishers*
Macken House, 39/40 Mayor Street Upper,
Dublin 1, Ireland D01 C9W8

This paperback edition 2022
1

First published in Great Britain by Hodder & Stoughton Ltd 1941

A catalogue record for this book is
available from the British Library

ISBN 978-0-00-855418-7

Set in Sabon Lt Std by Palimpsest Book Production Ltd, Falkirk, Stirlingshire

Printed and bound in the UK using 100% Renewable Energy at CPI Group (UK) Ltd

MIX
Paper | Supporting
responsible forestry
FSC™ C007454

This book is produced from independently certified FSC™
paper to ensure responsible forest management.

Find out more about HarperCollins and the environment at
www.harpercollins.co.uk/green

Contents

1

The Parlour of a Spider

Albert Reeve took a bunch of keys from his pocket, and after glancing at the window to make sure the curtains were properly drawn, unlocked his diminutive but extremely high-class Milner safe and extracted a small, square wooden box. This he placed on the table adjoining, and having adjusted the paraffin reading-lamp to his satisfaction, he opened it and began turning over the cards which it contained.

The room, though small and poorly furnished as a man's study and workroom, was not uncomfortable. The shape of the single window, nearly twice as high as it was wide, and the cheap cast-iron mantelpiece, showed that the house was neither modern nor really old. The paper on the walls was faded and the paint on the woodwork scratched and stained. Except for the expensive safe, the entire furnishings would have produced but a few shillings if put up for auction. But the coal fire burnt brightly, and the armchair drawn up to it, if dilapidated, looked easy and well padded.

Albert Reeve also looked somewhat dilapidated, due perhaps to the old lounge coat he was wearing over his more dressy waistcoat and trousers, and the frankly disreputable pair of red morocco slippers on his feet. He was a thin, undersized man of about sixty. His narrow, pallid face was still further lengthened by the small grey goatee which jutted aggressively out from his chin. Heavy-rimmed tortoiseshell spectacles covered his eyes, tending to hide how closely together these were set. His features generally were not prepossessing but his mouth was actually repellent. It was like a gash across his face, and its rough-hewn lips, drooping at the corners, proclaimed him ruthless and brutal and coarse.

But these qualities—ruthlessness, brutality and coarseness—were just those which Reeve required to carry on his business with success. For he was a moneylender, and to obtain their pounds of flesh on the appointed dates from those in his toils required something more than a mere knowledge of bookkeeping.

To give Reeve his due, he was less severe in his terms than many in his profession. Also he was straight, in as far as demanding the interest agreed on constitutes straightness. But he was pitiless to those who fell behind with their instalments. They paid or they went under. He lent to no one over whom he could not obtain some hold, and this he used without restraint if the need arose. No considerations of misfortune or ill health were accepted as an excuse. Failure to pay produced a letter to the victim's employer or to some other person, causing dismissal or trouble of an equally serious kind.

Some years before this particular evening a coincidence, lucky or unlucky according to the viewpoint, had opened up for Reeve a new and even more lucrative source of income. He had become a blackmailer. To understand how this came about, it will be necessary to give a very brief sketch of his life.

Albert Reeve was an Englishman who as a lad had emigrated to Australia in search of adventure. His somewhat obscure parents had given him the best education they could afford, and when he had knocked about for a few weeks and found that life in Sydney could be as hard and as humdrum as in London, he had the luck to be taken on as a junior clerk in the cashier's department of a large Sydney produce firm, Messrs Porter, Mayberry & Co. There he did reasonably well, obtaining promotion at somewhat widely spaced intervals. By the time he had reached the age of thirty he had risen to third in his department.

Then it was that the event took place which was to have such dire consequences for all concerned. Frank Peters, his immediate superior, getting into financial difficulties, helped himself to some £4,000 of the firm's money. This he had found possible owing to the slackness of his chief, who had indeed passed the age limit and was shortly retiring. Peters was caught, and his activities brought him a sentence of seven years' penal servitude. Reeve was an important witness in the trial.

For the cashier the affair meant immediate dismissal with the loss of his pension, but what worried Albert Reeve was not his chief's fate, but the fact that he did not himself escape scatheless. It was held that though he was not directly to blame, a more wide-awake attitude on his part would have discovered what was in progress. Against his will his connection with the firm also ceased, and he found himself alone in Sydney without a job or the testimonial necessary to obtain one. Needless to say, the one thing which he had gained from the episode was a lively and bitter hatred of Peters, the cause of all his misfortunes.

The war then breaking out, Reeve served in an Australian regiment. He was invalided out in 1917, returned to Australia, recovered his health, and began looking for a billet. This was not easy to find, and he drifted about from one temporary post to another, gradually descending in the social scale, till at last he got permanent work as a scullery man in a large restaurant. Here the work was hard and often distasteful, while the pay did little more than enable him to keep body and soul together. However, he stuck it because he couldn't find anything else to do. Then after some ten years, during which time he had risen to be a waiter, he received a letter which led to a change in his life.

At Christmas he was in the habit of exchanging greetings with his only surviving relative, his brother William, who had remained in London. On this occasion William's note was similar to its predecessors. It was curt, it was formal, and it gave but little information about the writer. Yet this year it did somehow seem to Albert to radiate an atmosphere of prosperity; He began to feel, what he had never thought of before, that compared to himself, William was well off.

The seed thus sown germinated and some weeks later bore fruit. Albert decided to go home and look his brother up. Perhaps William could put him in the way of something more worthwhile than waiting in a restaurant. For a time he considered writing to inform William of his purpose, then, concluding that the *fait accompli* of his appearance might have a more compelling effect, he decided to arrive unannounced.

The question of transport then occupied his mind. He had not the wherewithal to pay for even the cheapest passage, and he therefore sought another method. After several weeks of haunting the docks and steamer offices, he found it. He shipped as a steward on a P. & O. liner, and six weeks later walked ashore at Tilbury with a cheap suitcase in his hand and his savings of some £50 in his pocket.

To ensure the best possible results from the meeting with his brother, he felt he must look prosperous. His first proceeding in London was therefore to fit himself out from head to foot. His manners could be good enough when he chose, and new clothes and a haircut made him seem a very different person from the server in a steamer's second-class dining saloon. With an air he walked into William's tiny office and demanded of the single clerk an interview with the principal.

'Hullo, William,' he said casually, when the door had closed behind him. 'You didn't expect to see me, I'll be bound.'

William stared at him for some seconds without recognition, then slowly got to his feet.

'It's not—' he said with growing amazement, 'it's not by any chance Albert?'

'Albert it is,' returned the other easily, 'come round half the world to greet his brother. Well, how goes it, William?'

To Albert's very real surprise, his brother seemed glad to see him. Calling to his clerk that he would be back presently, William led the way to the nearest bar, and finding a secluded corner, ordered whiskies. At first the talk was of the trip home, which, William learnt, had been made in the first-class portion of the ship; then gradually the two men became more personal.

'Been doing pretty well?' William asked, running a speculative eye over Albert's turnout.

It appeared that Albert had been doing pretty well. He had, as William knew, left the produce office after that unpleasant business in his department, had served in Gallipoli, and after being demobilized, admitted that for a time he had not found anything which exactly suited him. Then things improved. 'Nothing spectacular, you know,' he admitted largely, 'but enough for my modest wants. Then I thought I'd come home and have a look around the old country. But we can't talk all the time about my doings,' he went on, making a virtue of the desirable. 'What about yourself? You're running a business of your own, I see.'

William did not seem anxious to discuss it. He briefly admitted that he had a small concern with which he managed to fill up his day, then returned to Albert. 'You never married, did you?' he asked.

Albert had never married. Nor, it appeared, had William. This gambit led them little further. Both men seemed to be fencing, each trying to keep his real position from the other. Had they not been where they were, they might have succeeded. But their very embarrassment caused them to drink, and this in its turn broke down to some extent the barriers of reserve. William did not discover that Albert had travelled home as one of the liner's stewards, but he did learn that no lucrative position awaited his return to Australia, and that he had come home in the hope that William would be able to put him in the way of something to live on.

To this, William at first made no reply. He eyed his brother more speculatively than ever and then said that it was now so late that they might as well go and have a bite of lunch. He added, with what Albert thought was rather ostentatious indifference, that he was afraid jobs were not so easily come by as Albert seemed to suppose, but that if he heard of anything he would mention it. Then he went on: 'Where are you staying? If you like to come home with me I can put you up for a night or two, but you mustn't expect much, for I live very simply.'

This was just what Albert had hoped for, and after adequate hesitation he accepted. Then his tact, of which he had a fair share, suggested that William had had enough of him for the time being.

'Very good of you, William,' he declared. 'Then, if you don't mind, I'll take myself off now. I've one or two calls to pay, and I'll meet you in the evening wherever you say.'

William seemed relieved. 'Right,' he said; 'then Number Six platform at Paddington at 5.45.'

Albert spent his afternoon in the purchase of a good second-hand suitcase and the outfit he would need at his brother's. The elder man turned up punctually and they travelled to Staining, a town on the Thames, some thirty miles above the capital.

'My little place, Myrtle Cottage, is a mile and a half out,' said William as they stepped from the train. 'I generally walk in and out; keeps me fit, you know; but as you have a bag we'd better drive.'

He hailed a taxi and they set off. Albert enjoyed every moment of the short run. It was a mild evening in September, and the country was looking charming. They left the town, which was on the south bank, and crossing the river, turned west through a residential suburb. The extraordinary stability, the settled peace, the unbounded prosperity of it all, filled him with wonder, as the beauty of the water backed by the rich foliage enchanted him. Even Myrtle Cottage, which proved smaller and in worse repair than he had expected, seemed like a minor palace after his Australian quarters.

They passed the evening in desultory talk, William still markedly avoiding the subject of his business. Next day Albert's tact told him he should not stay alone in the house, and he announced his intention of going to Town with William, 'to have a look around for a job'. William's evident relief showed him that he had done the right thing.

These somewhat unsatisfactory relations obtained for two more days. Then on the third evening William broached the subject which had evidently been in his mind.

'About that job you were talking about,' he began, apropos of nothing in particular. 'Have you got one in mind?'

Albert admitted that he had not.

'Would you be content with a small one?' went on William. 'Good enough to enable you to share the house with me if you cared to do so, but not to make you any kind of millionaire?'

'Why, yes that would suit me all right.' Albert spoke carelessly, but his heart leaped. 'Do you know of one?'

'Well,' William was cautious, 'I've been thinking.' Then as if suddenly deciding to burn his boats, he continued: 'The truth is, Albert, I'm not feeling as strong as I was, and I'm looking for a partner. The little business would bring in enough for us both, if we were content with simple living.'

'I'd be content all right. But you haven't told me what the business is. Is it something I could do?'

It came out at last, William's carefully guarded secret. He was a moneylender. He attended race meetings and made friends with bookmakers, who for a consideration recommended him to their unsuccessful clients. He treated these clients reasonably well, and they recommended him to their friends. In this way he had built up a connection. He was willing to take Albert into partnership on terms depending on the amount of Albert's available capital.

At this point Albert had the sense to tell his brother the truth. He would gladly join with William and work for what was fair, but he couldn't put in any capital for the simple reason that he hadn't any to put.

William apparently was neither surprised nor disappointed. 'I thought I would have heard more about your fellow passengers on the Poona if you had travelled with them,' he observed mildly. 'Then, seeing that I've put in all the capital and worked up the connection, would you be content with one-third of the profits, I to keep up the town office and meet all overhead? The amount varies, but it would bring you in from three to four hundred a year, and you would pay one-third of the cost of this house.'

Albert put out his hand. 'I agree,' he said. 'Shake on it.'

Two years later William died, and Albert took over the business and ran it as his own. The continual enlarging of his connection, so vital to success, he found hard work, but otherwise he carried on easily enough. It paid him reasonably well; there were few years in which he didn't clear a thousand pounds. But he was no more satisfied than when he had been working at the restaurant. Now he wanted provision for his old age. He wanted enough to buy an annuity, so that he could have first a little leisure in which to enjoy life, and then security for his declining years.

For some time he saw no way in which this could be achieved, and then an event happened which turned his thoughts into new channels, and seemed to bring the realization of his dreams within reasonable distance.

One evening in the refreshment room at Paddington he saw a man whose face seemed vaguely familiar. He was standing at the bar, slowly consuming a whisky and soda, and apparently lost in thought and oblivious of his surroundings. Albert was therefore able to watch him unobserved. For a time he could not place him; then the man made a little nervous movement of his fingers which Albert recognized. With a start of surprise he realized that he was staring at Frank Peters, his former superior at Porter, Mayberry's, the man who had absconded with the four thousand and paid for it with seven years' hard.

Peters was much changed in appearance, which accounted for Albert's tardy recognition. Partly this was due to the passage of time, but more particularly it had been deliberately brought about. A moustache, glasses, different clothes and hair trimming, a more upright carriage and a much more prosperous air, made an extraordinary difference. Indeed, except for that tell-tale gesture, Albert felt he might never have made his discovery.

He said nothing for the moment, but when Peters left the refreshment room, Albert passed through the door behind him. It is unnecessary to recount the interview which took place. Suffice it to say that at that and subsequent meetings agreement was reached between the two men. Peters admitted that he was in a good job and had connections which would be jeopardized if it became known that he was a convict. On his part Albert stated his appreciation of the fact, and in consideration of the sum of £300 per annum, paid in four equal quarterly instalments, he undertook to keep the knowledge to himself. So Albert became a blackmailer and made his first entry into serious crime.

This addition to his income whetted Albert's appetite and filled his mind with a host of new ideas. Never before had he dreamed of making money simply by sitting tight and doing nothing. The £300 a year made so much difference to him that it was not long before he was planning methods of increasing it.

By chance he had learnt a man's vital secret. He need not hope for a second miracle; so if he were to become possessed of any others he must find them out for himself.

Was there any way in which this could be done? Obviously only the secrets of those with money were valuable. How could he get in touch with them?

For a long time he was baffled by the problem, and then a possibility occurred to him. Among those to whom the 'firm' had lent money were certain butlers and ladies' maids. Albert took on new activities. In an assumed character he visited the various neighbourhoods where these were employed, drank at the pubs, and discoursed with the landlords on local topics. At the same time he became an earnest searcher for truth in those paragraph papers which live by innuendo and suggestion about the morals of our upper ten. For a time he obtained no results, then he struck what he thought might prove to be oil.

It did. Gallant and debonair Major X was carrying on a flirtation with young and sprightly Mrs Y under the noses of his wife and of her husband. Mrs X and Mr Y held the purse strings in their respective families. Discovery would undoubtedly mean a double divorce and financial ruin. Moreover, Mrs Y's maid was in debt to the firm, to the tune of £28.10.0. Albert asked her to call.

For a time he talked to her about her debt and her next instalment, suggesting that as the firm had had some losses, it might be necessary to require a larger amount, and when she declared she could not possibly pay more, hinting vaguely at police and prison. Then, the ground having been duly prepared, he went on to say that perhaps she could do him a small service. If so, he would in return cancel the debt, and she would be entirely free from further liability.

This was an attractive bait, and she eagerly inquired as to the service. When he told her that it was to provide him with a letter or other evidence of her mistress's intrigue she was at first horrified, declaring that she couldn't do anything of the kind. He agreed with disarming readiness.

'All right, my dear,' he said. 'just as you like. It's immaterial to me which way you pay. Then I'll have your next instalment on the first.'

He turned back to his correspondence to indicate that the interview was over. But she remained seated, and when next he glanced at her he saw that the bait had been swallowed. For a time she didn't speak; then in a low, distressed voice she asked how he thought she could do what he wanted.

'A matter for you,' he answered easily. 'I couldn't presume to dictate. But in a case like this, letters are usually kept. If you know where they're likely to be kept and look there, you might find one.'

A week later a highly compromising document was in his hands, and in still another week he had sold it for £250. The maid's cancelled instalment and his own expenses in the case came to £30; so here was a clear profit of £220.

The deal confirmed him in his new role. His great difficulty, of course, was to learn the necessary lucrative secrets, but here, as in moneylending, he found that a connection could be worked up. His next essay was indeed also due to Mrs Y's maid. She sent a housekeeper friend, who had already obtained a compromising letter, to know if he would buy it. When Albert very reasonably said that he would have to see it before he could answer her, he was rather shocked to find that this lady wouldn't trust him with it. She showed him a copy, and only parted with the original when he had handed her fifty one-pound notes. That deal, however, also proved profitable. He sold the letter for £400, making £350 clear.

Albert took endless precautions to keep this side of his activities secret. He feared a burglary at his office, and though he transacted blackmailing business there, he kept all his compromising papers and records at his home.

So things had gone on until, on this evening on which he was examining the nefarious records in his card index, Albert was making a minimum of £2,000 a year and saving against the time when he should be able to give up the work, which, to do him justice, he utterly loathed.

The house was the same Myrtle Cottage to which he had come home with William more than a dozen years earlier. It was a tiny structure, with a dining-room and kitchen on the ground floor, two bedrooms above, and the room in which he now sat in a back return over the scullery. Excepting for an occasional coat of paint to preserve the structure, he had spent no money on it, finding it good enough for his wants. One major expenditure he had made—the only one—was to buy three acres of the woodland surrounding it, to prevent building and preserve the seclusion he so much enjoyed. That had cost him well over £1,000, but he had not grudged it.

The house was run and his breakfast and supper prepared by a Mrs Porter, the wife of a gardener, his nearest neighbour. She came morning and evening, but the place was always empty in the daytime, and Albert was alone from eight every night until the same hour on the following morning.

As he turned over the little pile of cards, each of which represented one of his victims, his chief feeling was one of satisfaction. He was pleased not only with their number, but also with the substantial income which practically every one of them represented. A second set, marked by a diagonal red line ruled across the face, represented 'dead' transactions, persons who had paid off their debts or with whom he had had a single deal, such as the vendors of valuable documents.

By his inflexible methods Reeve had taught his clients, as he called them, to pay promptly. Of the thirty-seven at present in his toils, all but two were toeing the line satisfactorily. Of these two, one was trying to evade the repayment of a loan which was just about to mature; the other was questioning Reeve's terms for the repurchase of a compromising letter.

Curiously enough, both these persons lived close by, the first actually in the suburbs of Staining. This was a young detective novelist named Tony Meadows. He was one of Albert's most profitable types: a gambler. He was also one upon whom Albert would have no mercy whatever. There was no reason, except his own folly, why he should be hard up. He lived with his mother and sister, who, if not wealthy, were at least comfortably off. Probably he was not making much by his books—he was still too young—but his work must be bringing him in something. The silly young fool had got into a gaming set, and that was where his money was going. Well, if he was determined to be rid of it, Albert might as well have it as anyone else.

The other prospective defaulter was a Mrs Marjorie Broad, who lived some three miles farther up the Thames. Albert was not really worried about her. She would pay; a little persuasion only would be needed. He would see that she received it.

Deciding to summon these two clients to his presence in the Town office, Albert put away his cards and, taking up a novel, settled down to enjoy a couple of chapters before going to bed.

2

The Entry of a Fly

On this same evening on which Albert Reeve was thus meditating upon Marjorie Broad, that good lady's thoughts were equally centred on Albert Reeve.

Marjorie Gale, as she was before her marriage some six years earlier, had up till then lived with her mother and two brothers on the outskirts of Staining. Her father, Major Gale, had been killed in a motoring accident, leaving the family indifferently off. They lived quietly, taking part only to a restricted extent in the social life of the town.

Marjorie was then a pleasant-looking young woman of eight and twenty, with a bright, vivacious manner and a keen sense of humour. She was not exactly pretty, but she had a certain charm, added to by her pale, clear complexion, tawny yellow hair, little turned-up nose and sharply pointed chin. She was an entertaining companion, fond of games and dancing, and with plenty to say. Neither a reader nor a thinker, she took her opinions from the last speaker, but seeing the humorous side of every question and being without malice, she was welcome wherever she went.

It was strange that a woman of her personality should have reached the age of twenty-eight without a proposal. But so it was. It may have been that those with money and a settled position wanted something more stable than she could give them, while those who would have taken her as she was had to marry money. Now a fear was growing up in her heart, none the less poignant because it was shared by so many. Her youth was passing, and the prospect of a lonely life was growing more and more insistent. She could not deceive herself with the suggestion that she did not care. She cared very much, but so far she had met no one whom she wanted to marry or who wanted to marry her.

Then it was that Howard Broad appeared on her horizon. He was a shipping magnate, settled and wealthy, who lived alone in a large house on the river, some three miles above Staining. They met at a civic function at Staining, when the Minister of Health came to open a new wing of the local hospital. Marjorie was acting as one of the waitresses, and she so captivated him with her attentions and conversation that he insisted on renewing their talk after tea. Then he called on the Gales and invited the family to lunch at his home. In a heavy, pompous way he carried on his courtship, which duly culminated in a formal proposal of matrimony.

It proved a question of some difficulty for Marjorie. Here were offered to her all the material things which she had wanted. As Mrs Broad she would have money and position. She would be mistress of a large house, surrounded by acres of charming grounds falling to the Thames, with a staff of servants to attend to her every want. If she cared to travel— one of the dreams of her life—she could do so. And more than any of these things, fear both of poverty and of solitude would vanish. It seemed like a glimpse of heaven.

There was indeed but one snag, but that was fundamental: Howard Broad himself. Not that he wasn't everything that a man in his position should be. He was settled, not likely to run after other women; he was honest and well-meaning and kindly, and she was sure would do his best to make her happy. But whether he would succeed, and whether after a few months she could endure being near him, were much more doubtful questions. First, there was his age; he was fifty-six. Twenty-eight years older than she was; in fact, exactly double her age. Then he was strict, or she thought he would be. He had rigid religious views of the Calvinistic type, and these might make him censorious and unyielding. He was a stay-at-home, and she feared that their evenings would be a *tête-á-tête* over the fire instead of the theatres and dances for which she longed. Moreover, though she really did like him, she didn't deceive herself into thinking she loved him. To marry him would surely be as unfair to him as to herself.

In the end she took what she considered was the only honourable course: she told him the truth and let him make the decision. 'You know I don't really love you,' she declared. 'If I marry you I will do my utmost to be a good wife to you, but you must understand that it will be for what you can give me.'

At this he smiled and said that any doubts he might have had as to her complete suitability had been dispelled by her uncompromising honesty; that he couldn't expect her to love him as if he were a young man, but that he hoped to enjoy her friendship and esteem, and that if she gained material security, he would get the companionship and sympathy he so much needed. On this basis of mutual understanding the marriage seemed ideal, and shortly afterwards it took place.

*

It had been on the whole successful. They both obtained what they had bargained for, and because each knew the other's limitations, there was neither disillusionment nor any very serious disappointment. For five years they carried on as well as most couples. Then the inevitable happened. Marjorie fell in love.

At an afternoon concert in Staining which she attended alone— Howard Broad was in Town at his office, and in any case he did not care for music—she happened to sit beside a tall, dark young man with a thin, eager face and the most wonderful eyes she had ever seen. He was evidently musical, and when he particularly appreciated what was being played they lit up as with an inner fire of enthusiasm. He was alone, for the seat beyond him was vacant, but he seemed to want to talk, and kept on shooting little appraising glances at Marjorie. She was not surprised, therefore, when after an item he turned to her.

'Good old J.S. at his best,' he said, and she thought his voice was as charming as his eyes, rich and mellow and sympathetic. 'Are you a Bach fiend?'

'Oh, yes,' she said, 'and then of course there's Myra Hess.'

'Grand, isn't she?' His eyes lit up. 'But you know, I always think the performer is secondary, provided he's not actually had, of course. But it's the composition itself, the motifs and progressions and development and all that, which is so thrilling.'

'You mean the technique of composition?'

'Oh, much more than that, though that too. I mean the composer's expression of life rather than the executant's. Both necessary, of course, but to me the composer's is the more important.'

This was a new idea to Marjorie, who was inclined to take the popular view that it was the artist who mastered, irrespective of what he or she played. She would have replied, but just then the orchestra broke into a Vaughan Williams suite.

During the interval the stranger talked so earnestly that by the time it was over Marjorie felt as if she had known him for months. At the end of the concert they bade each other good night like old friends, though he neither told her his name nor made any attempt to learn hers.

During the next few days he remained a good deal in her thoughts. But she would probably soon have forgotten him, had it not been that within the week they met again. This time it was at a cocktail party in Staining, at the home of a certain Mrs Lambert, and this time, whether by chance or through his own engineering, he was properly introduced. His name, she learnt, was Nettlefold, Sinclair Nettlefold to be exact, and he wrote. What he wrote nobody seemed to know, but it appeared that he had taken rooms in a tiny cottage a mile out of the town, so that he could work undisturbed.

Marjorie learnt this after they had talked together and separated, but presently she saw him standing alone and drifted in his direction.

'I hear you write,' she said as he came up. 'How interesting!'

His eyes lit up, then he made a grimace. 'I do for my sins,' he answered, 'but sometimes I think I might save myself the trouble. So far people haven't tumbled over each other to get my work.'

'What do you do, if I may ask?'

'Good of you. I'm at a play now; my first attempt. It has a fair plot, I think, but I'm not sure of my technique. I've done a couple of novels, but neither has sold anything to speak of.'

She made him talk about himself and his work, which he was more than ready to do. But he was deprecating rather than boastful, though without any trace of false modesty. She felt more attracted to him than to anyone she had ever met and on the spur of the moment asked him to a cocktail party a week later.

'I see you've been talking to our new lion,' Mrs Lambert said, when a little later she went to say goodbye.

'Lion?' she repeated. 'I didn't know.'

'Oh, yes, he's published some books. Mr Jaques, the publisher, whom I know fairly well, says he's a coming man.'

That was the beginning and when they met a week later at her own cocktail party, Marjorie realized that she was in love.

For her a time of conflict now began. That he was attracted to her she was sure, but whether this amounted to actual love she was not so certain. About herself she had no doubt. The longing to meet him grew almost insupportable, but she felt that this would be treachery to her husband, who had been kind to her according to his lights and who trusted her.

Believing it to be right, she forced herself to continue her normal life without any attempt to get in touch with Nettlefold. Probably, as she hoped, her feelings would become blunted with the passage of time. Unhappily, before they did so, she met him again.

Some ten days after the cocktail party she went to Town to do some shopping. She had driven herself up in the small car—they had a Daimler and an Austin ten—and she was returning up Bond Street to the park where she had left it. Suddenly her heart leaped. A moment later he was walking by her side.

'Oh,' he exclaimed, 'how wonderful!' And then after a few remarks, 'What about a spot of tea? That would be more marvellous still.'

She said she thought some tea would be nice, though as a matter of fact she had just had it. She managed a second without realizing what she was doing. Then she asked him how he was going back.

'By the 5.45 from Paddington, and walk from Staining,' he told her.

It would, she felt, be churlish not to offer him a lift, since she was passing close to his cottage. Presently they were in the car.

During the drive she was preoccupied with the problem of what she should say if he asked for a further meeting. He did ask for it before she had made up her mind. 'This afternoon has been so wonderful,' he said, 'that I'm going to beg for another. I'm in Town quite often. Do you think you could possibly have tea again next time you're up?'

Again it would be churlish to refuse, but the thought of her duty to her husband kept her from accepting too readily. But as the days passed she felt that she just must see him, this wonderful new friend, and eventually a formal note, which she posted herself, signified that she was going to London on the following Tuesday, and if Mr Nettlefold happened to be there she would be glad to accept his kind offer to give her tea.

Since then several months had passed, and the affair had become an Affair. For Marjorie it was a period of alternating joy and sorrow: the thrill of her love was balanced by the naggings of her conscience and her hatred of the necessary deceit. She could not do what they would both have liked: confess the whole thing to Howard Broad and ask for a divorce, and if he refused it, simply go away with Nettlefold. Financial considerations forbade it. She had no money, and Nettlefold was making scarcely enough to support himself alone. All that they could achieve was occasional meetings during the day in London, and both were beginning to feel that under such conditions life was insupportable.

Then something happened which seemed to presage trouble.

One afternoon they had tea in Town and had just reached Berwick Street, where an obscure garage had suggested a safe parking place. They were turning out from it into the street when a man passed. Marjorie noticed him look at Nettlefold and then rapidly avert his head. But before he did so she had seen not only his face, but its expression.

It was Cullen, her butler, and it was obvious that he had appreciated what he had seen.

Thomas Cullen was an efficient butler, but personally Marjorie thoroughly disliked him. That he hated her she was convinced, though outwardly his manner had always been correct. He had been the head of the establishment for several years before Howard Broad's marriage and had then enjoyed almost complete liberty to run things as he saw fit. On Marjorie's becoming mistress of the house, he found his powers considerably curtailed, and for this he had never forgiven her. Now Marjorie realized that he was in a position to take his revenge.

She told Nettlefold what she had seen and they discussed the matter on the way home, but except that in future they would have to be even more careful than they had, they did not see what they could do about it. Indeed only Marjorie took it seriously.

'What has he discovered?' Nettlefold asked. 'Only that we met in Town and that you were giving me a lift home. What is there in that? The meeting might have been accidental, and whether or not, why shouldn't you offer me a seat?'

'It's just that he dislikes me,' Marjorie persisted. 'I don't trust him. I feel he would do me an injury if he could.'

'Perhaps; but he can't. All the same I suggest that you mention it to your husband. Say we ran into each other when you were going for your car and that you offered me a seat. Then if Cullen does bear tales, you'll have queered his pitch.'

'I don't like it. Still, I suppose it would be wise.'

'I'm sure it would.'

'There's another thing,' Marjorie went on dolefully. 'I'm afraid we mustn't meet for some little time. Cullen is an underhanded sort of man, and I'm sure he'll watch me.'

'Why not get rid of him?'

'Oh, Howard wouldn't stand for that. He thinks a lot of Cullen.'

'But what about me? I can't live without seeing you.'

'I know, dear; I feel like that too. But it's too dangerous. We'll have to write instead. My letters to you will be safe enough, because I can post them myself in the post office, and you put yours in cheap business envelopes and type the address. No one will then suspect.'

'I'm not so sure. I don't care for putting things in writing.'

'You needn't say anything illuminating to an outsider. I'll understand.'

After prolonged discussion Nettlefold agreed, against, as he said, his better judgment. They now met much less frequently and then with even greater precautions, though in between their meetings they exchanged an increasing number of letters. But this state of things was less satisfactory than ever, and at last Nettlefold tried to end it.

'We can't go on like this,' he wrote; 'life under these conditions is not worth living. I'm going to drop my writing and get a job of some kind, so that if you came away with me we'd have enough to live on. In the meantime we must meet; not for a couple of hours in Town, but for at least a weekend. I know a farm on the marshes in Essex where we could be put up. Make an excuse and let us meet there.'

Marjorie told herself that it would be madness; that not possibly could she lie to her husband in the direct way which would be necessary; that even if she were able, she could never invent and carry out a sufficiently ingenious plan. Many reasons she gave herself for refusing the proposal.

But for all that she accepted it. Her love and her longing were stronger than her reason. After a bitter struggle she wrote to say that if Nettlefold could suggest a plan, she would carry it out.

Her letter so thrilled him it threw him off his balance. As a result his reply was much less guarded than usual, much more outspoken than they had agreed was wise. He wrote:

DARLING,

Your letter has transformed hell into heaven.

Now here is what I suggest. You mentioned your friends in Saffron Walden. Tell your husband that you are going to spend the weekend with them, and drive off in your small car. Actually do call on them, but leave them after tea and drive to Braintree. I shall be waiting for you on the road at the entrance to the town. We shall then drive to the place I told you of, and on Monday you will return home as from Saffron Walden.

Till we meet,

S.N.

It was short and to the point, but terribly dangerous. She thought she ought immediately to destroy it; then, for fear of forgetting some of the details of her journey, she did not do so. Instead she locked it carefully in her dispatch box and locked the box in her davenport.

To get away was easy. Though Howard liked to have her with him, he never objected to her leaving home when she wished to do so. All she had to say was that she had been asked to visit friends, and would like to spend so many days with them. He invariably replied: 'All right, my dear. Have you plenty of money or would you like a cheque?'

But now, when it came to the point, an unexpected difficulty arose. She just couldn't do it. She couldn't bring herself to lie to him and deceive him so blatantly. He was I too good to her and too trustful. For some days she remained undecided, wretchedly unhappy, and knowing that whichever course she adopted would make her miserable. Then after lying awake almost all of one night, she reached a decision. She would not go. Bitterly she regretted the hurt to Sinclair Nettlefold, but even more would she regret the hurt to Howard. Her first action next day would be to write telling Sinclair of her change of plans.

But next morning's post brought a letter which made her former unhappiness seem like heaven by comparison. The envelope was marked 'Personal' and the letter 'Strictly private and confidential'. It read:

                                        1078e, Long Acre,
                                        London, WC2

Mrs Broad,
'The Limes,'
Merlock,
Staining.

MADAM,

I have the honour to inform you that through a singular accident a certain letter has come into my possession. It appears to be a valuable document and I am holding it pending the discovery of its owner and arrangements being made for its return. In case you should be interested I am taking the liberty of sending you a photographic copy, but as the reproduction may be too small for you to read, I give also its beginning and end. It begins: 'DARLING, Your letter has transformed hell into heaven.'

It continues about a visit to a certain place in the eastern counties and ends, 'On Monday you will return home as from S.W. Till we meet.'

This letter, as I said, is valuable, and is for sale. The price is £400 (four hundred pounds sterling), which includes the photographic negative and all prints.

Perhaps you will kindly let me know if you are interested, as if not I will offer it elsewhere.

Yrs respectfully,

ALBERT REEVE.

Marjorie's heart seemed to be playing queer tricks as she read this effusion. She grew cold as if a lump of ice had formed in the centre of her being. She had been standing before the fire in her sitting-room, but her knees suddenly began to tremble and she collapsed into a chair. For a moment she thought she was going to farm, then the blood rushed back into her head.

For the first time in her life she was in real trouble. Often she had read of men and women being caught in the blackmailer's net, just as she had read of murders and murderers. But these things did not happen to oneself or to one's friends. But there she had been wrong! They did happen to oneself.

It couldn't be true! There must be some way out. It could not be she who was caught in this ghastly trap!

Unsteadily she got up and crossed the room. Yes, the drawer of her davenport was locked. And the steel dispatch box inside it was locked. But the letter—feverishly she turned over the papers—the letter was gone.

She relocked box and drawer, and went down to the dining-room. There with trembling hands she poured herself out some whisky, a drink she normally loathed. But it did what she wanted. It pulled her together and made her normal. Going back to her sitting-room, she threw herself into a chair before the fire and began to think.

Oh, what a fool she had been! *What* a fool! That she had fallen in love was not foolish; it was her misfortune. No, dear Sinclair, not her misfortune: she could never be sorry it had happened! Her misfortune had been that she had married before it had happened. Where she had been a fool was to have taken half measures. She should either have been straight, told the whole thing to Howard and chanced the money, or else if she were going to lie, to have taken care that she was not found out. Oh, if she had only kept to her resolution and burnt the letter! How Reeve had got it out of her locked davenport she didn't know, but if she had burnt it, she would have been safe.

Now her situation was desperate. She couldn't, of course, pay the money: she didn't have it. And she didn't see how she could raise it. She had no jewels of her own which she might have sold: those she wore were old Broad family treasures. And of course Sinclair couldn't pay either, even if she would have let him.

But if she didn't pay, this Reeve would take the letter to Howard. That would be the end of her. Howard had been very good to her, according to his lights. But this he wouldn't forgive. In such a matter his peculiar views would make him absolutely relentless. He would not divorce her: of that she felt sure, but he would turn her out of his house. And she was sure he would refuse her the smallest allowance. He would tell her to go to her lover, and if she answered that her lover

27

couldn't support her—and her heart fell still further at the thought of such ignominy—he would say that she ought to have thought of that earlier.

If she did go to Sinclair they couldn't live. They would not exactly starve; she had a few pounds a year, and he made a little by his writing; but it would be stark, grinding poverty. In such an atmosphere love would quickly die. They would get to hate each other, and it would end up in misery and wretchedness, if not actual tragedy.

Then she told herself that she must not brood. The danger was pressing. She must act. A blackmailer was a criminal, and he or some of his agents had stolen her letter. Surely if all this were so, there must be a way of getting it back? Could she not invoke the law?

These were matters of which she knew little. But there was one thing she must do, and that immediately. She must tell Sinclair. He must see Reeve's letter. He might suggest some way out.

For an hour she sat thinking over ways and means. People were coming both to lunch and tea, and Howard, of course, would be back for dinner. Her only free time was in the morning or late at night. She decided she must break another of the rules they had adopted, and call at Sinclair's cottage. Great as was the risk, it had now become the lesser danger.

Putting on her things, she went out, walking off in the opposite direction. Then doubling round, she made her way to the cottage. It was a couple of miles, and she did it in forty minutes—she believed, entirely unseen.

Here she met with disappointment. An elderly woman who she presumed was Mrs Simpson, the landlady, opened the door. It appeared that Sinclair had gone out.

'Would you like to come in and wait?' the woman went

on, looking at her more keenly. 'I expect he'll be in by about twelve-thirty.'

Twelve-thirty! But Marjorie's guests were coming at one, and she had to change. 'No, thanks,' she answered, trying to speak easily, 'but if you would kindly give him this, I'd be grateful.' Quickly she drew a small block from her bag and wrote: 'Tonight in summer-house at our tennis court. 1.30 a.m. Very urgent.' She tore off the leaf, sealed it in an envelope which by a piece of luck was also in her bag, and handed it over.

It was melodramatic and it was dangerous, but she did not know what better she could do. They had not foreseen the possible need of an emergency meeting and had made no arrangements for it. Frightened and sick at heart, and bitterly regretting that the landlady had seen her, she turned back to her luncheon party.

3

The Tactics of a Schemer

'Like master, like man,' says the proverb, and 'like mistress, like man' is probably equally true. It was so at all events at The Limes. If Fate was leading Marjorie Broad into devious and thorny ways, the same was true of her butler, Thomas Cullen.

Marjorie was correct in thinking that Cullen disliked her, though she underestimated the strength of his hate. She had indeed injured his prospects much more severely than she realized.

Cullen was a capable butler and had been well trained as assistant in the house of a shipping magnate in one of the northern counties. Howard Broad had been an occasional guest, and when Cullen heard that he was looking for a butler, he applied for the job. He was appointed, gave satisfaction, and gradually achieved a position of power in the household. Broad had no objection to what saved him trouble. Cullen took more and more on his shoulders. When he obtained the right to appoint and discharge the staff he became a little god in the establishment, and when he was instructed to oversee the purchasing of household stores, it opened up some extremely lucrative connections. Before Howard's marriage Cullen's life was extraordinarily easy and comfortable, and more profitable than that of any other butler of his acquaintance.

Marjorie's coming changed all that. Her conscientious scruples told her that the running of Howard's house came within those wifely duties which she had pledged herself to perform to the utmost of her power. She took over the appointment of the staff and the placing of the household orders, and at once Cullen was reduced to a mere butler, a humiliation which the staff received in silent but none the less obvious ecstasy. At the same time, he lost those perquisites which had been so satisfactorily swelling his bank balance.

A further factor made the change more bitter still. Shortly before Marjorie's appearance Cullen had become engaged. He had not fallen in love with Dora Parkes, a lady's maid in a Mayfair house, whom he had met in Town: that was not his line. But he had discovered that Dora's dearest ambition was the same as his own: to save enough to retire from service and to buy a public house in some village within easy reach of London. Neither could do it alone: as man and wife the thing would be simple.

At the time of Marjorie's coming Cullen had estimated that in three years he should have saved enough for the venture. Now six years had passed, and thanks to her, he still had not reached the figure. No wonder he hated her!

One thing had interested him from the wedding day; indeed, at first it had filled him with a hopeful excitement. Marjorie was young. The gap between her and her husband was indeed greater than could be measured by their years. By temperament she was younger than her age, as Howard was older. Cullen had seen such marriages before, and he told himself that he knew what to expect. If it happened and if he played his cards well, he might make all the money he needed.

He watched Marjorie like a lynx, but for five years he had to admit that she remained the model with. But within the last year he noticed a change. It was not only in her appearance, her look of warm life, her almost beauty at times: her manner was equally suggestive. She was more absent-minded and did not give anything like the same attention to household affairs. But what finally convinced him was her visits to Town. She went much more frequently, setting off alone in the small car instead of being driven by Hughes in the Daimler. Moreover, before the visits she was excited and on edge, as if looking forward to them with anxiety as well as pleasure. After them she was sad and thoughtful.

Cullen set himself to find out the truth of what held out such exciting possibilities. For weeks he made no progress, then two slips on Marjorie's part gave him his information.

The first was that she omitted to remove a parking ticket from the pocket of her sports jacket, into which she had slipped it, an oversight for which he had continually been on the lookout. This gave him the name of a garage in Soho. The second was that shortly afterwards she went to Town on his afternoon off. He followed by the first train and took up his stand near the garage. That was when he saw Nettlefold in the car.

He recognized him at once. He had a good memory for faces, and he remembered his having been at one or two cocktail parties.

Cullen now made desperate efforts to obtain evidence which might be profitable, but without success. Marjorie and Nettlefold were too discreet.

His failure was the more exasperating as it chanced that

just at this time an ideal little property in public houses had come on to the market. It was within easy reach of London and in the kind of small village he and Dora admired. They had gone out to see it and had been charmed, but when they inquired the price it was some £300 more than they could afford. In a kind of desperation, both looked about for some way of raising the money, but neither could find it.

Then it was that, as a result of this urgency, Dora made an extraordinary break. It proved important apart from its direct results, because it furnished Tom Cullen with a new idea and set him on the line which he believed would lead him to his goal.

Dora was really the last person to run off the rails in any such way, because she was unusually hard-headed and incredulous of easy-money tales, but her action was undoubtedly due to that wishful thinking of which in these days we hear so much.

The first thing that Cullen noticed was her repressed excitement, together with the strenuous way in which she denied its existence. He knew there was something on her mind, though he could not find out what it was. Then she did not turn up on their next day of meeting, writing that her employer, Lady Wymbleton, was entertaining and that she could not get away. He began to wonder was she going to throw him over.

When at last they did meet he was shocked at her appearance. Her face was pale, with dark shadows under her eyes, and her features registered the deepest gloom.

'Why, Dora, what on earth's up?' he exclaimed.

At this her lips began to tremble. She shook her head and refused to speak, but as soon as they had reached a lonely part of the park in which they were meeting, she broke down, sobbing as if her heart would break.

'Oh, Tom,' she wailed, 'I've been such a fool! You'll never forgive me! I can never forgive myself!'

He tried to comfort her, but when he had heard what she had done, he found it hard not to curse her to her face.

It seemed that she had been out to supper with a friend who was visiting London and whose husband had afterwards seen her home. The meal had been festive, and they had all taken more than was good for them. On the way her escort grew amorous, and he presently asked her did she want to make some money. She said she had no objection, whereupon he declared he knew how it could be done. He was employed in a big training stables near Newmarket, and he had inside knowledge of the horses. He could tell her how she could make seven-to-one profit on the big race of the next meeting. It was an absolutely dead cert, and the price would be only a few kisses. Was she on?

It was not a tale for which she normally would have fallen, but at the moment she was not normal; she was disposed to take an unduly rosy view of life. She knew, moreover, nothing whatever about horse racing and supposed that from such a source, information would be impeccable. The stableman was presentable enough, and she paid her fees with more readiness than she pretended. In return she was told that for the 2.30, Golden Pepperpot was the goods. He was not the favourite: on the contrary the odds were seven to one against. But that was because his secret had been well kept. No outsider had any idea what he could do, and the entire outfit at the stables were putting their shirts on him.

Three hundred pounds, added to what Tom Cullen had, would buy the pub, and if what her friend's husband had told her was true, as she never for a moment doubted, £45 put on Golden Pepperpot would produce the cash.

It was in a way to Dora's credit that she had not the money herself. She could easily have saved it and more from her salary, had it not been that she had spent her surplus on her mother, now a helpless invalid and, except for Dora, alone in the world. She tried to borrow it, but failed. She thought then of passing the tip on to Tom, but she decided that she could not deny herself the pleasure of producing the cash by her own unaided efforts. She pictured his amazement and delight when she handed it over and imagined the compliment he would pay her. 'Wouldn't have believed you had it in you!' she could hear him saying. 'We'll go right now and get the deal settled, and it'll be your house as well as mine.'

This charming picture, however, seemed an impossibility until a sudden idea struck her. At first she rejected it, telling herself that it was dishonest and that she had always been straight. But it kept forcing itself back into her mind, and at last, after a prolonged struggle, she gave way.

In the picture gallery were several cases with glass tops containing various small curios and objects of art. Many of these were of considerable value. Once when Sir Harold and his wife were discussing their insurance with an official valuer, she had had occasion to take a note to Lady Wymbleton and await her reply. She was then amazed to hear what some of the specimens were worth. On another occasion she had made the equally surprising discovery that the cases were not locked. Except that Sir Harold was extremely wealthy and careless about money, she could not understand such a lapse. However, there it was.

Why not, she now asked herself, borrow one of these objects, pawn it, and return it after the race? It was in the highest degree unlikely that the cases would be looked at during the necessary couple of days, as only on the rare occasions when visitors were being shown the gallery did Sir Harold or Lady Wymbleton open them. Once a month when the collection was dusted by the housekeeper the inventory was checked, but this had just been done. The risk was really negligible, and she presently decided to act. She was usually free in the afternoon, which would give her the opportunities she required.

Two days before the race, while the family were at dinner, she slipped into the gallery and extracted a jewelled Buddha, which she had heard the valuers price at £130. It was small and at a distance not very striking, and when she had moved the surrounding pieces together so as to leave no space, she felt sure that its absence would not be noticed. Rolling it in a duster, she carried it to her bedroom and locked it in a suitcase.

To her astonishment, she felt no fear and was able to carry on in a perfectly normal and unsuspicious manner. It was only when she reached the pawnbroker's, a high-class establishment in Long Acre, that a momentary panic seized her.

The assistant to whom she offered the Buddha looked first at it and then at her.

'A valuable piece,' he said, weighing it absently in his hand.

'I'm told it's worth £130,' she answered.

'Is that so? Excuse me a moment.'

He vanished and stayed away for ten minutes. 'I'm sorry for keeping you,' he said when he came back, 'but Mr Joyce handles that sort of work. Will you come to his office, and he'll fix you up?'

The young man spoke naturally, but he frightened Dora. Somehow going to an office seemed. ominous. Mr Joyce proved to be elderly and stern-looking. He pointed to a chair, while the young man withdrew, shutting the door with an air of finality. Dora's nervousness increased.

'This is a rare and beautiful piece of work,' Mr Joyce pronounced, fingering the Buddha. 'Do you want to pledge it for any time?'

'No, only for a few days. I'm not going to sell it. It's only to meet a sudden call until other money comes in.'

His stern expression relaxed somewhat. 'I see,' he returned slowly. 'I don't think I caught your name?'

'Miss Annie Seabright.'

He wrote rapidly. 'And the address?'

'1260, Lenington Avenue, Brighton.'

She had foreseen the question and thought out her answer. The house was close to that of some friends, and she knew it was occupied by a Captain Seabright, retired from the merchant service.

'Thank you. Now in the case of an article of this sort, we have to ask certain purely formal questions. Is this object your own property?'

Dora hesitated to what she thought was the proper extent. 'Well, no,' she admitted. 'It's really a family possession. My father's a sea captain, now retired, and he brought it home with him on one of his voyages.'

'And I take it your family approve of this action?'

'Well, naturally.' She achieved a grin. 'Do you think I stole it?'

'Of course not. I told you my questions were purely formal. Will you please wait a moment till I consult my partner as to the sum we can advance?'

Her fear had subsided. He had obviously accepted her word, and if he looked up the address in a Brighton directory, as she expected he was doing, he would find the name.

He returned in five minutes. 'We can advance you £60 on this,' he said. 'I hope that will be satisfactory?'

'That will do, thank you. I'll come back for it in three or four days.' As she walked to the address of the bookmaker mentioned by her friend's husband, her mind was filled with the question whether to stake the whole £60, or only the £45 she had thought of originally. Four hundred and twenty pounds or only three hundred? How splendid to get the larger sum! How usefully they could spend the extra money in repairs and decorations! Yes! In for a penny, in for a pound! She would stake the whole of it.

Then, of course, happened what anyone but herself would have foreseen. Golden Pepperpot, instead of heading the list, came in eighth. Instead of having the gratifying figure of £420 to hand to Tom, her £60 was gone, and her employers' Buddha was as far beyond her reach as if it had been at the North Pole.

For a whole day she was prostrate from fear and worry and had to simulate a bilious attack to account for her appearance. Then her native common sense reasserted itself. She went back to the bookmaker and asked him if he knew of an honest moneylender.

The bookmaker took this as a joke, but he recommended Albert Reeve; and to Albert, Dora went. She was wise enough to tell him no tales about retired sea captains. She gave her true name and address and said she had been betting and couldn't pay her debts. She added that she had learnt her lesson and would throw away no more money. Albert, having warned her that if she failed to pay her instalments he would apply to her employers, made her the advance. That evening during dinner-time she replaced the Buddha in its show case.

She had met the immediate peril, but her activities had landed her with a drain of something like £3 a month for two years. Now both she and her mother would have to go without a good deal that they were accustomed to. And Tom! If Tom were to raise the £300 and buy the pub, instead of a help to him, she would be an actual hindrance. Bitterly Dora wept, but tears did not ease her position.

Three days later there was a note from Albert asking her to call. She did so that afternoon.

'Tell me,' he said, when she was seated before him in his little office, 'are you going to find it inconvenient to pay your instalments?'

She was at once on her guard. 'Well, yes,' she admitted cautiously, 'but I can manage it all right.'

'Of course,' he returned, 'I wasn't questioning that. But it might be possible for you to discharge your liability in another way. Would you care to consider that?'

Dora, somewhat mystified, told him that she would be glad to consider anything which would obviate her payments.

He peered at her appraisingly. 'Very well. But first I need scarcely tell you that every word spoken in this room is strictly confidential.' His glance grew sharp. 'You understand that?'

'Yes, that's all right.' Her surprise deepened.

He leant forward and lowered his voice. 'Did you ever hear of a Captain Maurice Hope?'

'Yes, he visits at my employers' house.'

As a matter of fact she knew a good deal more than this about the gallant captain. He did visit at her employers' house, but it was only when its master was absent. Dora had long suspected that he and Lady Wymbleton were lovers.

This, it appeared, was what Albert Reeve also believed, and it was in this that he was interested. 'You get me', he explained, 'evidence to prove their relation, and I'll hand you a full receipt for your debt.'

So that was it! Blackmail! Dora felt indignant, but she was

in the man's power. She replied that she had no such evidence and no way of obtaining it. In due course he suggested the search of the hypothetical letter.

But the 'borrowing' of the Buddha had produced in Dora a sharp revulsion from underhand and illegal methods. Besides, she was at heart an honest woman and was attached to Lady Wymbleton. Politely she rejected Albert's proposal.

He took her refusal without comment, merely saying that it was as she felt, and that if she wished later to change her mind the offer still stood. She thanked him, and with some courteous phrases he bowed her out.

All this story she poured into Tom Cullen's astonished ears as they paced the more secluded areas of the park. The man was immensely impressed: first, by her folly about the bet, which was utterly beyond his comprehension; next, by the resource with which she had extricated herself from her immediate difficulties, and lastly, by her inconceivable imbecility in refusing Albert's alternative. That he said little of what he thought was not due to regard for her feelings, but to the fact that her story had suggested to him a method of turning his own discoveries into cash.

A compromising letter! That was it! To find such a letter, if one existed, must be his first move.

But there was a second hint: how to use it when found. He had intended to blackmail Marjorie direct, though he fully realized the formidable objections to such a plan. Now he could act through this Reeve. If he could obtain his document and sell it to Reeve, he could make his profit without losing either his job or his employers' goodwill.

Full of these thrilling ideas, he got rid of Dora early and searched Town for some small blocks of wax. With these he returned to The Limes and began his watch.

A week later Marjorie made another fatal slip. She had made many similar in the past, but at that time Cullen had not developed his plan. She went out to get some flowers, leaving her bunch of keys on her desk. Cullen's heart leaped. He hurried to his room, took out his pieces of wax, and before Marjorie's return he possessed admirable impressions of all the keys.

On his next free afternoon he brought his trophies to a jobbing locksmith in Town, and a week later a replica of the bunch was in his pocket. From that time he kept himself intimately acquainted with Marjorie's private correspondence. Unhappily for him, she was extremely wary, and for a considerable time he could lay his hands on nothing of value.

Then came the lovers' feeling of desperation and Nettlefold's proposal of the weekend in Essex, followed by his letter referring to Marjorie's reply and giving directions for her journey. It will be remembered that this was the one letter Marjorie did not at once destroy, owing to a fear of forgetting its details. Cullen, always closely watching her, and believing from her manner that something special was afoot, promptly investigated. At last he saw that he had got what he wanted. That night he wrote making an appointment with Albert Reeve, and on his next free afternoon he called. Albert met him courteously but coolly.

'And what can I do for you, Mr Cullen?' he asked, without any particular show of interest.

His calmness irritated Cullen, keyed up as he was by his own eagerness. 'I called,' he explained, 'because of something my friend, Miss Dora Parkes, told me. She said—'

'Miss Dora Parkes? Excuse me a moment.' Albert pulled out an index drawer and without haste took from it a card. 'Ah, yes,' he went on as he glanced at the entries. 'I remember her. Yes, Mr Cullen?'

41

'I take it,' Cullen paused uncertainly, 'that anything I say will be treated confidentially?'

Albert seemed shocked. 'Like doctors, bankers, Stockbrokers, and other professional men, I naturally keep my clients'—er—business—inviolate.'

Cullen nodded shortly. 'I gather from Miss Parkes that you were prepared to buy certain letters?' he plunged.

Albert smiled. 'That depends on the definition of the word "certain". Provided a document has some definite value or interest to me, and provided everything in connection with its offer is correct and above board, I might be prepared to buy.'

'I have a letter here that I would be willing to sell, if you were interested.'

'Oh, yes? What is it about?' Albert stretched out his hand. 'I should rather know where I stand before passing it over.'

Albert made a gesture of mild exasperation. 'But, my dear man, isn't that rather melodramatic? How can I possibly tell if the letter is worth anything to me unless I read it?'

'I'll tell you what it is, and then you could say if you would deal.'

Albert shrugged. 'As you will.'

'I'm butler to Mr Howard Broad, of Merlock, near Staining. He's an elderly man, with very rigid views, particularly about the sanctity of marriage. His wife is young and lively. The letter proves that she is intending to spend a weekend with her lover at some place in Essex.'

'And how do you imagine that could be of value to me?'

Cullen felt exasperated. 'I thought that perhaps you could sell it at a profit.'

'You mean that I could sell it for more than I gave you for it?'

'That's what I mean.'

'Then why don't you sell it yourself and get my profit as well as your own?'

The interview was not going according to plan. Cullen folded the letter. 'Perhaps I'd better do so, if you don't wish a deal,' he said shortly.

'What you really mean,' Albert returned, 'is that you don't like the job of dealing with it yourself and that you think I might do the dirty work for you?'

Cullen hesitated. 'For a consideration, of course.'

'It would have to be a thundering big consideration. How did this letter come into your possession?'

'I—er—found it.'

'Accidentally?'

'Well, no, I wouldn't say that altogether: no. The truth is, I suspected that it might exist, and I looked for it.'

'Show it to me.' Albert's voice was partly authoritative and partly scornful. After a moment Cullen handed it across. Albert sat thinking deeply.

'I'll give you £50 for this,' he said at last.

'Fifty pounds!' Cullen stared. 'Why, it's worth five hundred!'

Albert handed it back. 'Then get five hundred for it,' he suggested.

'But it is worth—ten times what you offer!'

'It's worth,' said Albert dryly, 'precisely what you can get for it: neither a penny more nor a penny less. You can get £50 from me. If you can get more elsewhere, then go there.'

Cullen argued: first he stormed and then he besought, but nothing could move Albert. 'You recognize that there may be difficulty and unpleasantness in negotiating a sale,' he presently pointed out. 'You funk it yourself and you want me to do it for nothing. I don't think so, Mr Cullen. My offer of £50 stands, but I don't ask you to sell.'

On the one hand the certainty of fifty and no questions asked and no risk to his job: on the other the chance of more, added to every kind of trouble? Tom Cullen felt himself exasperated, frustrated, cheated; but he was unable to better the terms.

Ten minutes later he left the office with fifty one-pound notes in his pocket and bitter rage in his heart.

4

The Discussion of a Dilemma

The more Tom Cullen thought over his deal, the more intense became his feelings of exasperation. He had risked his job, his prospects, even his liberty; he had put himself in the power of Reeve, and for what? A beggarly £50! When he had said that the letter was worth £500, it had been no bargain counter. He was positive that he could have obtained that sum from the lovers. But by going to Reeve he had lost nine-tenths of it. And such a marvellous opportunity would not recur. The gods had offered him a cup of wine, and he had thrown away all but a spoonful of the dregs.

What made it infinitely worse was that, having applied to Reeve, he could not now withdraw his proposal. Reeve had him in his power. If he refused to accept Reeve's offer and used the letter himself, Reeve could give him away to his victims.

All this was on top of that other ghastly worry, Dora's idiocy. Cullen groaned as he realized that he would not now get even his £50: it would have to go to pay her debt. The net result of the whole affair would be merely that they were jointly £10 out of pocket! No wonder Cullen was feeling fed up with life!

By next morning he had somewhat regained his balance. He scarcely supposed that there could still be pickings for him in the affair; all the same he determined to watch its development, in case something useful should present itself.

When, therefore, after the arrival of the post three mornings later, Marjorie showed extreme perturbation and dismay, he had no difficulty in diagnosing the cause. He watched her surreptitiously and noted that she presently went out with a casual air, returning hurriedly in time to change for luncheon. She carried on normally enough in the presence of her guests; yet he could have sworn she was not at ease. The same occurred to a more marked extent at dinner.

It did not occur to him to keep a watch on her room after she had retired for the night, but here again Fate or his particular luck stepped in. Thinking that it might be wise to find out what had upset her, he built up a larger fire than usual in his pantry and sat up over it until the small hours, intending, as soon as it was safe, to have another look through the davenport in her sitting-room. By half-past one he judged that the time had arrived.

As he silently left the room, he heard a step, light and stealthy, but unmistakable. Someone was coming downstairs. He stood rigid. Then he saw the flickering of an electric torch. The light, faintly reflected from the polished woodwork, showed him that the figure was Marjorie's. She reached the hall, turned noiselessly, and flitted down a passage leading to a side door.

This door was locked at night, but the key was left in the lock. She turned it gently, passed outside, and the door softly closed behind her.

Cullen, seizing a dark felt hat and overcoat from the rack in the passage, was at the door in five seconds. Silently he opened it and peeped out, fearful that she would have halted on the step. It was dark, but there was a thin crescent moon, and he could see at least that she had gone on. He drew the door to, and as he did so he heard a light step on the gravel. Then all sound ceased.

He crept along the grass at the edge of the path which stretched from the door down to the tennis courts. Some twenty feet from the door was a side path, and he guessed that it was while Marjorie was crossing this that he had heard her step. He followed more quickly; then as his eyes grew more accustomed to the light, he saw her.

She was now walking normally across the grass, as if satisfied that she had here nothing to fear. The night was calm and very still, but cold. He could now see the black masses of trees and shrubs and the gravel on the path.

Presently Marjorie turned round some flower beds, and he realized that she was making for a small summer-house whose open side faced the tennis courts. He moved up a little closer, keeping close beneath the overhanging bushes.

'That you, my darling?' A man's voice sounded softly. Cullen froze into immobility.

There was the murmur of her reply; then the man said: 'Let's go into the shelter. Pity there's no door. I'm afraid you'll be cold.'

'I have a thick coat,' Cullen heard. Then their voices dropped, and he lost the next remarks.

Stepping quietly back and making a detour, he came up behind the summer-house. Then, scarcely daring to breathe, he advanced till he reached its open front. A faint light came from the interior. With the utmost caution he peeped in. They

47

were standing together with their backs to the opening, the man reading a letter by the light of a torch. Presently he turned towards Marjorie, and Cullen saw that it was Nettlefold. Nettlefold swore as he switched off the light.

'That puts the lid on things all right,' he declared. 'When did you get it?'

'This morning.' Cullen could sense the fright in her voice. 'That's why I went over to see you. I couldn't wait till you got back, because there were people for lunch.'

'By Jove, it's more than a mystery. Who is this Albert Reeve? Do you know him?'

'I? No. I never heard of him. I supposed you did.'

'Never heard of him either, though he evidently knows us. But how did he get the letter? You can't have destroyed it as we arranged.'

'I didn't. Oh, Sinclair, I was terribly wrong.' She began to sob as if in spite of herself. 'But I was afraid of forgetting the directions.'

There was the sound of movement and then of kisses. 'My poor darling,' came in Nettlefold's voice. 'Don't worry. We'll fix this all right. Come, let's sit down and talk it over.'

'I'm frightened, Sinclair. I'm afraid Howard will take it terribly badly.'

'Broad's not going to know. Come close to me, and we'll keep each other warm while we decide what to do. No one will miss you from the house, I suppose?'

'Oh, no; everybody's in bed long ago. I slipped out without waking anyone.'

'Right, then. Now, not to criticize—you know it's not that, sweetheart, but just to know what took place: where did you leave the letter?'

'Locked up!' Her voice expressed the mystification she so

evidently felt. 'That's just it. It was perfectly safe. I locked it first in my deed-box, a very strong steel box, and I locked the box in the drawer of my davenport.'

'Did you leave your keys about?'

'No, I was specially careful. They weren't out of my possession for a single moment.'

'Were the locks broken?'

'No: neither.'

'But that's extraordinary. They must have been forced.'

'I assure you they weren't: at least, there were no signs of it.'

'Then they have been opened with wires or skeleton keys. But why should anyone want to search your davenport? You're absolutely positive, darling, that you couldn't have made a mistake and locked up some other letter instead of this one?'

'Absolutely! Oh, Sinclair, I was so careful.'

'I'm sure you were, but I just wanted to know. It's very puzzling. Who could have done such a thing?'

'That's what I've been asking myself ever since.'

'No one knows about—us?'

'Well,' she spoke with hesitation, 'Cullen did see us. You know, coming out of the garage; I told you. And I know he dislikes me.'

'A mere casual meeting between us.'

'No; he suspected. I could tell from his expression.'

'A dangerous game for him to play.'

'I don't say it was he. But he's the only person I can think of.'

'Well, I expect we can find out through this Reeve.'

'But what does it matter? Even if it was Cullen, we can't do anything about it.'

'If it was he, and if we can prove it, I think we can get him a long stretch in prison.'

Cullen stiffened. This conversation was not going as it ought to. It was disconcerting to learn that he had been seen in Town. The slightest error, and they would be on to him like dogs on to a rat. Of course up to the present he hadn't made an error; he had been extraordinarily discreet. But perhaps after all it was just as well that he had sheltered behind Reeve.

'I don't see how,' went on Marjorie's voice. 'If we act, he can threaten to tell Howard.'

'But don't you think, darling, that that's what we should do ourselves? Then his teeth would be drawn.'

'What does it matter whether he is punished or not? It's ourselves that we have to think about.'

'Darling, I am thinking about ourselves. You know how we both hate all these subterfuges and underhand dealings. Let's be finished with them. After all, we haven't done anything to be ashamed of. We've fallen in love. We didn't do it purposely, and we can't help ourselves. Broad should divorce you so that we could be married.'

'Ah, dear heart, what's the good of bringing up that again? You know we've discussed it till our brains have reeled. You don't know Howard. He wouldn't divorce me, and he wouldn't let me have any money. Besides, I couldn't take it even if he offered it. I have none of my own, and you haven't enough. Then how could we live? Only in a poverty that would kill our love in six months.'

'We could manage. I'd get another job.'

'But you haven't got another job. Don't let's consider it, Sinclair. If Howard was normal in his views, yes, I'd agree then. But as it is, it would only lead to greater misery.'

'I wouldn't accept that answer from you, darling, except

that I know in my heart of hearts that you're right. I feel most terribly humiliated, but it's true that I couldn't at present support you as I would like.'

'Dear Sinclair! I feel such a coward by not being willing to face it. It would be all right for a time, but I know what would happen.'

There was a silence. Cullen was less and less pleased with the turn the conversation was taking. If they changed their minds and told the truth to Broad, the blackmailing profits would vanish. Would Reeve then grudge the £50 he had paid and demand it back? If so, could he enforce his demand? And if these two prosecuted Reeve for blackmail, would he try to share the blame? In spite of the cold perspiration formed on Cullen's forehead. It would be—

But Nettlefold was speaking again. 'I suppose we couldn't deny that the letter referred to us. No names were mentioned.'

'A forgery! It's not really like my ordinary hand. I wrote in a hurry and badly. That's an idea, Marjorie. What about saying it's a frame-up: a blackmailing frame-up? Could we carry it off?'

'How exactly do you mean?'

'Could we not say that someone was trying to blackmail us? Cullen had reported our harmless meeting in Town, and this Reeve had seen his chance; had forged a compromising letter, photographed it, and sent it to you as a threat. You indignantly show it to Broad, and I am called in to substantiate your story. After consultation between the three of us we hand the letter to the police. How would that work?'

'But, Sinclair, it would be a lie from beginning to end.'

'Darling, isn't every part of this hateful secrecy a lie? All the same, in dealing with a blackmailer anything is justified.'

'I couldn't lie to Howard so directly as that.'

For some minutes they discussed the idea, to Cullen's relief eventually rejecting it.

'Well, then, what about paying?' Nettlefold went on. 'I take it that's the only alternative.'

'Four hundred pounds!' Marjorie laughed bitterly. 'I don't see that we need discuss that when neither of us has the money.'

When Cullen heard the sum which Reeve was demanding, fury took possession of his mind. Four hundred pounds! Four hundred pounds for what Reeve had paid him only fifty! That was to say, he had had all the work and worry and danger for one-eighth of what his efforts were worth! That money would have bought the Jolly Farmer with a good slice over. Cullen was not a passionate man, but now he felt that the only thing he wanted was to kill Reeve. With his fingers itching to be about the other's throat, he was so carried away by his passion that he no longer heard the droning of the voices. Then suddenly his mind jerked itself back to the present. Nettlefold was again speaking.

'Of course, a man like Reeve, a blackmailer, wouldn't accept that excuse. He would say that the wife of a man like Broad must be able to raise four hundred. He would ask, hasn't she any jewellery?'

'None of my own: only old family belongings of Howard's mother.'

'Reeve would say, "Let her get paste copies made and sell the originals."'

'But I couldn't do that. I simply couldn't. It would be stealing from Howard.'

'I know, sweetheart, but that's the kind of suggestion a blackmailer would make. Very well, we'll not pay, for the very good reason that we can't. Well! Not very hopeful is it?'

'It's just ruin.'

'No, no, don't say that. We'll think of something. Steady a moment! By Jove, I believe I have thought of something!'

'What is it?' Marjorie's tone was urgent.

'The simplest thing possible. To get the letter back!'

Marjorie laughed bitterly. 'If only we could! Do you imagine he'd give it to you?'

'My idea wasn't to ask him.'

'What then?'

'I suggest this. To ring him up from a call box and say that we're prepared to deal and that I'll take the money to some place where I can be sure our meeting is not overlooked. I'll tell him that I'm not going to risk being seen going to his office. When we meet I'll show him a roll of notes and say I'll hand them over when I see the letter. Directly I'm sure that it's the original I'll knock him out and take it from him. I'm a bit of a boxer, as you know, and I can give him one on the chin that'll put him down, without doing him any real harm.'

'Oh, Sinclair, do you think that would be wise? He could have you up for assault.'

'That's just what he couldn't do. He wouldn't dare to approach the police. Besides, assault is a small matter, but blackmail is a penal servitude job.'

'Do you really think you could do it?' Her voice sounded unhappy. 'It seems a desperate remedy.'

'I can try. The snag, of course, is the private place. If he's wise, nothing will induce him to get out of reach of help. I may fail there; but otherwise I'd be all right.'

'I don't like it.'

'You don't suppose I like it, do you? But everything else would be worse. I'll have to think about that snag. I might find out where he lives and see him at his home.'

Still Marjorie sounded dissatisfied. 'There's no chance I suppose, of your really hurting him? Oh, Sinclair, there's no chance of your *killing* him?'

Nettlefold laughed mirthfully. 'Kill him, my precious? Don't fill your head with nonsense of that kind. Trust me to know how to knock a man temporarily out. I'll not hurt him.'

'It's just that I've read stories about men falling with their heads on fenders and places.'

'Stories! This is real life! Seriously, darling, don't give that a thought. It'll be all right.'

'Very well, but I'll be terrified for you till I know it's done. Oh, but you can't!' Marjorie's voice rose shrilly. 'You've forgotten the photograph!'

'No, I haven't. The photograph is not evidence. No one could prove it's not the picture of a forgery. Darling, you must trust me. There's nothing else for it.'

'Oh, Sinclair, you know I trust you! I'd trust you with my life and everything I have. It's only that I'm afraid for you.'

'But that's not trusting me.'

'Well, I'll say no more. When can we meet again?'

'Let's see, this is Tuesday. I should want three or four days. What about Friday?'

'In Town or here?'

'Town is safer. I don't like this night business. Suppose someone got ill and you were called?'

'Yes, I suppose you're right.'

There were movements in the summer-house. Cullen Slipped back to the rear of the building and then followed the two figures as they walked towards the house. He decided to remain out of doors for a few minutes, so as to give Marjorie plenty of time to settle down. Fortunately the key of the back door which he had made for use on former, amorous excursions was in his pocket.

Pacing among the shrubs, he was dominated by resentment, furious and bitter; against Marjorie because, but for her interference, he might now have been the landlord of the Jolly Farmer, against Nettlefold as his enemy in the blackmailing scheme, against Dora for the imbecile folly which had robbed him of even the miserable profit he had made, and most of all against Reeve, for cheating him of the one chance he had had of establishing his fortune. But nothing was to be got out of resentment, and soon his crafty brain was again at work to see if he could wrest some shreds of victory out of defeat.

Would it, he wondered, be possible to short-circuit Reeve? He knew, but Reeve didn't, about Marjorie's clandestine meeting. What about asking her for £100 to keep it secret from her husband? But could he prove it? It would only be his word against hers. He didn't think that she could lie directly, but he couldn't be sure. Or could he—here was an idea!—could he take some small object out of her room and say he had found it in the summer-house? He didn't know. The scheme was dangerous, and he didn't. like it.

Could he, he then thought, get anything out of Reeve in return for warning him about what was in contemplation? It would be worth a tidy sum to the blackmailer to know. But how could he recover the money? Reeve would not pay before he received the information, and once it had been given him, its value would be gone.

But did he want Reeve to be warned? No, of course he did not! Quite the reverse! Nothing would please him better than to know that the old thief had been robbed of his evil gains and had a sore jaw for a week or two. Cullen hoped that it would hurt like hell.

Then he told himself this was being merely silly. Revenge was sweet and all that, but what he wanted was money. And there would be no money for him in Reeve's being knocked out.

But wouldn't there? Cullen grew rigid as a much more promising idea flashed into his mind. What if he were to follow Nettlefold to his secret meeting, watch him knock out Reeve and take the letter, and then reveal himself. Nettlefold would surely pay to have the episode kept secret!

This was certainly better. It would, he believed, be both safe and certain. And yet there was a serious snag. Nettlefold was a poor man!

Then at last he thought of something else, and instantly he knew that he had found what he was looking for. It was something that would fulfil all his desires—and more than all. It would not only give him his revenge on all three of his enemies, on Reeve, on Nettlefold, and on Marjorie, but there might be money in it—possibly even big money.

Before applying to Reeve he had found out something about him. He knew where he lived; he had been to see his little cottage and had been impressed by its isolation. In the bar of the local pub he had listened to gossip about the old man. The husband of the woman who cooked Reeve's meals had been there and had been the authority. An occasional discreet question had been all that was necessary, as the man evidently loved to hear himself talk. It seemed that Reeve lived alone, and so far as was known, had neither relatives nor callers. He lived rather poorly, but the thing which had captured the charwoman's imagination was the one piece of really expensive furniture in the cottage: the safe, massive and shining and invariably locked.

The safe loomed large in Cullen's thoughts. What would a

safe like that be for if not to contain money? Reeve would require for his purchases large numbers of one pound notes, which could not be traced. Probably he would prefer to collect these over a long period rather than obtain them in blocks from his bank. In the safe there might be hundreds of pounds!

Cullen now thought that if Reeve agreed to see Nettlefold in private, his cottage would be the meeting place. If so, why not follow Nettlefold there secretly, let him knock the old man out, take the compromising letter, and make off? Then go in, and while Reeve was still unconscious, find his keys and clear out the safe? As easy as falling off a log!

If Nettlefold were to nurse Reeve back to consciousness before leaving, it would not be so simple, though still it would be perfectly feasible. To meet this contingency he would have to wear a mask and either knock Reeve out again or use chloroform. Even if Reeve saw him, his testimony that there was a second assailant would be unlikely, owing to his condition, to carry much weight.

With Reeve suffering physically and robbed of his blackmailing profits, with Nettlefold in prison on a charge of burglary, and with Marjorie's dreams of happiness destroyed, revenge would be complete. And if his idea about the safe were correct, he himself might be the owner of the Jolly Farmer and have a good balance in the bank as well!

Cullen hugged himself over the idea, then suddenly was brought up all standing.

Suppose Nettlefold decided to act promptly. Was there anything to prevent his going this very night—indeed he might be on his way at this very moment—to Myrtle Cottage and settling up his account?

Perhaps it was not very likely, but it was possible. It was at least the kind of impulsive thing that Nettlefold would do.

Cullen felt he could not risk missing his chance. If he hurried, he could overtake Nettlefold and shadow him either to his own house or to Reeve's.

With long, noiseless strides, like some stealthy pursuing animal, Cullen broke into a loping trot.

5

The Trials of a Gambler

Some hours earlier on this same evening on which Albert Reeve considered his machinations over his card index and Marjorie Broad and Sinclair Nettlefold discussed the same at their nocturnal conference, another pawn in the great game which was slowly developing made his first move. This was the young detective story writer, Tony Meadowes, the second of the two 'clients' upon whom Reeve's attention had been specially and unfavourably focused.

Tony was looking worried, and the cause of his worry was Albert Reeve—or rather the whole series of events which had brought him in touch with Reeve and into his present impasse. Seated in the 5.45 train from Paddington, on his way back to Staining after a visit to Town, he let his paper fall on his knee and stared vacantly before him into space, while for the hundredth time be reviewed his unhappy position.

He was a good-looking young fellow with a penchant for long hair and slightly untidy clothes. Tall and slight and fair, he had a good forehead, dreamy blue eyes, which on occasion could light up with extraordinary intelligence, a rather petulant mouth now drooping dolefully at the corners, and a chin not quite up to the standard of the other features. The artistic temperament and weak, the casual observer would have said, and the casual observer would have been right. To the former, Tony owed his literary success; to the latter, his connection with Reeve.

He was the son of a Staining architect who had died some ten years earlier, leaving his widow comfortably off and able to continue without a break her education of their two children, Tony and his sister Cecily. A couple of years later Tony passed from school to Cambridge, and it was there, during his third year, that he wrote his first book. It was a detective novel, and it met with a gratifying success. In spite of all that his mother could say, he threw up the career in the diplomatic service which had been mapped out for him, and began to write another book. This was acclaimed an improvement on his first, and from then the die was cast. He came home to Staining, fitted up a room with a desk and bookshelves, and settled down as a detective novelist. He had persevered in the work, and now, at the age of twenty-five, he had six books to his credit.

But the pursuit of literature, even in such a form, has its drawbacks. It is a lonely occupation, and Tony soon found the need for outside companionship. There was tennis, of course, and golf and boating at Staining, but Tony gradually convinced himself that he wanted livelier social contacts. He got into the habit of going up to Town in the evenings.

Now this would probably have been all to the good if he had confined his attentions to a spot of dancing and so on with some crowd of other young things also seeking relief from life's monotony. But unhappily for himself, Tony did not do so. One evening at his club he met a fellow novelist, a

60

much bigger man than himself, whose acquaintanceship was a thing to be prized—or Tony thought so. They had some talk, and the big man asked him to dine. Tony jumped at it. Three or four other men joined the party, and after dinner they all moved on to a 'club' where gambling was in progress. Tony at first decided to confine himself to looking on, but pressure was presently brought on him to play. Not having the courage to appear less a man of the world than the others, he eventually did so. He found that further meetings were unavoidable. It was necessary to return his friend's hospitality, and this involved offering him his revenge. Finally Tony was caught.

At first he enjoyed it. The men were good company, at least so long as there was no shortage of money and drink, though their goodwill was inclined to take the form of a back-slapping heartiness. All the same, at times of depression Tony saw clearly enough that he was not obtaining any real value for his money, and that he could have had far better friends had he sought them elsewhere.

At first the luck favoured him. Then it turned—not suddenly: there were evenings of gain as well as of loss. But gradually he found he was losing more than he was winning. Inevitably he reached the stage of debt.

At this time, however, some two years before the present, a small debt was not a serious matter. Tony's books were bringing him in between three and four hundred a year, most of which he was spending as pocket money. In lieu of an allowance, he was living at home free of charge, and as his other necessary expenses were trifling, he was quite well-to-do. His mother, though not wealthy, was comfortably off, and he knew that at the cost of an unpleasant half hour, he could obtain the £350 he owed. But unfortunately for him, at just this time occurred the failure of a large industrial concern in which a considerable portion of his mother's money was invested. It soon became clear that instead of receiving the gift he needed, Tony would have to make a contribution to keep the establishment going. Indeed for a time they feared they would have to leave their pleasant house on the river.

This proved unnecessary, though Tony knew that it could not have been avoided had he pressed his claim.

It was then, when he had borrowed all he could from friendly sources, that his novelist friend mentioned the name of Reeve. It was hard luck, he sympathized, that Tony had lost, but that happened to everyone, and when it did, they all went to Reeve. Reeve was a decent fellow, straight as money-lenders go, and his terms were easy. Tony reluctantly called to see him.

He was favourably impressed. Albert was quiet, polite, and businesslike. He would, he said, be glad to do business with Mr Meadowes, and he was sure they could come to satisfactory terms. He lent at a lower rate of interest than most of his rivals, but against this he required better security. What could Mr Meadowes offer?

It may be admitted that in this case Albert was not anxious about the security. He knew the Meadowes' house, which occupied a valuable site in Staining, and he knew the family by repute. From Mrs Meadowes he had no doubt that he could recover any sum he was likely to lend. But to say so wouldn't be business.

Tony found the question embarrassing. He had imagined that Reeve would lend without security—other than that of his position. If legal security were required, he could as easily get what he wanted through his bank. He intimated as much.

Albert called his bluff. 'Then if I were in your place, Mr

Meadowes,' he answered promptly, 'I would go to my bank. For one thing, your own security would be greater.'

This again was not what Tony had expected. He was well aware that he could not offer his bank any security without raising the very difficulties from which he was trying to escape. Albert noted his hesitation and was sympathetic.

'I wonder if I could help you, Mr Meadowes,' he said, with a faintly deprecating air. 'Your finances are not my business, and I don't wish to pry into them, but if you cared to tell me how you are situated, I might be able to suggest something.'

He did. When, after some beating about the bush, Tony had explained his circumstances, Albert went on: 'I think the case can be met quite simply. I suggest that I now hand you £350, which will meet your immediate difficulties. You will in return sign an agreement to pay me £400 on this day two years; that is, of course, principal and interest.'

'And the security?'

'Your literary royalties. It's quite a simple matter, which I've arranged on various occasions.'

Tony was relieved. It was a way of escape and less irksome than he had expected. He agreed readily.

Albert seemed quietly pleased. 'Very well,' he approved, 'if you're satisfied, that's all right. But we'd better have it in writing. Will you wait and sign it and get the money now, or would you prefer to call back later?'

'I'll wait.'

Albert wrote rapidly for some minutes, then sent his notes to be typed. Furious clacking followed in the outer office, and presently two copies of the agreement materialized. Albert handed one to Tony.

'Pretty stiff, that Clause 7, isn't it?' Tony protested, when he had glanced down the sheet.

Clause 7 stated that in the event of a failure by Tony to pay any part of the £400 on the date mentioned, Tony empowered Reeve to recover from his agent or publishers or both, by legal proceedings if necessary, any moneys which might then be due to him or might subsequently become so, until the whole debt, together with interest calculated at 10 per cent per annum, was paid.

Albert glanced at his copy. 'A matter of form in your case,' he answered easily. 'It's a standard clause for such circumstances. But if you don't like it, it's not too late. You haven't signed.'

Tony saw that he couldn't help himself. 'I'll sign,' he returned, and did so.

He had had his lesson, and he really did turn over a new leaf. He settled all his outstanding debts, gave up the 'club', and began to save. In spite of his payments at home, his balance grew satisfactorily. But such a high standard of virtue was hard to maintain. Gradually his first ardour passed, and the balance suffered. Then after some sixteen months, a new complication arose. He fell in love.

Grace Farson's parents had always lived in a small way, and she was anything but exacting; yet Tony found that his courtship required money. But for his debt he could have spent as he felt he should, now he found himself crippled. He had to appear mean when he felt that an appearance of meanness might wreck his prospects. Again and again he considered telling Grace the facts, but each time he funked it, lest the story should itself undo him.

Till the debt was paid Tony had not intended to propose, but six months later during a tramp up the Thames he was carried away by his feelings, did so, and was accepted. In his resulting exuberance, he spent as he ought not. And now, six days before the repayment was due, he found himself with little more than half of the required sum.

Realizing what was about to occur, he had three weeks earlier gone to Albert in the hope of persuading him to accept a part payment. He found a much less accommodating Albert. Briefly he was told that a bargain was a bargain, that Albert had kept his part of it, and he expected Tony to do the same. Tony was left in no doubt that if he failed, the penal clause in the agreement would be put in force. This was the prospect which, as he sat on this late September evening in the 5.45 train, was causing him so much anxiety.

He shrank from making another appeal to Albert, but he did not see any other possible course. Perhaps if he paid what he could the man might not go to extremes. He decided he would call on him next day and once again try his luck.

It was getting on towards seven when he reached Staining. He walked home, turning his back on the town and recrossing to the north bank of the Thames and then sharp to the left along the same road as Albert Reeve passed each morning and evening. The Meadowes' house, Riverview, lay between the road and the Thames. It was a low, rambling cottage of old russet brick with heavy gables and chimneys. Wisteria and climbing roses covered its walls, and it was screened from the road behind and its neighbours on either side by tall, close-growing shrubs. Though small, its privacy, its position on the river, and its proximity to the town made it a valuable property.

Tony's arrival brought the maid into the hall.

'The mistress has one of her attacks, Mr Tony,' she said. 'I think she's asleep. And Miss Cecily's dining out. She'll not be back till late.'

Tony unsuccessfully hid his disappointment. 'Oh, all right, Kate. Then I'll have dinner when it's ready.'

The family consisted of the three members only. Mrs Meadowes had been until recently an energetic woman, managing her house with efficiency and yet finding time to occupy herself with social and philanthropic pursuits. She had been a member of the hospital and other committees and generally had taken an active part in the life of the town. Then some four years earlier she had had a breakdown in health, gradually becoming a chronic invalid, and being now practically confined to bed. Her outside interests had had to be given up, and she had found even housekeeping beyond her powers.

Her illness had made a great difference to her daughter. Cecily was a pretty young woman of some three and twenty when it started. She was as good-hearted as she was pretty and as intelligent as she was good. Her chief interest was in acting, and she had always had a wish to go on the stage, though she had never taken any steps in that direction. It happened that just then the way had opened up, as a result of a meeting with a celebrated actor-manager during a tour in Italy. Cecily was confronted with a cruel decision. Here was her first and probably her last chance of making a career for herself, but to avail herself of it would mean the break-up of their home. She was devoted both to her mother and to Tony, and rightly or wrongly she decided to sacrifice herself for their sakes. She took over the running of the house and tried to blunt her disappointment by throwing herself into the work of the local Repertory Company. She became its secretary, and under her enthusiastic guidance the standard of its performances notably improved.

It had been a puzzle to all who knew her how such a gifted and charming young woman had remained so long single, but within the last few months this problem, if not solved, had lost its point. A new assistant had been transferred to one of the local banks. Ronald Barrymore had met Cecily at tennis and had promptly fallen for her, so wholeheartedly that even Tony, who usually was blind to such matters, had seen it. Tony had watched with interest the working out of Barrymore's plan of campaign. Occasional meetings with Cecily at tennis would get him nowhere: something to bring him constantly in touch with her was required. Only the Repertory Company could supply this need, but unhappily Barrymore was no actor. He was, however, both handy and resourceful, and the next show saw him installed as scene-shifter and stage carpenter. This gave him the opportunities he required, but Tony could not tell what use he had made of them. So far no hint of marriage had come Tony's way.

Having made sure that his mother really was asleep, Tony sat down to his meal. He felt a grievance against his sister for being out. Though he ragged her as a brother should, he leant on her a good deal more than he realized. She was capable and dependable and unselfish. Now he felt it would have been a relief to talk to her. Not to tell her about the debt: he intended to keep that a secret, but just to discuss anything which would take his mind off his troubles.

Of course the person he really wanted was Grace Farson. If he could only be with her he could forget his worries, and Albert Reeve or no Albert Reeve, he would be happy for a time. But that evening Grace had an engagement and had told him she could not see him. His depression still further increased.

Grace was an only child, and she lived with her parents in the next-door house on the Staining side of Riverview. She was a sturdy, direct-mannered girl of some four and twenty, not at all pretty, but pleasant and wholesome-looking. She was private secretary to the managing director of a large multiple stores and went up to Town every day.

It was through Cecily that she and Tony had first met. Grace also was a member of the Repertory Company, and though not much of an actress, was very keen. Being utterly dependable, she was always in request, though for small parts only. But she realized her limitations and did what she was asked without jealousy. As a result she was popular and enjoyed the association.

On different occasions Cecily brought her home to discuss Repertory affairs, and it was not long before Tony sat up and began to take notice. Then he found himself up against Ronald Barrymore's problem. He had no histrionic ability and until now had treated the Repertory Company with the scorn he felt it deserved. But Grace's membership altered his ideas, as Cecily's had Barrymore's. He saw that membership was the channel through which to reach Grace's heart. The company acquired another scene-shifter.

The Farsons, some years earlier, had had a financial reverse and domestic upheaval. They had kept a small private hotel in the Peak District, intended principally for fishermen. Mrs Farson ran the place well. Her husband George was little use as an executive and did not interfere with her direction, but he was good at figures and handled the clerical side. For a time the venture had done well; then the fishing had deteriorated and the place had gone down. The couple struggled on hoping for an improvement, but at

last they had to acknowledge defeat. They decided to close down and get what they could for the premises.

For a time it looked as if bad times were in store for them, though they knew that a small annuity of George Farson's would keep them from absolute want. Then a prospect had opened up which, though it meant a loss of prestige, would ensure them comfort and a reasonable competence.

One of their patrons, a Mr Cornell, had been staying at the hotel just before it closed, and had thus learnt of their difficulties. He said nothing at the time, but came back a few days later and made them a somewhat unusual proposal. He was alone in the world, and because of the difficulty of running a bachelor establishment, he had been living in hotels. Of this he was now utterly sick. He wanted a home, and he had thought of a plan by which he might obtain it. The plan required their co-operation, and this, he believed, they would find it advantageous to give. In short, would they share a house with him? He knew of a cottage at Staining-on-Thames which could be made into two flats: the larger ground-floor area for them, and the first floor for himself. He was fond of boating hence his choice of the locality. Incidentally he would have a boat of his own, which they might use when he was not himself requiring it. He would bear the entire cost of the house, and in return they would do the work of both flats, cooking for him and making him comfortable as they had in their hotel.

The Farsons jumped at it. With lodging found, George Farson's annuity would give them comparative affluence. They would be able to afford a maid to take the heavy work off Mrs Farson. Grace, moreover, could live at home. Altogether they would be more comfortable and care-free than for many a day. Cornell had the alterations made, and a week after they had given up the hotel, they moved to their new home.

The arrangement worked well. Cornell fulfilled to the letter his part of the bargain, and Mrs Farson saw to it that he had no complaints to make about theirs. He proved an ideal lodger. Evidently a solitary, he spent most of his evenings alone in his flat or in his boat. Until recently he had seldom gone out, still less frequently entertaining. In spite of this they saw little of him. He did not seek their company, though he was always pleasant enough when they met.

Tony continued brooding over his difficulties as he sat at his solitary dinner. His depression had steadily increased with the progress of the meal and by the time he had finished had reached such a pitch that he determined at all costs to see Grace. He would call and risk her displeasure. If she were engaged she could say so, and if she were going out he might perhaps walk with her. On the other hand, if she were already gone, no harm would be done.

It was easier to go up to the road and down the Farsons' drive than to pass through the hedge dividing the two properties, and this Tony did. The night was cold for the time of year and rather dark, though a thin crescent moon would presently appear. A breeze rustled the bushes and the sound of traffic came from across the river. Tony walked quickly, to enter upon what was to be for him, though he didn't know it, the most eventful and momentous evening of his life.

6

The Discovery of a Tragedy

Three minutes after leaving home, Tony reached Brown Eaves. The excitement he always felt at the prospect of seeing Grace was not unmixed with anxiety, for tonight he was acting directly contrary to her expressed wishes. To butt in when she had said she wanted to be alone was taking a risk.

However, he was not now going to draw back, and he knocked firmly. Presently shuffling steps approached the door. It opened, and George Farson's figure became revealed. He was a thin old man, round-shouldered and frail, with a pale, narrow face of which the most striking feature was a large pair of tortoiseshell spectacles. A whimsical mouth betokened a sense of humour. When in the vein he could be entertaining enough, his observation being shrewd and his wit sharp. He was inclined to rag Tony in a detached and superior way, but his remarks were free from venom, and Tony got on well with him.

'I wondered if Grace was about?' Tony insinuated when greetings had been exchanged.

Farson pulled the door further open. 'She's in the back room with your sister. Cecily had supper with us, as I suppose you know. Then the calls of art intervened. They've gone off to say their lines.'

'Repertory?'

'Repertory. Some upheaval in the cast, and Grace pitch-forked into a part she can't play.'

'Of course she can play it, Mr Farson.' Tony was indignant. 'Grace could play any part.'

The old man led the way to the dining-room. 'You may be right,' he admitted, 'though I've never seen anything to make me think so. I'm just finishing my coffee. Have some?'

'I've just finished, myself, thanks. Who in the cast has done the dirty?'

'Someone called Grainger, I believe. I know nothing about it, but I hear the girls talk.'

'Connie Grainger! Why, she was doing the lead in *Yesterday's Tomorrow*: Elise, you know. And is Grace taking that on? My word, that's fine!'

Farson nodded. 'Yes, but as Grace can play any part, your surprise is surely out of place.'

Tony smiled. 'Good for Grace! It's a difficult part, and she hasn't done anything like it before.'

'It'll be child's play to her, I'm sure.'

'I mean there's so little time. Hang it all, here's Tuesday, and the show's on Friday and Saturday.'

'I rather gathered so from your sister. Very keen, she is: your sister, I mean. Delightful to meet people who are young.'

'She's not such a chicken,' Tony retorted; 'she's twenty-seven.'

'Young in mind, Meadowes; young in mind. Eager, energetic, enthusiastic, delightful!'

Tony was unsympathetic. 'I'd like to see Grace,' he persisted stubbornly.

'As much as your life's worth to interrupt them, I should think, but you can try. Ever seen a cat spit?'

Tony thought the simile ill-judged, but before he could protest the door opened and Mrs Farson entered, bearing a tray.

'Good evening, Tony,' she said as she deposited it on a side table. 'Your sister's here. Did you want to see her?'

'I wanted to see Grace if I might.'

'They're in the back room.' She turned to her husband. 'He has scarcely touched his dinner, and I was so careful to have it nice for him.'

'Mr Cornell ill?' Tony asked.

'Yes. He came home early, as he wasn't feeling too well. Now he hasn't eaten his dinner. I wanted to send for the doctor, but he wouldn't hear of it. Said all he wanted was to sit quiet and not to be disturbed. Quite short, he was, and you know that's not like him. It shows he's pretty bad.'

'I shouldn't worry,' Farson advised. 'He'll be all right in the morning.'

'Oh, yes,' Tony added, with equally facile optimism. 'Eaten something that's disagreed with him, I expect. Well, I'll go and ask Grace.'

He walked down the passage, the sound of Grace's voice growing louder as he proceeded. It was raised as if in indignation. 'I'll bet it's true,' he heard her say. 'It's—it's—why, his wife left him!'

'Not for nothing,' came a murmur from Cecily.

'It's not for nothing his wife has left him,' repeated Grace, with the same indignant intonation. 'Do you think I don't know what's being said?'

Tony knocked and the voice stopped. 'What is it?' came in ordinary tones. He opened the door, remaining outside.

73

'Please, may I come in?'

'No, no; you can't! Go away!' Wrath seemed to surge from the room.

'I'll be very quiet,' he pleaded, putting an eye round the door. Grace was in the middle of the room, evidently declaiming, Cecily lolling before the fire with a book in her hand.

'No, no,' Grace declared again. 'He'd be on my mind. Send him home, Cecily.'

'Home, John!' Cecily ordered. 'You may perhaps come tomorrow night. Or may he, Grace?'

'I suppose so, if he must. But get him to go away now.'

Tony, seeing it was hopeless, retreated according to plan. Mrs Farson, small and bright and perky, like a bird, was still talking vivaciously about her lodger's attack, her husband looking bored. She talked vivaciously about everything, and Farson nearly always looked bored.

'Got a flea in your ear?' he grinned.

'Not worth waiting,' Tony explained loftily. 'Can't get any sense out of either. They're crackers about the play.'

Farson chaffed him good-humouredly, then dropped his bantering manner and spoke to his wife. 'If you don't want to go out, I'm sure Meadowes would take your parcel.'

'Yes, of course,' Tony answered. 'What is it?'

Mrs Farson hesitated, 'I don't know that I could ask him,' she said, weighing Tony with an appraising eye.

'The scientific attitude,' her husband recommended. 'When in doubt, don't speculate: experiment.'

'Of course,' interposed Tony again. 'What is it, Mrs Farson?'

The little woman nodded her head as if to peck a crumb. 'Well, it's Mr Cornell really. At least, there would have been no difficulty if he had been as usual. But as it is, I don't like to go out, in case he gets really ill. You see, it's Clara Hepworth:

Mrs Hepworth who lives in Cross Street. You've met her here, I think?'

Tony had met the lady and was not anxious to do so again. Patiently he waited till from the tangled web of Mrs Farson's discourse he was able to extract her meaning. It appeared that Mrs Hepworth was suffering from a cold, for which malady Mrs Parson had an infallible remedy. This remedy she had promised her that evening. Maggie, the daily help, would normally have taken it on her way home, but by an inscrutable decree of Fate she also was ill and had not been at work that day. Hence Mrs Farson's personal preoccupation with her lodger's tray. Under these circumstances she had intended to take the remedy herself, being prevented as aforesaid.

'Of course I'll take it,' said Tony. 'I'll row across in Cornell's boat. If he's ill, he won't want it. I'll not be ten minutes.'

Cross Street was in the town, a little downstream from Brown Eaves. It would be less trouble to take the boat than to go back to Riverview and get out Cecily's car.

'It's very good of you,' Mrs Farson said doubtfully. 'I'm more than grateful.'

Tony let himself out and walked down the narrow strip of garden to the river. Though he could only faintly see the shimmering of the water, he was fully conscious of its presence. It was strange how the Thames dominated the entire area, not merely as a physical barrier which could only be crossed by bridges or boats, but in some less tangible way, as if it had some kind of life in itself which influenced the minds of those living near it. Brown Eaves and its neighbour Riverview were on the outside bank of a gentle curve between two straights, with the result that from both gardens one could see end on down two reaches. That to the left ended in the grey stone arches of the Staining bridge, while in the other direction the wooded banks appeared to close in, forming a long and narrow lake, seemingly landlocked and without exit. In these northern gardens there was privacy, the towpath running along the opposite bank.

Tony felt vaguely that he ought to use his own boat, which was in the Riverview boathouse next door, but Cornell's was much lighter and easier to pull, and as Cornell allowed the Farsons to use it, Tony decided that he would do so while on the Farsons' business. He therefore turned towards the boathouse, which stood at the opposite side of the garden from Riverview.

It was a tiny structure, long and narrow, and but little larger than the skiff it was built to shelter. From the door, which was in the centre of one side, three or four steep steps led down into the water, and from these one stepped directly into the boat. This was all right for the person who was getting it out, but for the convenience of others a narrow slip with a single handrail ran out from the end of the house into the water.

Tony felt under the eaves for the key, opened the door, and with a flash or two from his torch, stepped into the boat. In ten seconds he had lifted down the oars from their rack and pushed out on to the river through the open gable. Another ten seconds, and he was pulling with easy strokes over the smooth dark water.

He was making for Coulter's Wharf, a public landing place some two hundred yards downstream on the south bank and just at the end of the town. From this a lane led up to the main road going west, really the extension of the High Street. Cross Street was close by, and he quickly delivered his parcel. Mrs Hepworth herself opened the door, and was duly grateful when she learnt his errand.

'I feel it's a shame to impose on your good nature,' she went on, 'but if you're going back it would be a great convenience if you'd take this other small parcel to Mrs Farson. It's something I intended to give her before this, but I had no opportunity to take it across. Would you mind?'

Tony did not mind. It normally gave him pleasure to oblige people, if this could be done without undue exertion. Particularly was this so in the case of Mrs Farson, with whom the more favour he could earn, the better for his future prospects.

He took the parcel, and in due course arrived back at Brown Eaves. His reception by Mrs Farson was gratifying. He felt he had done himself no harm.

He refused to sit down, but remained for a moment chatting. As he was doing so they heard the distant strains of a military band. Mrs Farson looked relieved.

'That's Mr Cornell,' she explained. 'Turned on his set for the news. He can't be too bad if he's interested in that.'

Tony glanced at the grandfather's clock, ticking solemnly in the corner. It was just two minutes to nine.

'That's good,' he said as he went out. 'It'll be a relief to your mind.'

He thought afterwards what an example all this was of the way in which vitally important events hinge on trifles. There are alternative routes to a destination. A man takes one and meets his future wife; had he gone by the other he might never have married. So tonight it was Mrs Hepworth's cold and Mr Cornell's internal attack, neither of which actually concerned himself, which indirectly led to the most dreadful experience of his life.

Nine had only just struck when Tony reached home. He looked in on his mother, who was awake, though disinclined for conversation. He therefore went down to the sitting-room. Kate was there, making up the fire.

'That's all right, Kate, thank you,' he said. 'I'll be here for the rest of the evening, and I'll look after it. You go to bed when you want to.' He threw himself into an armchair and picked up a book.

But he could not read. The visits to Brown Eaves and to Mrs Hepworth had taken him out of himself but now that he was once more alone, his troubles surged back into his mind. Should he tell his mother and ask her help? He would get it, of course, but unhappily the request would tip the balance in the house controversy. He decided that this must be the last resource.

Would anyone else lend the money? He racked his brains, but the only persons he could think of were those from whom he had already borrowed.

No, it looked as if the only hope was tomorrow's appeal to Reeve. Tony began to plan his tactics: how he could most convincingly put his case.

Then an idea flashed into his mind. Why go to the office? Reeve lived close by. Why not see him at his house? Perhaps in a less formal atmosphere the man would be easier to deal with.

If so, could any time be better than the present? It was not too late. And *what* an overwhelming relief it would be to know his fate!

In the end it was this desire to know the worst which decided him. He would go at once. He would plead his engagement as the cause of his having spent too much. Such a plea would surely soften Reeve's heart.

Of course he must keep his visit to himself. If it became known, all kind of stories would get about. Well, the night was dark, and if he took care he should not be seen.

Already he had a kind of alibi. His mother and Kate knew that he had come in, and Kate had seen him settle himself at the fire for the evening. Moreover, he had told her that he would be in for the rest of the evening. All he had to do was to slip out quietly. He should be back long before Cecily. He knew the kind of hours she kept when her blessed Repertory was in question.

He got up and tiptoed towards the door. Then he stopped, retraced his steps, and switched on the wireless. A prop for the alibi! He crept silently into the hall and noiselessly let himself out of the house.

Though it was still dark, the crescent moon was just coming up, and it was not difficult to see. Keeping on the grass verge, he passed up the drive. The road was deserted, and he stepped out with more confidence. Reeve's cottage was about a mile away, farther from the town. He should be there by half-past nine.

Doubts as to the wisdom of his expedition now assailed him. Perhaps instead of making Reeve more sympathetic, the visit at such an hour would irritate him. After all, the place to do business is at one's office. This evening call was obviously to make Reeve his host, as to enlist on his side the man's polite inhibitions. But Reeve was no fool. He would see the motive and might well resent it.

All the same, Tony's desire to get the matter settled overcame his fears. He *must* know where he stood. He walked on more quickly.

It was lonely out here. So far he had not met a soul; not even a car had passed him. The road had left the houses and now ran through a wood, the branches meeting overhead. From childhood Tony had disliked being beneath trees at night. Somehow it gave him a creepy feeling. The wind was moaning eerily among the twigs, and an owl hooted mournfully. His creepy feeling deepened to foreboding. A desire to turn began to possess him, to give up this call. Then once again he told himself not to be a fool. Now that he had come so far, he was damned if he was going to turn back.

Presently he reached the approach to Myrtle Cottage. Why Reeve had so named it, Tony could not imagine. It was surrounded by birches and tall, dark pines, and there were no myrtles anywhere near. The drive was a mere track winding through the trees. Grass grew between the wheel-ruts, and he walked in complete silence.

The moon was now a little higher in the sky, and Tony's eyes being by this time accustomed to the light, he could see reasonably clearly. Presently the cottage came into view. It was very secluded; out of sight of other houses. There was a little clearing beyond it, and it showed as a dark mass against the sky.

As Tony walked forward his eye caught a movement at the porch. He did not want to be seen, and he crept off the drive behind some bushes. If Reeve were going out he would have to postpone his call, but if it were someone else he could go on as soon as the coast was clear.

He could now see that the unknown was a man. He was bending down, either doing something to the door or looking in through the keyhole. For a moment he remained motionless; then straightening himself up, he hurried off at top speed. In a few seconds he had passed down the drive and vanished from sight.

Tony waited for three or four minutes, then walked to the door and knocked. There was no reply, and he began to fear that his journey had been wasted. However, he knocked again, and feeling for the bell, pressed it for several seconds. It sounded faintly in the distance, and he was satisfied that anyone in the house who was not deaf must have heard it.

He was turning away when it occurred to him to copy the unknown and have a look through the keyhole. He put his eye to it, then gave a gasp. The interior was faintly lighted, and he could see an area of floor, obviously part of the hall, for the stairs went up from it. The steps ended to the left in a wall and to the right in banisters. They looked steep and narrow and were covered by a drab carpet.

But it was not on these details that Tony's horrified eyes were fixed. On the bottom step was a human foot, a naked foot, apparently a man's. The leg stretched out forward and towards the right till it passed out of Tony's view. A red bedroom slipper lay beside the foot. The leg was clothed in pyjamas, with the corner of what looked like a red dressing-gown just appearing. The foot was horribly white and horribly motionless. The heel was uppermost, showing that the man was lying on his face. It was evident that he was either unconscious or dead.

Tony recoiled in horror. Here was the disaster which he had felt was coming! His heart beat fast, and an unreasoning dread filled his mind. He tried to keep calm while he considered his proper course.

He wondered whether the man were Reeve. He knew that Reeve lived alone, but this evening he might have had a visitor. Whoever it was presumably had been ill: if not, why had he gone to bed so early? Tony glanced at his watch; it was only twenty minutes to ten. It looked as if the man had fallen downstairs and injured himself, perhaps due to his illness having left him weak or giddy.

But Tony saw that he must not stand there theorizing. Whatever had happened, the man could not be left lying where he was. If he were alive he would require immediate medical attention, and if he were dead the police must be informed.

Tony seized the knob and shook the door, then put his shoulder to it. But it was immovable. He walked round the house, trying the windows and the back door, but these also were fast. He considered smashing a window but was inhibited by the idea of housebreaking.

While he was hesitating he remembered that the unknown who had hurried away had also looked through the keyhole—he was now sure that this was what he had done—and at once a wave of relief. swept over him. The affair was already known. The unknown had seen what was wrong and presumably had gone for help. Assistance was doubtless on the way, and if so, there was nothing he himself need do.

But if there was nothing he need do, there was no reason why he should advertise the fact that he had been there. On the other hand, there was an excellent one for keeping it dark. His visit at this hour to such a man could be for one purpose and for one purpose only. If he wanted to keep his secret, he must clear out at once.

Tony was too much agitated to think clearly. If he had, he might have seen that other considerations were involved which demanded a different action. Now he thought only of how to escape his immediate embarrassments. Like his predecessor, he turned from the door and hurried away.

7

The Correction of an Error

Tony's one desire was now to get home without being seen. He ran lightly down the drive, his senses keenly alert for car lights or the sounds of approaching men. He was ready on the least alarm to slip off among the trees, behind which he would hide till the danger passed.

To his relief he reached the road without incident. Here he did not think he would be challenged, but if he were, no one could prove that he had been at Reeve's.

All the same he was glad when, without having met anyone, he reached the Riverview gate. A few seconds more, and unseen and unheard, he had regained the sitting-room.

His first care was to switch off the radio. This would be heard by Kate if she were still downstairs and would stiffen his alibi. He decided to go to bed early, not so early as to cause comment if Kate heard him, but early enough to miss Cecily, who was as sharp as a needle and would notice the least strain in his manner.

He timed his movements well. He was undressing when he heard his sister come in, and he demonstrated his normal condition by calling softly to ask how the coaching had gone on.

His experience had, however, shaken him, and he could not sleep. He was satisfied not only that he had not been seen, but that he had left no traces at Reeve's cottage. If he kept silence and carried on as usual, nothing would ever be known.

Would the accident, he wondered, affect his own position? If Reeve were merely temporarily knocked out, it would of course make no difference. But suppose Reeve were dead. If there were no other partner, would that mean the cancellation of his debt?

For a moment Tony felt carried away by the splendour of his idea, then again he grew sober. Even if there were no partner, there would be executors. Besides, to do him justice, he did not want to evade his liability: all he wanted was time to pay.

His thoughts turned to the future. Tomorrow—today—now—he had intended to call at Reeve's office. Should he still do so?

He believed it would be wise. First, it would show that he expected Reeve to be there, a still further boost to his alibi, and second, he might learn about a partner.

Though it seemed as if the affair was going to fall out to his advantage, Tony remained worried and unhappy. And now, thinking over the circumstances more dispassionately, he began to see why. He was increasingly ashamed of the part he had played. If Reeve had fallen downstairs and been hurt, he required assistance. It was up to Tony to see that he got it. To have run away as he had was not playing the game.

He could see now what had happened. The man was ill, and when the unknown had knocked, he had got up to open the door. He had fallen on the stairs, hurt himself, and been unable to get up.

Tony grew more and more horror-stricken at his own lapse. He had thought only of himself when perhaps the poor old man was dying for want of assistance. It was no excuse, he now saw, to have assumed that the unknown had gone for help. If Reeve had been hurt by his fall and died there at the bottom of the stairs, he, Tony, would be morally responsible for his death.

His conscience told him that even now at this late hour he should give the alarm. He looked at his watch. It was nearly four: six hours since he had made the discovery. Still, if the man was lying there hurt . . .

Tony shivered at the very idea. He would have to ring up the police, and then, *then* he would have to explain this? He could not! He had been terribly stupid and selfish, no doubt. But would not further action merely make things worse?

For a time moral right and self-interest struggled in Tony's mind, and at last self-interest won. Better sit tight and say nothing. His connection with the affair could never be known, and he would be worse than a fool to stir up trouble. Reassured, though at heart still unconvinced, he turned over and dropped into a troubled sleep.

Next morning he felt better. He was able to greet Cecily normally and to chat creditably during breakfast. His journey to Town was easier still. He made it behind his newspaper in a compartment of strangers.

At Reeve's the clerk remembered him and smiled a superior smile.

'Mr Reeve has not come in this morning,' he replied to Tony's request for an interview.

'Do you know when he'll be here?'

'I know no more than you do, Mr Meadowes.' Tony shivered

at the unfortunate phrase. 'It's not like him not to turn up, but I don't expect he'll be long.'

'Oh, well, I'll call again in a day or two.'

He need not do it, of course, because in a day or two he would have heard of the accident. Tony was pleased. The call had been the right thing. Moreover, he had been natural in manner, and the clerk had obviously suspected nothing. By now indeed his fears had largely evaporated, but at lunch he had a shock which more than revived them, leaving him in a much worse state than before.

As luck would have it, on entering his usual restaurant, he was hailed by an acquaintance named Richards, a solicitor who lived in Staining. The man was alone at a table for two, and Tony could not refuse to sit with him.

They chatted harmlessly for some time, then Richards remarked: 'Nasty business that, last night: that fire, I mean.'

'Fire?' Tony repeated. 'I didn't hear of it.'

'Didn't you?' Richards brightened up on finding a fresh listener. 'It was out your way too. Old man living alone in a cottage about a mile out. Burnt down in the night.'

Tony gasped, then pulled himself together. 'Good Lord! And the old man?'

'Burnt to death, I'm afraid. Ghastly business.'

'Ghastly.' Tony slowly blew his nose. It gave him time to think. 'I wonder if I know the place. Where was it?'

'Place called Myrtle Cottage. Man's name Reed, I think. Had some business in Town and went up every day.'

Tony put down his knife. 'I know the cottage. It stands alone among trees. But I didn't know who lived there.'

'Nor I. Pretty ghastly fate though, poor devil.'

Was Richards looking at him curiously? Tony felt perspiration breaking out on his forehead.

'Horrible,' he returned. 'When was it discovered?'

Between three and four this morning, I believe. Someone saw the light in the sky and rang up the brigade. They were there, I heard, in just over seven minutes. Not too bad for Staining.'

This was more hideous than anything Tony could have imagined. He could see clearly enough what must have happened. Reeve, disabled by his fall, had lain unconscious for a considerable time. Then he had revived and had tried to get back to bed. In his weakness he had upset his lamp and set fire to the house—Tony didn't expect electric light would be laid in so far from the road. Owing to Reeve's injuries he could not escape . . .

And *he*, Tony, was to blame. If he had reported his discovery Reeve would have been saved from this ghastly fate. But while he was with Richards, he must not think of that. He *must not* think of it.

There was no doubt that Richards was looking at him curiously now. Tony felt he must account for his manner.

'It's given me a bit of a shock, all that,' he said, a little tremulously. 'As a matter of fact,' he leant forward and became confidential, 'that's been a nightmare of my own—being caught in a burning house. Got a fright when I was a kid, and it affects me ever since.'

Richards nodded. 'You seemed a bit upset, but that explains it. But as I've often said, no one should be alone in a house. Any sort of accident might happen, and there should always be a second person.'

Tony agreed, and presently the talk turned to the theatre. He felt when he left the restaurant that he hadn't done too badly. Richards suspected nothing.

But on the journey home the full horror of what he had

done came down on his mind like a physical weight. He just couldn't bear to think of Reeve's last moments. Trying to escape from the fire, perhaps with a broken leg or some even worse injury! And if he hadn't been such a cowardly fool it wouldn't have happened!

When he reached Staining he suddenly felt he could not face his mother and sister. They would notice his manner and question him, when all he wanted was to be left alone.

Alone! But was that what he wanted? He was alone! And no matter who was with him he would be, fundamentally, alone. This thing would be a barrier between himself and all the people he really cared about.

Then it was that he understood what he really needed. Sympathy! To tell someone! If he could talk the thing over with someone, someone who would understand and sympathize instead of condemning, it would just make all the difference.

He could not tell his mother. She was too ill. But Cecily. Could he tell Cecily?

He saw at once that this was what he must do. Cecily was annoying at times, but beneath that she was a good pal. Cecily would sympathize. She would hear what he had to say and wouldn't preach. Oh, yes, it would be a relief to confide in Cecily.

When he reached home his luck, for once, was in. Cecily was there alone in the sitting-room. She glanced at him; then her eyes halted on his face and grew keen.

'What's wrong?' she asked in a slightly tense voice.

'Well—' he began unhappily.

'Wait,' she interrupted. 'Here's Kate with tea. You look as if you'd be glad of it too.'

It wasn't exactly tea that he wanted, but he let that go. He threw himself into a chair. Now that he had come to the point, confession wasn't going to be so easy. He began to consider gambits.

When Kate had departed, Cecily returned to the attack. 'There's something wrong, Tony. What is it?'

He avoided her eye. 'Just a spot of trouble.'

'What is it? Tell me, Tony.'

For a moment he did not answer. Then he plunged. 'It's about—that fire.'

'That fire? I don't understand.'

'You'll keep it to yourself, Cecily? You'll promise?'

'I can't repeat what I haven't heard.'

'No, but you will promise?'

'Very well.'

'It was that fire last night—at Reeve's. I—I was there.'

She stared. 'Tony, what *are* you talking about? You were there—at the fire?'

'No, no. I'll tell you.'

Slowly the tale came out, helped at intervals by judicious promptings. The invitation to dinner by the successful novelist with its unexpected sequel, the need for a return game, the continued gambling and its result. The loan from Reeve, the impossibility of repaying the debt, the visit to Myrtle Cottage and what happened there.

'I feel so badly about it,' he ended up. 'I feel that if I had only reported what I had seen, the fellow's life might have been saved.'

That she was overwhelmed with horror he could see. For a while she did not reply. He waited, suspicious of her silence, fearful of her condemnation, and with bitter resentment surging in his mind, ready to overflow at the first word of criticism.

Then at last she spoke. 'Poor old Tony! What a ghastly time you must have had!'

In Tony the remark produced a revolution of feeling. His bitterness dissolved like frost crystals in a bright sun. He felt a sudden relief. Cecily was a real pal. This was what he had hoped for when he came home.

'But you know,' she went on, 'you were terribly, terribly wrong not to tell me before: and Mother too. We could have helped you with the debt. I'm sure Mother could have paid it right off, and then you wouldn't have had to go to Mr Reeve at all. Oh, Tony, why didn't you trust us?'

'I know, I know. I've been a fool. But, you see, there was this house. It would have just made the difference. We would have had to go.'

'Better to have gone than that you should have been unhappy all that time, and Mother would have said the same.'

'I dare say she would. But that's not it. The debt will be repaid. I can do it, given more time. It's about not having got help last night that I'm so worried.'

She shook her head sadly. 'I know. I can't say anything about it. We needn't pretend it wasn't bad.'

'Then you blame me?'

'Blame? Who can blame anybody else? I would probably have done the same thing in your place. But that doesn't make it right.'

'I know. I feel it dreadfully. But it's done. I can't do anything about it now.'

She hesitated. 'If you feel it on your conscience, what about telling the police?'

'Now?'

'Yes.'

'But—I mean, it's too late now.'

'Well, but is it?'

'I thought of it at four in the morning, and I saw that it was too late even then. Why, at that very time the place was on fire.'

'If it would ease your mind?'

'But wouldn't it make things worse? I'm out of it now: shouldn't I stay out of it?'

'Then you'll have to bear the weight of it.'

'I know, but there's no help for that.'

Once again Cecily did not immediately reply.

'From the moral point of view and also for your own happiness, I think you should tell the police even now; in fact, I'm sure you should. But it's easy for me to say so. If I were in your place I don't suppose I'd do it. You'd object to it very much?'

Tony made a gesture. 'Well, what do you think? Of course I'd hate it. And what good would it do now?'

'I don't know. Are you going to tell Grace?'

'Why should I? It wouldn't help matters.'

'You'd be happier if she knew.'

'No, I wouldn't. Besides, Cecily, it's true that a secret known to more than two is no longer a secret. No, no: I'll tell no one else.'

Cecily didn't answer. She sat staring into the fire, her expression troubled. Then she started on a new line.

'I wonder what about the inquest? I suppose it's over by now?'

'Don't know, I'm sure. I hadn't thought of it, but we ought to find out what's been done.'

'You don't know anyone who'll be there?'

Tony swung round and spoke with emphasis. 'No, and I couldn't ask him if I did. And you couldn't either. Don't you see, neither of us can show any interest in it.'

'I'll tell you.' Cecily got up. 'I'll go round now and change a book at the library. There's usually a parliament in the Reading Room, as you know. I expect I'll hear what's happened.'

Tony nodded. 'Good idea. But for Heaven's sake be careful. Don't ask questions or show too much interest.'

'You leave it to me.'

It was an hour before Cecily returned. She looked mystified. 'I had no difficulty in hearing,' she said; 'they were all full of it. The inquest's just over. Mrs Brierley's husband was on the jury and he's just home.'

'And what happened?' Tony spoke impatiently.

'They didn't finish it. It's been adjourned.'

Tony stared. 'What! You're sure?'

'Of course I'm sure. I saw Mrs Brierley herself.'

'But—good God, Cecily, don't you see? It means there's something wrong!'

Cecily stared in her turn. 'Wrong? How do you mean, wrong?'

'Why, that they're not satisfied, of course! What else?' Tony's heart was turning to water. 'It couldn't be,' he halted as a dreadful idea flashed into his mind, then whispered, 'that they suspect—foul play?'

Cecily was tolerant. 'Oh, no, don't be morbid. How could it be? It's some small technical point. What's the matter with you, Tony? You seem all on edge.'

'You'd be on edge if you were in my position. Suppose they do fear foul play. See where I come in! I was there—secretly. I didn't report what I had seen. Why not? Don't you see, those are the sort of questions that they might ask.'

'But they don't know you were there.'

'No.' Tony no longer felt so satisfied. An accident was one thing, but if any ghastly suspicions should arise, it would lead to an inquiry. Tony's knowledge of police methods, amateurish though it was, told him that there wasn't much that could be kept secret from them.

'What do you mean by saying "No" like that? Aren't you sure? Is there something more you haven't told me?' Cecily sounded exasperated.

'No, no; nothing. I expect it's all right, only—'

'Only what?'

'You see, if there's suspicion, there'll be a full-fledged investigation, and they do find out the most wonderful things.'

Cecily was silent. 'This is important,' she said at last. 'Think, Tony, carefully. Is there any way they could find out that you had been there?'

Tony did not believe there was. It was only that the police were so clever. They traced people from cloakroom tickets and other unlikely things in ways that seemed miraculous to the ordinary man.

'Go over it in detail. Did you step on soft ground anywhere?' Cecily had read her brother's stories.

'No, I'm sure I didn't. I walked on the grassy part of the drive, and where I stepped aside there were pine needles. Round the house it was all grass or gravel.'

'Did you touch anything?'

Tony thought. 'Well, I rang and knocked. And I shook the door by the knob.'

'Wearing gloves?'

'No.'

Then if they made dustings of the knocker and knob they might get his prints! Tony hadn't thought of this, and it gave him a further shock. Cecily's pause showed that she also appreciated the point.

'Well,' she said presently, 'I'll tell you what I think. If there's the slightest chance that the police may learn you were there, and apparently there's quite a good one, you must go and report to them at once.'

'Oh, no, I couldn't. How could I explain not going before?'

'You'll have to tell the truth.' Cecily's manner had grown short. 'No matter how bad it looks, it's the best thing now. And make it clear that it wasn't till you heard that the inquest had been adjourned that you realized it might be serious. Say that directly you realized that, you went.'

'A ghastly job.'

'Much better than having them find it out and then calling you to the station to answer questions. Go on, Tony, don't be a fool!'

Though Tony grumbled he allowed himself to be persuaded. By this time it was after six. He took out his boat and rowed across to Coulter's Wharf.

8

The Safeguarding of a Suspect

Tony was looking forward to the coming interview with positive dread. If only he had gone at the time! Then his story would have been convincing. But now, after all this delay, it would sound very different. If there really had been foul play, they might easily suspect him. He had a motive all right for doing away with Reeve. Moreover, with these thoughts in his mind his manner would not do him justice. He felt he would give a great deal to evade the ordeal, but he saw that further delay would make things look worse. It was therefore with something of the courage of despair that he turned into the station's open door.

A notice on an inner door adjured him to 'Knock and Enter.' Tony did both and found himself in a bare room, with a table and some chairs and a barred counter behind which a policeman was writing at a desk.

'Yes, sir?' said the policeman without getting up.

'It's about that fire,' Tony said, trying to overcome his nervousness, 'the fire last night at Myrtle Cottage.'

The policeman looked at him more keenly. He put down

his pen, rose slowly, and approached the counter. 'And what about the fire?' he asked.

'Well—just that I was at the cottage last evening, and saw something—unusual, and I thought I ought to tell about it.'

The policeman picked up a small block. 'I see. What's the name? And address? Quite. Well, just take a seat there for a moment, until I find someone to take your statement.' He tore off the sheet and disappeared through a door, shutting it behind him.

Tony breathed more freely. There was something reassuring about the man's manner, so matter-of-fact and devoid of emotion. If the interview could be carried through on that level he would be all right. In spite of his stories, Tony had never had any dealings with the police, and he really knew little of their methods.

Presently the policeman returned. 'The superintendent will see you in a few minutes. He's engaged at present. Seen the evening paper?' He pushed a *Standard* beneath the bars, reseated himself, and went stolidly on with his writing.

Tony thanked him and took the paper. He looked eagerly for a paragraph about the affair, but could find none. The rest of the news he simply could not read. However, he held the paper before him as if he found it interesting.

He did not know the superintendent, but he had heard that he was an able man, much respected in the town. This was comforting. He was a senior officer, moreover, and would have experience of people in Tony's position. Probably he would be easy to talk to.

Presently a buzzer sounded. The policeman once more got up, and opening a door, invited Tony to enter. They traversed a dingy passage with doors at both sides, at one of which the policeman knocked. He flung it open, said 'Mr Anthony

Meadowes,' motioned Tony to pass in, and withdrew, closing it behind him.

The room was small and plainly furnished with a table desk, file cabinet, bookshelves, and other office fittings. A hat and waterproof hung on a solitary hook. At the desk sat a heavy man, with a large clean-shaven face, from which two extremely wide-awake little eyes looked at Tony.

'Good evening,' he said, leaning back in his chair. 'You wanted to see someone about the Myrtle Cottage fire? Just sit down there and tell me all about it.'

Here was the same quiet matter-of-fact tone, neither cordial nor hostile, but pleasant enough. It helped Tony, and yet he found it hard to begin.

'I was up at the cottage last night,' eventually he plunged. 'I looked through the keyhole, and I—I saw a—a human foot.'

The superintendent's expression changed slightly. His little eyes grew keener, and Tony felt as if they were boring through his face into his mind. But all he said was: 'In that case I think we'd better have Inspector Jackson here. He's in charge of the case, and he might want to ask you some questions.' He picked up a desk telephone, touched a switch, and spoke. 'Is Jackson there? . . . Tell him I should like to see him.' Then to Tony: 'Save you repeating your story twice.'

'Thanks,' said Tony.

'You live on the other side of the river? I think I know the house. A nice property.' Whether this was meant to put him at his ease Tony didn't know, but it certainly had that effect. He began to feel that at this man's hands he would have a fair deal, though he was sure he could be ruthless when once he had made up his mind.

In a few seconds another man entered the room. He was younger and thinner and had a more good-natured expression than the superintendent. Like the elder man, he was in civilian clothes.

'Inspector Jackson,' said the superintendent, introducing them. 'This is Mr Anthony Meadowes, and he has something to tell us about the Reeve affair. Sit down, Jackson. Now, Mr Meadowes, will you begin at the beginning and tell us what you know?'

'I had some little business with Mr Reeve,' Tony answered, 'and shortly after nine last night I decided to go to Myrtle Cottage to talk to him. As I reached the house I saw a man looking in through the keyhole of the hall door. I got behind a bush to watch, and he went off down the drive. I went then to the door and knocked, but I couldn't get in. Then I looked through the keyhole,' and he described what he had seen.

Jackson had been writing, presumably shorthand. Now he and his chief exchanged glances.

'That sounds as if it would be helpful,' the big man said, with an evident attempt at geniality. 'But I'm afraid we must have it in more detail. We'll have to ask some questions, but we'll not keep you longer than we can help. You go ahead, Jackson.'

Jackson, who had been eyeing his chief interrogatively, now nodded briefly and turned to Tony.

'It'll save trouble in the end if we get all the particulars now, so as to avoid having to ask you to come back. Now, Mr Meadowes, what was the business you had with the deceased?'

Tony thought it wise to avoid any appearance of prevarication. 'Well,' he said, 'he was a moneylender, you know. I had borrowed from him.'

That was all right as far as it went, but it did not go far

enough. Question followed question, all scrupulously polite, but so searching that before long there was nothing of Tony's finances which was not known to these men. His writing, his home circumstances, his gambling, his debt, all lay naked and open before them.

'You went to see the deceased to try to induce him to give you more time to pay. But hadn't he already said he wouldn't?'

'That was a month earlier. I thought perhaps he would change his mind.'

Jackson and the superintendent exchanged rapid glances, and Tony thought the latter shook his head.

'I follow,' said Jackson easily. 'Now just tell us why you chose—what time did you say, about half-past nine last night?—to pay your call?'

'It was just a sudden idea. I wasn't doing anything, and it occurred to me that Reeve might be easier to deal with in his own house. I looked at the clock and saw that if I went at once it wouldn't be too late.'

'Did you tell anyone you were going?'

'No.'

'Why not?'

'As a matter of fact, I didn't want anyone to know,' Tony answered, then added: 'But apart from that there was no one to tell. My mother was asleep, my sister was out, it was no business of the maid, and there was no one else in the house.'

'Did you pass anyone on the way out?'

'No.'

'Then you saw the figure at the door and hid. It was a man, you said. Can you describe him?'

'No, it was too dark.'

'Was he tall or short? How did he walk? Energetic? Slouching? Shoulders thrown back or poked forward?'

Tony shook his head. 'I couldn't really say, except that he walked quickly. I thought he was a man, but I'm not sure of anything else.'

The questions about the details of what he saw through the keyhole Tony found easy. Then Jackson came to the point he had feared.

'Did you think the man was dead?'

'Yes.' Tony was now not very sure what he had thought, but this seemed the best answer. 'I supposed so.'

'But you didn't know for sure?'

'No.'

'There was a chance of his being only unconscious?'

'Yes, I saw that afterwards. But at the time I took it that he was dead. I was a good deal upset, and I'm afraid I didn't think very clearly.'

'Did you suspect foul play?'

'Oh, no, no! Never! I thought it was an accident.'

'Did it occur to you that you ought to report what you had seen immediately?'

'Yes, it did,' Tony admitted without hesitation.

'Then why did you not do so?'

This was easy; he had prepared for it. 'Well,' he answered, not too readily. 'I didn't want to be dragged into it, of course, because it would have brought out all about my debt, but I would have reported it only for the other man.'

'The other man?'

'Yes, the man I had seen at the keyhole. I thought he was hurrying off to do it.'

'Oh.' This seemed to give Jackson food for thought. 'Did you not make any other investigations or inquiries?'

'None except trying the windows and the back door, as I said.'

'You took the risk that the man might be alive and might die if he didn't have help, and you said nothing about it?'

Tony hung his head. 'I thought of that when it was too late, not at the time.'

'Did you tell anyone what you had seen?'

'No, not then.'

'Then when did you tell anyone else and who did you tell?'

Tony paused. 'It was like this,' he said. 'I didn't hear about the fire till lunchtime,' and he told what had happened. 'Then I began to wonder whether there could be more in it than I had thought. I was uneasy, and when I came home I consulted my sister.'

'And what did she say?'

'She said she would find out if the inquest was over and what the verdict was. When we heard it had been adjourned it seemed to us that the affair might be more serious than I had thought. I therefore came immediately to report to you.'

For some seconds the superintendent had been sketching on a piece of paper. Now he handed this across.

'That's a rough plan of Myrtle Cottage,' he explained. 'Would you mark on it the place where you stood while watching the man at the door? Here'—he handed over a book—'write on that. Thank you.'

Tony heaved an inward sigh of relief when he realized that this concluded the examination. It hadn't been so bad. There had been nothing like a third degree; in fact both men had been considerate and polite. They had asked nothing that he had not been able to answer, and answer easily. He wondered intensely what they thought about it all, but he felt it was unlikely that they would tell him. They didn't seem to have any suspicion of him, but he supposed they wouldn't show it if they had.

In any case Jackson's next words were a further immense relief. 'Now I'll get this run off on the typewriter, and then you can check it over and sign it, and that will be all. Sorry to keep you, but you can understand that a statement's no good unless it's signed.' With an almost friendly nod he went out.

Tony plucked up his courage. 'What do you think took place at the cottage?' he asked. 'Is there really doubt of its being an accident?'

The superintendent's keen eyes once again bored deep into his mind. 'We don't know,' he said pleasantly enough. 'It's a rather puzzling affair. Now we've got to fit this statement of yours into it. I think it'll probably help us. And that reminds me that in case some further question arises we'd like to be able to get in touch with you. Do you propose leaving home in the early future?'

'No—oh, no.'

'Then that's all right. Now if you'll excuse me, I have some letters to finish up. I want to get home as much as I expect you do.'

It was all infinitely reassuring. Soon Tony had read over and signed the statement and was outside the building. They had warned him that he would probably be required at the adjourned inquest, but he now had no fear of that. He felt an absolutely different being. He marvelled at the change. It was as if he had just awakened and found the dreadful position he had been in was only a nightmare.

Cecily's relief when he told her seemed just as great as his own. 'I knew it was the right thing to do,' she said, 'but I didn't know how they'd take it. I'm so glad, Tony. You may have to give evidence at the inquest, but that's all you'll hear of it.'

'I think I'm well out of it.'

'I'm sure you are. Look sharp now while I tell Kate you're in. I suppose it hasn't occurred to you that dinner's nearly an hour late?'

'Never thought of it. But I'm ready for it now.'

'In two minutes.'

'You know,' Tony went on when they were at the table, 'I've been thinking it out, and I believe you were right about telling Grace. I wouldn't like her to feel that I was keeping this secret from her, as if I didn't trust her.'

'I'm glad you feel that way.'

'I'll go over after dinner.'

'As a matter of fact I'm going too: another rehearsal. Grace was coming here, but she rang up to say that she couldn't. What with Mr Cornell's illness and their maid being away, she had to help with supper. Would you like to go alone, and I'd follow in half an hour.'

'Just like you, Cecily,' he said gratefully. 'No, let's go together. I'll tell her and then clear out, and you can go ahead with the part.'

Grace opened the door to them. 'Oh,' she cried with well simulated disappointment, 'are *you* here too? Why did you bring him, Cecily? He can't come in, you know.'

'Oh, yes, he can,' Cecily answered. 'He has something to tell you. Very private: don't say anything before the others.'

Grace sighed with fervour. 'Very well, on this occasion only.' She led the way to what was usually called the back room.

'Such an excitement has been agitating the house of Farson all day,' she went on as she pulled a third chair up to the fire. 'I don't know if you understood over the phone, but Mr Cornell has been really ill.'

'I didn't grasp that,' Cecily answered. 'Hard lines on your mother.'

'He's been quite bad. He called Mother about two this morning, and she was so frightened she phoned for Dr Hewitt. He thought so badly of him that he came back again this afternoon.'

'Oh, Grace, I'm so sorry. It's not—dangerous, I suppose?'

'Oh, very much so. Fortunately he doesn't seem worse this evening.'

'What's the trouble?' Tony put in, feeling more than virtuous in discussing the affairs of another person.

'Acute enteritis, I believe. Dr Hewitt was inquiring if he had anything to eat that we hadn't.'

'And had he?'

'Not in this house. But his illness raised the problem of whether we should send for Mrs Lambert.'

'And did you?'

'Well, we told her that he was ill.'

'And did she come?'

'She did, and stayed for ten minutes.'

This referred to the fact that Cornell and Mrs Lambert had recently become engaged. Cornell had told Mrs Farson himself, saying the wedding would take place in three months' time. It was a severe blow to the Farsons, who, if Cornell left, would be unable to keep on the house.

Mrs Lambert was a tall, well-preserved woman with an aggressive face and a domineering manner. Her husband, now ten years deceased, had made a fortune in the City, and had left her Holt End, a charming Staining residence, with plenty of money to keep it up. Holt End was on the Thames, nearly opposite Riverview, but some half-mile farther from town. While it was a large and pretentious place, its situation was not perfect, in that the towpath separated its grounds from the water's edge. Owing to her money and position Bertha Lambert was considered a great catch, and quite a number of men had hoped that they might induce her once again to change her name.

When the engagement was announced, most people's reaction was surprise. Not that there was any mystery about Robert Cornell. It was known that he was an Englishman who had lived for many years in the Argentine and who had come home from there as the London representative of a large produce business. But he mixed so little in the social life of the town that few knew him to speak to. That this semi-recluse should land the town's most famous matrimonial prize set the local tongues wagging.

'It seems,' Cecily declared, 'to be a day of problems. You haven't heard Tony's.'

'No, of course not. You were going to tell me something. Forge ahead, Tony.'

Cecily got up. 'I'll be tactful and go and commiserate with your mother about Mr Cornell. Tony'll tell you himself.'

Even with all this help Tony found it hard to begin. But when he had at last unburdened himself, he had no complaint to make as to his story's reception. Grace was more impressed even than Cecily had been. But he was pained to find that she took a much more serious view, both of his failure to report to the police at the time, and of possible future developments.

'Oh, Tony, you should have told them *at once*. Oh, dear, it's easy to say so now, of course, and I *don't* mean to criticize, but you really should.'

'I know that, of course; but there it is, I didn't. The police didn't seem to think anything of it.'

'I'm glad at least you went this evening, and the adjournment of the inquest certainly did give a reason. Poor old boy, what a ghastly time you've had!'

This was what he had hoped to hear. Grace was not going

to hold it against him. It was just like her. She was absolutely it! You knew where you were with Grace and what she would do. Once again he experienced the relief of confession. For some time they discussed the tragedy, and then Grace turned to another point.

'You've been bad about that money too,' she declared, and when he seemed taken aback at the unexpected onslaught, she went on: 'Not for getting into debt. Of course that was silly. But when you got into trouble about the repayment, you were really bad. Tony, old thing, why didn't you tell me? I could have helped.'

No upbraidings could have made Tony feel more of a worm. How hideously he had misjudged Grace! He had been afraid to tell her lest she might throw him over, or he had thought so. Now he saw that this was not his true motive. It was his stupid pride. He wanted to pretend to her that he was stronger and wiser than he really was: to conceal his weakness and folly. In either case his want of trust had hurt them both. It had hurt her: he could see it in her manner, though she did not reproach him. And as for himself, he might have saved himself an infinity of distress by merely sharing his burden with her. Indeed he realized that what he had done was the way, not to preserve, but to lose, her love.

Her attitude broke down this pride of Tony's, and during the next few minutes they drew nearer to each other than ever before. Never had Tony been so thankful that Grace had accepted him and that she was what she was.

'Who will you pay to now?' she presently asked.

'That's just what I've been wondering. Perhaps to no one.'

'But, Tony, if you owe it?'

'If Reeve constituted the firm, and he has no relatives, I don't see why I should pay.'

'I think you should, since you owe it. There are sure to be executors. But you'll probably get what you wanted—time to pay.'

'Oh, rather. I'll wait now till I get a demand.'

'I should go to the office again and ask. There may be a partner after all.'

This was what Tony did. The next day he called, to find the place shut up. He told himself then that he need make no further move. In any case, if there were executors, they would not be slow to approach him.

But the rest of that week passed, and no demand was made. Tony began to settle down, while the nightmare of his experiences receded. He told himself that he had learnt his lesson. No more gambling, no more hiding of important matters from Grace. His thoughts indeed turned to another matter: how soon could he afford to marry?

Then, just as he was beginning to think that this unhappy period of his life was over and that he might forget his terrors and look forward to a happier future, an utterly overwhelming blow fell.

On the following Monday evening, six days after the fire, he was alone in the sitting-room at Riverview, Cecily having gone with Grace to a Repertory rehearsal. He had been writing some letters and was now deep in a novel.

It had just struck ten when there was a ring at the door. Tony wondered if Kate had gone to bed; then he heard her in the hall. There were deep bass murmurings, followed by heavy steps in the hall, and the door was thrown open.

'Inspector Jackson to see you, sir,' Kate said. The inspector he had met at the police station entered, followed by two constables. Tony stood up.

'Good evening, Inspector,' he said, surprised.

The men had moved quickly across the room. Before he realized it they were at his elbow. Their faces were grave, and he experienced a sudden stab of panic. But before he had further time to think, he knew the worst.

'I'm sorry, Mr Meadowes,' said the Inspector, 'to have to carry out an unpleasant duty. I arrest you on the charge of murdering Albert Reeve at Myrtle Cottage on the evening of Tuesday, the twenty-fifth of September last. It is my duty to warn you that anything you say will be taken down and may be used as evidence.'

Tony had often read of a person's blood running cold—in fact in his books he had more than once used the phrase himself—and had supposed it was mere poetic licence. Now he knew he had been wrong. No more fitting description of his sensations could be found. Stunned, he was unable to reply and stood staring helplessly at the officers. He must have looked as he felt, for Jackson tried to minimize the shock.

'There now,' he said, looking as if he hated his job, 'don't take it too much to heart. You'll probably have a good defence. I see some whisky on the side table. Would you like a drink before we start?'

Tony nodded, and as if by magic a glass was in his hand. The spirit pulled him together.

'This is a terrible surprise, Inspector,' he said. 'Does it mean that I have to go with you now?'

'I'm afraid it does, Mr Meadowes. You'd like a coat, and we'll get it for you if you tell us where. In the meantime, the less you say, the better for yourself.'

Still partly stunned, Tony found that things arranged themselves without any volition on his part. A policeman was holding his coat for him, and another handed him his hat. They were in the hall. He was telling Kate—or was it one of the officers?—that he was going with them, but that he hoped to be back soon. They were in a car. The car was travelling through the night as he sat in the back seat, wedged between the inspector and a constable. They were getting out. They were at the police station: in a bare room with a desk and wooden seats. The policeman whom he had seen on his previous visit was at the desk. He was speaking. Tony could scarcely follow his words. But he could hear 'charged with the offence of murder', 'Albert Reeve', 'the twenty-fifth day of September of this year'. Then, 'Do you wish to make any statement? You need not do so unless you like. But anything you say will be taken down and will be used in evidence.'

Mechanically Tony shook his head. He was then conscious of being in another room. Hands were passing over him. His possessions, money, watch, knife, were lying on the table in front of him.

'Now just come this way,' said a constable. They passed through a door into a passage with doors on either side. The constable opened one and motioned to him to enter.

It was a cell about ten feet by five with a plain bed against one wall and a stool and a can in the other corners.

'There's a bell if you want anything,' said the constable. 'You can see your solicitor in the morning. Don't be upset; you'll find things won't be so bad.'

Tony, in a daze, thanked him. The man said good night in a friendly way, then went out, locking the door.

Locking the door! As Tony gazed at its smooth surface, his heart sank as it never had done before.

9

The Repercussions of an Arrest

That evening had been a tiring one for Cecily. The Repertory was putting on Galsworthy's *Escape*, and the man who was playing Matt Denant had got 'flu and had had to drop out. Ever since dinner Cecily had been chasing round in her car, looking for a substitute. Now, close on eleven, she had found one, and after fixing up with him for special coachings and rehearsals, she was driving home, weary, but with the satisfying consciousness of having met an emergency with competence.

She was surprised to find the outer hall door open and Kate waiting for her on the threshold.

'Oh, Miss Cecily!' she exclaimed. 'I—I heard your car.'

Cecily realized that something serious had happened. Kate was fond of her bed and bitterly resented being kept up after ten.

'Oh, Kate,' she cried, 'whatever is the matter? It's not Mother?'

'No, Miss. It's—it's—Mr Tony.'

'Tony!' Though Cecily was careful not to show it too openly, she idolized Tony. Now visions of accident, road or river, flashed through her mind. 'What's happened? He's not hurt?'

'No, Miss. It's—the police. They've—taken him.'

Cecily stared, while her heart seemed to stop. 'Taken him? You don't mean that he's—*arrested*?'

Kate nodded emphatically. 'About an hour ago. He's gone with them.'

Cecily staggered to a chair. 'Did you hear what for?' Her voice was low and hoarse.

'Yes, Miss.' Kate's eyes seemed to start still further from her head. 'For murder! Albert Reeve!'

Cecily groaned. Then the blow which she had at first feared, but afterwards thought they would escape, had really fallen! Tony! Her own brother, of whom she was so fond! Arrested for murder! She could scarcely believe it.

'Was he terribly upset?' she asked tremulously.

'No, Miss. He just said he was going with the police and hoped he would soon be back.'

'Does Mother know?'

'No, Miss. I didn't like to tell her.'

Cecily felt absolutely stunned. She sat there in the hall fighting for self-control and dimly conscious that Kate had gone and that she was alone. Poor Tony! He was also alone. Perhaps in a cell and locked up. Locked up! Locked away from his friends and from anyone who would help him!

Then her common sense began to reassert itself. There was some ghastly mistake. Tony was innocent, and they couldn't therefore prove him guilty. But couldn't they? Cases had been known . . .

Kate was there again, carrying a small tray. 'I thought you might like a cup of tea, Miss Cecily,' she explained, 'so I had the kettle on. There's a nice fire in the sitting-room.'

'Oh, Kate, that's good of you. But I don't feel that I could take anything.'

111

'You try the tea, Miss. It'll help you, and then you'll see better what to do for Mr Tony.'

Cecily absently took the tray. What *could* she do for Tony? She did not suppose that there was anything except to go and see him, but she did not know if that would be allowed.

What she wanted was advice. To talk it over with someone. At this hour whom could she find? The Farsons, of course! In any case she must tell Grace at once, and Mr Farson knew how things were done and could be capable enough when the occasion required it.

More for Kate's sake than her own she gulped down the tea. Five minutes later she was knocking at the Farsons' door. Grace presently appeared.

'Oh, Grace, I've got some terrible news. Prepare yourself for a shock. Tony—has been arrested!'

They were greatly distressed, all three of them. Grace said little, though her pale, strained face showed her feelings. Mrs Farson was voluble, though unconstructive, but George was really helpful.

'Don't get upset,' he told them; 'you're making far too much of it. You talk as if he had been convicted. The police have made a mistake. None of us believe that Tony would commit such a crime, and if he's innocent, no one can prove him guilty.'

'That's just what I was wondering,' put in Cecily. 'Aren't innocent people ever convicted?'

George Farson shook his head. 'Not once in a million times. I don't say that such a thing has never happened, but with a properly handled defence you may say that the chances are entirely negligible. No, no, don't begin to worry about imaginary evils. But that doesn't mean that we must sit down under this real one. You've done nothing yet, of course?'

'Nothing,' Cecily answered. 'I've only just heard.'

'Quite. Then let's see: who are your solicitors?'

'Messrs East, Burlington & East.'

'I know them. Good people,' they'll handle this all right. What about ringing up Mr East now? It's not too late. Do you know him?'

'Oh, yes, I've met him several times.'

'Tony knows young East—Trevor East. I've heard him speak of him,' said Grace.

'I know them both,' said George. 'If you like I'll ring the old man up on your behalf.'

'That would be splendid. I'd be so grateful.'

'Yes, do, George; get on with it at once,' put in Mrs Farson. 'Don't you think so, Grace?'

Grace eagerly agreed, but George Farson was not to be hurried. 'I think we should ring up the police station first and find out if Tony has already done anything.' Without waiting for the unanimous approval with which this was greeted, he put through the call.

'Mr Meadowes has done nothing about a solicitor yet, sir,' came the answer.

'Would it be possible for you to consult him? Say that his sister proposes to instruct Mr East, of East, Burlington & East, to act for him, and she wants to know if he's agreeable?'

'Yes, that can be done. Will you hold on?'

The answer soon came. It was just what Tony would like. George then rang up East. The solicitor was thunderstruck at the news. He reiterated that there must be some mistake. He promised to take up the case and see that everything necessary was done.

'No one who knows Meadowes,' he went on, almost in the words of George Farson, 'could believe him guilty, and if he's innocent, his defence should be straightforward.'

113

'Then we need do nothing more about it?'

'Not in the meantime. I'll see Meadowes in the morning and have him represented before the magistrates. Then later we can have a conference.'

This was satisfactory so far as it went, and Cecily was soon convinced that nothing more could be done that night. Till far into the small hours she sat talking over the affair, obtaining much comfort from the Farsons' sane and sympathetic attitude.

Next day, with George Farson, she was present when Tony was brought before the magistrates. She was surprised at the brevity of the proceedings: just Mr East's statement that he appeared for the accused, evidence of arrest, and an application for a week's remand, which was granted. As she put it to her mother later, Tony had scarcely appeared before he was gone again, but there had at least been time for her to give him the most reassuring smile of which she was capable.

After tea that day, as Cecily sat chatting to her mother, Ronald Barrymore was announced. Barrymore was the bank clerk who so obviously wanted to marry her, but who had not yet screwed up his courage to the point of proposal. Cecily was fond of him, but she had not yet made up her mind what she would say when the moment arrived.

'Oh, Cecily,' he greeted her, 'I just came to say how terribly sorry I was to hear the news and to ask if there was anything I could do.'

'Good of you, Ronald, but I don't think there is. East and Burlington are acting for Tony, and they'll see to everything.'

'It's beyond belief that the police could have made such a bloomer,' he went on. 'A ghastly shock it must have been to you.'

Barrymore was tall, well built and athletic-looking. He had

been a football blue at his college and was only a little less excellent as a boxer and oarsman. He had been intended for the civil service, but owing to the early death of his parents, he had to take up something more immediately lucrative. Now at eight and twenty he had already advanced some steps up the ladder of banking fame. He was a rather commonplace young man, but steady-going and with a backing of sound common sense. His manner was precise and elderly for his years, but he was decent and kindly. Cecily believed that he was of the type that would make a good husband, but though she liked him, she was not actually in love with him, and she was old-fashioned enough to believe that without this require-ment a happy marriage was unlikely.

'I wonder what sort of case they've got against Tony,' he went on. 'When will you know?'

'Mr East hadn't heard when I saw him this morning, but he said he would find out at once, and then we are to have a meeting to discuss what's to be done. Mr Farson's being splendid. He fixed up everything.'

'Well, if there's anything left that I can do, you will tell me, Cecily? There's nothing I would like more than to help you. You know that, don't you?'

'Of course I know it,' she said warmly, 'and there's no one I'd rather ask.'

His quiet, unobtrusive sympathy was comforting, and she felt more drawn to him than ever before.

After dinner she went back to the Farsons. There had been a long discussion that morning as to whether Grace should or should not go to work, her father holding that she should and her mother that she should not. Grace, however, had announced her intention of going, and Cecily had therefore waited till she was home again to pay her call.

115

Grace seemed tired and more subdued than usual, but when Cecily asked her, she said she was all right.

Mrs Farson was also depressed and, for her, almost silent. Only George was in his usual form.

'I met East this afternoon,' he told Cecily, 'just by chance, you know. We had a chat. He wants us to call at his office at ten tomorrow. Just you and me.'

'And me,' put in Grace with resolution.

'And what about your office?' her father asked.

'The chief can learn my value by doing without me once in a way,' retorted Grace. 'I'll ring him up in the morning.'

Seeing that she was determined, Farson said no more. Cecily was delighted. She had been sorry that Grace had gone to Town that morning, for she thought that her appearance at the remand would have cheered Tony. But this showed that she was taking the affair to heart.

For some time they discussed the morning interview, and then Cecily changed the subject. 'One thing which has been rather worrying me is the Repertory. I don't know whether it would be fair of me to leave all those people in the lurch, and yet I can't bring myself even to think of carrying on.'

'I can't either,' said Grace. 'I'm going to give up, at least till Tony's back again. But of course it's different for me. I'm not in the next show.'

'Nor am I,' Cecily replied; 'there's no trouble there. It's the secretarial work I'm thinking of. There's a good deal to be done, and none of the others know just how things stand.'

Grace shrugged. 'If you were ill, they'd have to learn.'

'I suppose I could explain it to Kitty Armstrong. She's the only one that would take the trouble.'

'It's not a matter for me, of course,' said George. 'but I do think, Cecily, you'd be well advised to give over the job in the meantime. What about Ronald Barrymore? He would be able to do secretarial work.'

'I know he would, but he's too much of a newcomer. The old stagers would think they were being passed over. But Ronald could help Kitty Armstrong.'

George nodded. 'You mean he could do the work and she could take the kudos?'

Cecily smiled. 'Well, yes, that's about it.'

'I'm sure Daddy's right,' Grace declared. 'If I were you I'd give it up.'

'I'll do it tomorrow. But tell me, Grace, why you're so keen about it?'

'I'm not keen about it,' Grace returned, but Cecily sensed a hesitation in her manner.

'Oh, yes, you are. What is it?'

For a moment Grace did not answer. Then with apparent embarrassment she said: 'Has it not occurred to you that people mayn't be so friendly now? A lot won't want to have anything to do with a man who's been tried for murder, or with his friends.'

'But if he's innocent—' Cecily was beginning indignantly, but Grace interrupted her.

'That won't matter.' She spoke a little bitterly. 'A lot of people are so righteous that association with you or me or Tony will contaminate them. You'll find it's so.'

'I don't believe it!'

'If you take my advice, you won't leave yourself open to snubs.'

Cecily was horrified. Surely people would not be so evil and so cruel? But Grace had spoken as if she knew. Cecily wondered had she already experienced it. Depressed, she went home to see her mother before she settled down for the night.

East, Burlington & East's office was in the High Street, which ran westwards from Staining Bridge parallel to the river. Mr East, Senior, was waiting for them when they arrived next morning. He was elderly, dry and formal in manner. His room was large and light and admirably proportioned with an Adam fireplace, garlanded ceiling, and decorated panelling. It must have been a fine apartment when the houses of the High Street were residences on a semi-country road. Now its day was past, it wanted paint and the walls were hidden by shelves of dingy coloured books. However, a good fire blazed in the grate, and three chairs were set close to it.

Mr East did not waste time in preliminaries. He expressed just enough of sympathy for his clients to avoid positive ill manners and then got to business.

'I have now received an outline of the police case,' he began. 'Further information is still to come, and until it does, I shall be unable to express my opinion as to the seriousness of the charge. But as it is, there are certain decisions which must be taken.'

He paused, looking from one to the other. He evidently intended to hold the floor and was about to proceed when Grace thrust in her oar.

'What is the case against Tony?' she asked.

East frowned. Such a direct approach was not in accordance with the best legal traditions. 'The outline only I can tell you,' he answered, 'but of course without details this may be misleading.'

But Grace was not to be put off. 'I understand that all right,' she persisted. 'I meant in outline: not in detail.'

'Well,' East said doubtfully, 'I'll tell you. But I hope you do understand that its seriousness depends on the details and that you therefore won't jump to conclusions. The police case is that—er—Tony was in financial difficulties which would have been solved by the death of Reeve, that he had the opportunity to murder him, that he was at Myrtle Cottage on the night in question, and so far as has yet been discovered, no one else could have committed the crime.'

Cecily was listening intently. 'Surely that last point is not evidence?' she said. 'It doesn't seem to me to have any weight at all.'

East leaned back in his chair and put his fingertips together. 'It depends on what I said: the details. At first sight our strong point would seem to be that they have not definitely connected Tony with the affair. So far as we know at present they appear to be able to prove that he could have committed the crime, not that he did so. Inquiries are doubtless still in progress, and we shall do well to reserve judgment until these are concluded.'

'But,' said Cecily, not wishing to interrupt, but feeling that some answer to this must be made, 'since he's innocent, they won't be able to find any proof of guilt.'

'That we all hope, Miss Meadowes. But I would be failing in my duty if I didn't warn you that they may find something which may appear very like proof. I don't think they will. I myself believe in—er—Tony's innocence just as you do. But there is the possibility, and we must be prepared for it.'

George Farson made a gesture of assent. 'That's right, Mr East. Now what do you advise?'

This again was going too fast. East nodded gravely. 'I'll come to that presently,' he said, 'but first I should like to be sure that you all understand the procedure which will be adopted. Are you clear on that point, Miss Meadowes?'

'Indeed no,' Cecily answered; 'I know very little about it.'

'Then it's only right that you should know what to expect.'

He spoke with more satisfaction, as if pleased to be once again holding the floor. 'In the first place you must understand that Tony will almost certainly he returned for trial. The police never, or practically never, bring a charge such as this unless they have sufficient evidence to justify an appeal to the Assizes. It would be unfair of me not to tell you this at once.'

His three listeners looked glum, but did not reply. 'Furthermore,' resumed East, 'it is usually wise to reserve the defence at the hearing before the magistrates. It may or may not be so in this case: the point will require serious study, but here again you should be forewarned. You must not think that if the defence is reserved, it means that it is inadequate.'

'I follow that, Mr East,' said Farson.

'I'm afraid I don't,' Cecily exclaimed. 'What exactly is the difference between the hearing before the magistrates and the Assizes.?'

East unbent still further. 'The procedure is not difficult to follow,' he assured her. 'As you know, Tony was brought before the magistrates this morning and at the request of the police was remanded for a week. That really means that their case against him is not ready. On Tony's behalf I raised no objection, because we also want time to prepare the defence. In fact, if the police had not asked for a remand, I should have had to do so.'

'I follow. And will everything be ready in a week?'

'It's most improbable. In that case Tony will be brought up and remanded for another week—perhaps two or three or four times.'

'But'—Cecily was really puzzled—'I still don't quite understand. What's the object of that being done each week? Why can't they say, "This is going to take us so long," and have done with it?'

'Probably neither side knows how long it will take. But apart from that, it's a safeguard for accused people. In this country no one can be arrested and just disappear and be forgotten. Unless the magistrates are satisfied that the request is reasonable, they won't remand. The case must then go on at once, or else the accused must be released.'

'It's a wise provision,' George Farson commented.

'Yes, it prevents the abuses that obtain in certain other countries which we could name. English justice is far from perfect, but it's as good, if not better, than any other in the world.'

'I follow that,' said Cecily. 'What happens then?'

'Eventually the police state the case against the accused before the magistrates. If these think there is a reasonable probability of his guilt, they return him for trial—that is, a detailed hearing before a judge and jury at the Assizes. If they don't think so, they release him then and there.'

'You said something about reserving the defence?'

'Yes. If counsel for the defence is pretty sure that the case will go for trial in any event, he often reserves the defence, which means that he does not attempt to defend the accused until the Assizes. There may be several reasons for this. It may be simply to save expense which can do no good. Or it may be to keep the prosecution in ignorance of the line the defence is going to take.' Mr East paused and looked round his little audience. 'Perhaps you're wondering why I should have gone into all this? Apart from answering Miss Meadowes' question, it was that you might reconcile yourselves to the fact that there's little hope of Tony being released before the Assizes.'

'That's in about three months?' Farson asked.

'I'm afraid so, yes.'

To both Grace and Cecily this was a heavy blow. They

121

discussed it for some time, till Mr East once again took charge of the conversation.

'All this doesn't mean that we can delay taking our steps for the defence. One essential which must be settled at once is the question of counsel.'

'Whom do you suggest?' East hesitated. 'Sir Redvers Grandison is undoubtedly the best man,' he said doubtfully, 'but he's very expensive. With a junior, say Maurice White, it would run into a lot of money. Of course we could let Edgar Griffiths lead. That would come to a lot less, and he's very good.'

'We must have the best, no matter what it costs,' Cecily declared. 'We'll meet it somehow.'

'It'll be a joint business,' Farson added. 'Can you give us an idea of the amounts?'

Cecily felt her heart warm to him. What good people these Farsons were! Many people in their position would have drawn back from contact with such a form of trouble. But not the Farsons. They were out to do the kind thing and the decent thing, irrespective of how they might themselves suffer by it. Tony was lucky, and as Tony's sister, so was she!

'One other question,' said Cecily, as East indicated that their business was complete; 'when can I see Tony?'

'I also,' added Grace. 'I want to visit him as soon as it can be arranged.'

East hummed and hawed. He did not think that this would be a wise move. But both girls were insistent, and eventually he undertook to see what could be done. Presently, depressed and partly conscious of the fight which lay before them, the little party left the solicitor's.

10

The Worth of a Sister

Now began for Cecily a period which, when she afterwards looked back upon it, seemed the worst she had ever experienced. The days, dragging heavily by as if weighted with lead, yet passed with a relentless and appalling swiftness. Each morning she awoke hopeful that before evening something would happen to help Tony, but when after interminable hours the evening came, she found that nothing had. And this period which was slipping away so rapidly was the only time they had in which to save Tony. A little more delay, and it might be too late. Gradually she grew almost desperate.

A week after the arrest there was a second remand. Mr East had of course told her that there would be, and she was therefore not disappointed. But during that week she could not discover what had been done about the defence. Sir Redvers Grandison and Mr Maurice White had been approached and had accepted the briefs, but so far as she knew, no meeting with them had taken place. Cecily haunted Mr East's office. The solicitor was always polite, but he did not tell her much. She assumed that he was doing everything possible, but there was no outward evidence of initiative or drive, and it was this that she so much resented.

Grace felt exactly the same. For Grace this period of waiting was in a way even harder. It was true that she had her work to take her mind off the affair, but on the other hand she had to keep up a cheerful front, irrespective of her feelings. The two girls met practically every evening, and practically only one subject was discussed.

Things had become more normal in the Farson household, the maid having returned to duty and Cornell being better, though not yet well enough to return to business. George was always optimistic, and Cecily found it a pleasure to talk to him, but Mrs Farson seldom spoke of Tony, as if she shared the young people's doubts.

'One feels so helpless,' Grace bemoaned one evening when she and Cecily were deep in one of their discussions. 'If one could do anything, it wouldn't be so bad. But this continuous inaction is maddening.'

'That's it. How I wish we knew what was happening! Mr East's very kind and all that, but he won't tell us what he's doing.'

Grace mournfully agreed.

Cecily hesitated and then went on to put into words the fear which had been haunting her. 'I suppose, Grace, they *have* a good defence? Sometimes, you know one gets worrying . . .'

Grace clasped her hands in an unconscious gesture. 'Oh, Cecily, that's what's been terrifying me: that there might be some hitch. If one was sure it was all right, one could bear it better.'

'I've asked Mr East—I'm sure if I've done it once, I've done it a dozen times—but he will never say anything definite. Do you know, George, I've scarcely admitted it even to myself, but sometimes I've thought he wasn't very hopeful himself.'

'So you've thought so too, Cecily! Oh, how I wish we could do something!'

'You couldn't do anything because of your job. But I've got all day. And I can't find anything to do.'

'My job! I would chuck it tomorrow if it would be any use. But as it is, what would be the good?'

A day or two later Grace took another holiday and with Cecily bearded East in his den and asked him the straight question: Was he absolutely confident of victory at the trial?

He was not too reassuring. 'Oh, well, you know, my dear young ladies, one can never feel that about any trial. As I have said before, the police will not put up a case unless it is at least plausible. And here their case is more than plausible. But I feel that Tony has an excellent chance.'

'Then you have got more details?'

'Oh, yes, I have now received its broad outline. It's very much what I expected.'

Cecily felt a little shiver of excitement. 'Oh, Mr East,' she begged, 'do tell us!'

'Oh, yes, do, please,' put in Grace. 'It's what we've been longing to know.'

East hesitated. 'It's extremely confidential, you know,' he said at last. 'I need scarcely occupy our time by explaining why, but you may take it from me that if the details were to leak out, it might gravely prejudice Tony's position. You understand that?' He looked at them quite sharply.

'We'll be discretion itself,' Cecily answered. 'Do you think that either of us would do *anything* that might injure Tony?'

East nodded. 'Very well, I'll trust you.' He sat back in his chair and cleared his throat. Apparently he found gratifying the breathless way in which the girls hung on his words, and as his tale developed his manner grew more and more genial.

But when Cecily heard what he had to say, it shocked her profoundly. The Crown case was immeasurably stronger than she had anticipated; indeed, with horror she had to admit that to anyone who did not know Tony, it might almost sound convincing.

'First of all,' East began, 'take motive. There is, of course, the debt to Reeve, which fell due on the first of October, six days after the murder. There's the fact that Tony hadn't the money to pay it and that Reeve would therefore have made things extremely unpleasant for him. The police know that Mrs Meadowes had had financial losses. and that Tony would have had difficulty in obtaining the money from her, and they also suggest that he probably feared that if there was a scandal, he would lose you, Miss Farson.'

'Oh, *no!*' cried Grace. 'That does you much credit'—East's voice was slightly dry—'but I assure you there are a good many young ladies who in such circumstances would take a very different view. Now if Reeve were dead, all this would be changed. At the worst Tony would gain invaluable time, and at the best, if Reeve had run his business alone, the debt might never be collected at all.

'Next, the Crown will bring Reeve's clerk to swear that some three weeks prior to the murder, Tony called at Reeve's office and begged him to accept a part payment when the debt fell due. He will swear that Reeve turned this down and that Tony was upset in consequence. So, you see, without labouring the point, I'm afraid it can be proved that Tony had a strong motive for wishing Reeve to be dead.'

'Horrible!'

'No doubt, but there it is. The police then point out that

Tony went to Myrtle Cottage on the evening of the murder secretly and that he said nothing about it till he realized that his visit must become known in any case.'

'But that was all explained!'

East shrugged. 'The police don't accept the explanation. They say that it is unlikely that he went to make a second appeal to Reeve, owing to the final way in which he had been turned down on the first occasion. However, that's a point for counsel to argue.'

'This is ghastly!'

'I'm afraid,' East said grimly, 'there's worse to follow. You see, I'm doing what you asked. I'm telling you the exact truth.'

The girls, both now pale and troubled, assured him that it was what they wished.

East nodded. 'The fire,' he resumed, 'as you know, was discovered shortly before four in the morning, and it is believed to have broken out some half an hour earlier. But here is a serious point. Reeve did not meet his death in the fire. He was dead when the flames reached his body. The exact hour of his death is not known with certainty, but the medical evidence suggests that it was about half-past nine, the very time at which Tony was at the cottage.'

'But that explains what Tony saw: the foot at the bottom of the stairs!'

'Yes, if the jury believe Tony's statement, as I hope they will. The police further suggest that the fire was caused by the murderer by means of a delayed action mechanism, and it's very unfortunate, but some notes of Tony's were found dealing with this very subject.'

'That would be for one of his books.'

'Of course, and that will be the defence on this point. But I'm afraid the police will try to make capital out of it. They argue that his specialty was in ingenious methods of murder, and that the plan adopted in the case of Reeve was typical of those described in his books. They claim therefore that it is reasonable to suppose that he could have been its author. Further, they say that as this type of inventive ability is very rare, its exhibition is a definite pointer to Tony. So you see, the case is not negligible.'

Cecily's mouth was dry with panic. 'It's worse than anything I could have imagined,' she declared brokenly. 'Oh, Mr East, what are we to do?'

'Well, we're doing everything that we can. We're trying to work up arguments to counter those of the Crown. I think we shall succeed.'

To Cecily it was terribly unsatisfactory. She did not see what more she could say, and yet she was loath to leave the matter where it stood.

'And is there *nothing* that Grace or I could do?' she asked desperately.

East forbore to make the obvious reply that it might be a help if they could find a real murderer and get him to confess. Instead he looked searchingly at Cecily. 'What could you do?' he asked. 'Could you get some helpful evidence? You know Tony's habits. Think over them. Something useful might occur to you.'

That night as she lay awake, East's question recurred to Cecily. Was there really nothing that she could do? After all, what East had said was true: she was in a better position than anyone else to suggest something helpful, owing to her knowledge of Tony's mind and ways. Surely, *surely* there must be some fact which would save him?

But though she spent half the night racking her brains, she found her thoughts merely retracing the path they had so often traversed. No, there was nothing which was not already known.

Could she, she wondered, get anyone to help her, anyone accustomed to these problems of evidence and proof? How Tony would have loved to help someone else in such a difficulty, had their positions been reversed. His writing of all these stories was such splendid training for that sort of thing.

But was there not an idea there? Why not consult one of his fellow writers? They had some kind of club in Town, and he went up to dinners. Surely one of the other members would be willing?

Cecily's excitement grew as she developed this idea. Her plan would be to see Ian Lane, who was unbeatable at the very same kind of problems. She had met him—Tony had taken her once or twice to their annual dinner—and she knew that he would hear her, for he was kindness itself. Whether he could do anything she didn't know, but it would at least be an immense relief to talk the matter over with him.

Then just as she reached the stage of making plans, another idea shot into her mind. It was revolutionary. Long before she went to sleep, as the early traffic began to pass the house, she had decided that come what would, she would carry it out.

During that first summer of her mother's illness, all three members of the family had had an unusual holiday. They had gone for a month's cruise in the *Hellénique*, the huge floating casino which for a year and more had circled the British Isles.*
None of them had gambled; they had gone simply for rest and change, which, it was hoped, would set

Mrs Meadowes up in health. It was expensive, but money had not then bulked as large among their problems as it did

---

* Described in the author's *Fatal Venture*.

now. They had gone aboard while the ship was coming down the west coast of Scotland, and had then worked round Ireland, doing shore excursions almost every day. For Cecily it had been a gorgeous time. But for one unpleasant episode she had enjoyed every minute of it.

That episode was the murder which had taken place near Portrush. The tragedy and the inquiries which were subsequently made, had cast a gloom over the whole ship. But now Cecily realized that it was just that murder and those inquiries which had made possible the action that she proposed.

During the cruise she had made the acquaintance of a Mr and Mrs French. They had been on board as ordinary passengers before the murder, but when this took place, Mr French had begun to investigate it, and it then became known that he was a chief detective inspector from Scotland Yard.

They were nice, quiet, homely people, and Cecily had liked them both. But it was not till some little time after the murder that she had learnt how really kind and good they were. She had made friends also with another passenger, a young woman of about her own age, who had fallen in love with one of the ship's officers. This man came under suspicion of the murder, and it was the Frenches' kindness to her friend during this trying period which had particularly struck her.

Now she wondered if she could possibly interest Mr French in Tony's fate. If she could tell him the circumstances, he might be able to advise her on some line of action. With his immense knowledge and experience he might see a weak point in the prosecution's case which she might follow up. If it was something that she herself could not do, she might perhaps employ a private detective.

It would be asking a lot, because Mr French was a busy man with his own problems and difficulties, but the worst that he could do would be to refuse, and for Tony's sake she would gladly risk a rebuff.

She began to consider ways and means. She thought it would be unwise to call at his office. That would make it formal, and besides, there he might grudge her his time. Better go to his home. Then she wondered whether she would be well advised first to enlist Mrs French's aid. Mr French could turn her down easily enough, but if her request were backed up by his wife, he would find it more difficult. The only snag was that she did not know their private address.

It proved so difficult to find this that at last she decided to go and see French at the Yard, and that morning after breakfast she set out. With some trepidation she walked in through the open gates and was directed by a constable to a certain door. Inside, another constable asked her business.

'I want to see Chief Inspector French, please,' she explained. 'Would you say it's Miss Meadowes and that we met on the *Hellénique*?'

'I don't think he's here today,' the man answered. 'Have you an appointment?'

'No. I really want to see Mrs French, but I don't know her address. I was going to ask the chief inspector.'

He gave her a keen glance and without further reply made a telephone inquiry. 'I'm sorry; he's away for the day.'

'Then could you give me Mrs French's address?'

The man shook his head. 'I'm sorry, Miss, but we're not allowed to do that. Against the regulations.'

This was what Cecily had expected, but she was prepared for it. On a scrap of paper she wrote down a telephone number and handed it to the constable with half a crown. 'In that case, I wonder if you could do me a kindness? Would you ring up Mrs French and say that Miss Meadowes of the

Hellénique wants to get in touch with her, and will she please ring up that number at twelve o'clock today?'

Rather to her surprise the man agreed, and she went along to her hairdresser's, whose number was the one she had given.

In due course Mrs French rang up. 'Oh, Mrs French,' Cecily explained, 'I'm so anxious to ask Mr French a question. It's about my brother, who has been arrested for a murder he didn't commit. I'm almost distracted, as you can imagine, but I'm sure he could help me with his advice: he's so very kind. I'm ashamed to bother him, but it's really a matter of life and death. Do you think I might come out to see you both on Saturday or Sunday?'

Em French's reply was warmly sympathetic. 'Come on Sunday,' she said; 'he won't be home till late on Saturday. Will you put up with pot luck and have lunch with us?'

'How good of you! But I feel I'm giving you enough trouble without that. I think, if I may, I'll come after lunch, but if you'd let me stay for tea, I'd love it.'

This evidently suited Mrs French better, and when she had obtained the address, Cecily rang off.

Until Sunday afternoon the hours dragged more heavily than ever, but at length three o'clock came and she presented herself at 16, Alford Terrace. French opened the door, and if his wife had told him what was in store for him, no sign of annoyance showed in his manner.

'This is very nice of you, Miss Meadowes,' he said. 'I'm sorry you had so much trouble finding the address.'

Mrs French welcomed her almost with affection. 'I can't say how sorry I am to hear of your trouble,' she exclaimed. 'No one who knew Mr Meadowes could imagine he could be guilty of such a crime. Just tell Joe all about it, and if he can help you, he will.'

French shook his head. 'Now, Em, you mustn't raise Miss Meadowes' hopes in that way. I'd be only too glad to be of use, but I fear there's no chance of it. You know I couldn't interfere unless the local police applied for help to the Yard, and then only if I happened to be sent.'

'And then,' Cecily smiled, 'you'd be acting for the enemy?'

French smiled back. 'I hope I'd be trying to find out the truth.'

'I was joking, Mr French, though I really don't feel very like it. But I never expected that you could actually do anything, just for the reason that you've given. What I hoped was that perhaps you would see some line which might be investigated, either by Tony's solicitors or by a private detective. To be quite candid, I'm not convinced that enough is being done about the defence.'

French thought this over. 'I'm afraid, Miss Meadowes, even that would be rather outside my province,' he said slowly. 'You see, you're asking me to try and defeat the efforts of another police force. I don't know that I could do that, at least behind their backs.'

Cecily felt a little desperate. 'Oh, but I'm not wanting that. I'm wanting only what you've just said yourself: to find out the truth. You wouldn't let professional etiquette prevent you from speaking if Tony was—was—found guilty and you knew he was innocent!'

Then Mrs French came to her assistance. 'Don't you mind him, Miss Meadowes,' she advised; 'that's only his nonsense. Hear her story, Joe; then if you think you can't interfere, you can say so.'

French shrugged. 'It's more than mere professional etiquette, I'm afraid. I think it's most unlikely that I shall be able to help you. However, with these reservations clearly understood, I'll be glad to hear what you have to say.'

Mrs French snorted. 'You might be a little more gracious over it. As I said, don't mind him, Miss Meadowes; for some reason he thinks it necessary to talk like that. But he'll do all he can to help you all the same. Now I'll leave you while I get tea ready, and you tell him the whole story.'

'If I'm not able to help you it won't be through unwillingness,' said French, when she had gone. 'Just let me get my pipe going. I can listen better when I'm smoking.'

Cecily was really grateful. She understood his hesitation and felt mean about her persistence. However, it was for Tony!

'I do think it's good of you,' she declared warmly. 'I'll not be longer than I can help. Well, it all began with Tony being idiot enough to get into a gambling set and start playing for money,' and she went on to tell the story. She had made notes of what she was going to say, so that she was able to give a reasonably concise statement. French listened carefully, only occasionally putting in a question. These delighted Cecily, for they showed how carefully he was following the tale.

'Well,' she said when she had finished, 'there it is. What do you think of it, Mr French? Can you suggest anything, *anything*, that I could do to help Tony?'

For a few moments he did not reply, sitting there pulling heavily at his pipe. 'I'm afraid it's as I thought,' he said at last, 'that you don't know, and therefore can't tell me, the details upon which the police decision was taken. As I have heard it, I imagine the trial might go either way. It would depend which of the counsel made the greatest impression on the jury and what view the judge took: things like that. It's really the details and what can be made of them that matter.'

'Is there any way, then, of getting more information?'

French shook his head. 'I doubt it. Who's the superintendent there? I ought to know him, but I've forgotten his name.'

'Mr Edgar.'

'Oh, yes, I've met him. He's a good sort, is Edgar: very straight and decent too. Tony will be all right in his hands.'

Cecily's heart was falling lower and lower. 'I had hoped,' she said as brightly as she could, 'that perhaps you would see some line of defence which might be investigated or worked up. You can't suggest anything?'

'The obvious defence is one that your solicitors evidently can't take, or they would have done so: I mean, to find the real criminal. If you could prove someone else guilty, that would of course end the matter for Tony.'

It was very much what East had told her, and it made her tend to withdraw her criticism of the senior partner. But it was no more helpful than he had been. She could as easily hold back the sun in its course as carry out French's suggestion.

They chatted for a little longer, and then Mrs French brought in tea. But before Cecily left, French had relented so far as to say that he would think over her story, and if anything occurred to him that might be useful, he would let her know. 'I hate to discourage you,' he went on, 'but I fear it is unlikely that anything will come of it.'

With this Cecily had to be content. In spite of their kindness, she left the Frenches' more despondent of the outcome than she had yet been.

11

The Enlistment of an Ally

Cecily's story had made a much greater impression on French than he had given her to believe. First, he liked and admired Cecily, who had been very nice both to himself and Mrs French on the *Hellénique*. Next, he had learnt he had also liked Tony, if not to the same extent. When he had learnt of Tony's detective stories, he had given him some information about the Yard and detection in real life and had been pleased by Tony's gratitude. Through these talks he had come to know the young man fairly well, and he now admitted to himself that he did not think he was of the type to carry through a premeditated and cold-blooded murder.

But there was a third reason why the story weighed on his mind. A few months earlier he had been in charge of a case in which a miscarriage of justice had very nearly taken place.* It was as a result of his work that an innocent young woman had been arrested for murder, tried, found guilty, and sentenced to death. True, he had not himself been satisfied as to her

---

* See the author's *James Tarrant, Adventurer*.

guilt, but unhappily those for whom he was working refused to share his doubts. Worse still, the final discovery which, just in time, had led to her reprieve and release, had been made, not as a result of his efforts, but of those of her lover. The case had given French a terrible shock, though both technically and morally his actions throughout had been justified. As a result he had registered a vow never to turn a deaf ear to suggestions as to the possibility of a similar error.

He had, of course, meant this in connection with his own cases. Such a contingency as that suggested by Cecily Meadowes had not entered his mind. Now he found himself confronted by a wholly unforeseen situation, and he was worried as to the action, if any, he should take.

He told himself that the affair was nothing to him, but he could not convince himself that such was the case. He had been appealed to for help: could he turn a deaf ear? If he did nothing, would he bear no responsibility should Tony be executed and his innocence afterwards established?

Technically, of course, it was not his business, but what about morally? French really did not know. Legally the responsibility was Superintendent Edgar's and that of his chief constable, as well as of the judge and to a lesser extent of the jury who were to try the case. There was no reason whatever to suppose that these, or any of them, would make a mistake.

And yet the superintendent and chief constable, the judge and jury, in the case which hung so heavily in his memory, had all made a mistake. What had happened before might happen again. If he were right about Tony's character, it looked as if it was already happening.

But even supposing he wished to take some action, what could he do? He had not invented the difficulties he had mentioned to Cecily: they were real. He had no *locus standi* in the case. Not only could he not appear officially, but even a private application to Edgar would be resented. Edgar was his superior in rank, and he just could not approach him, while to make inquiries behind his back would be more unpardonable still.

All that night and the next day the problem weighed naggingly on his conscience, like an aching tooth which, though forgotten at intervals, is always there. He made no deliberate decision, but by the time his work at the Yard was over, he realized that unless he did something about it, he would not again know a really easy mind. On his way home he took the plunge. From a street call box he rang up Superintendent Edgar to ask whether he could see him on a private matter if he were to call at his house that evening.

Fortunately he had once worked under Edgar, and their relations had been excellent. He had liked and respected the super, and as he had really helped him, and that tactfully, he believed the feeling was mutual. He could at least approach Edgar in a way impossible to a stranger.

French was not a nervous man and would have gone for an armed criminal without turning a hair, but on this unwonted errand he was conscious of some anxiety. However, he felt that all would depend on the line he took, and he determined that he would give no cause for offence.

Edgar received him in a friendly way, not as a superior, but as man to man, offered him a drink, and pushed over his tobacco pouch, while he talked about the case in which they had collaborated. But French wished to make his position clear without loss of time, and at the first opportunity he changed the subject.

'You've met me extraordinarily kindly, Mr Edgar,' he began, 'but I'm afraid when you hear what I want to ask you about, you won't be so pleased with me. I admit I've no right whatever to approach you on the matter, and if you simply tell me to go to a warm place, it's what I shall deserve. It's about young Tony Meadowes.'

Edgar raised his eyebrows. 'Meadowes? What about him?'

'I should like to explain that my interest in the case is not professional but private. I know the young fellow personally, and I know his family. You remember that job I had on the *Hellénique*? They were on board for a month, and through special circumstances which I needn't worry you with, the daughter and my wife got to be friends. Then when it got out who I was, Meadowes talked to me about his detective novels and asked me some questions. I'm afraid I didn't tell him very much, but I got to know him pretty well, and I must admit that I liked him. In fact they were all friendly and pleasant.'

Edgar seemed slightly puzzled. 'I'm sorry to hear that, Mr French,' he returned. 'In these matters you and I try to keep our personal feelings out of it—we have to or we couldn't carry on—so I sympathize with you now.'

French was not quite sure that this was not a rebuke. However, he decided to assume the contrary. 'Very kind of you to say so, sir. But I think I must make a full confession while I'm on the subject. Yesterday afternoon we had a visit from Miss Meadowes. She was very much upset, as you can imagine, principally because she thought the defence wasn't being pushed energetically enough. She begged me to advise her what to do. I told her it was impossible, that it was no business of mine, and that I couldn't interfere. She went away very much distressed.'

Edgar's manner grew slightly stiffer. He hesitated as if to choose his words, and French hurried on before he could speak.

'Of course I don't know the details of the case, but I couldn't get out of my mind two points which seemed to me to be in the man's favour. I thought I'd like to put them to you, sir, for your consideration. I wonder if you can bring yourself to hear them?'

'Oh, yes, certainly, go ahead,' and there was now no hesitation in Edgar's manner. 'If you have any ideas, by all means let's have 'em.'

'It's very good of you, sir, to appreciate that I'm neither attempting to criticize nor to butt in. The points are these. First, I understand the Crown is going to make a good deal out of Meadowes' books and his ingenuity, with the idea of showing that he could have worked out this murder?'

'I don't know about a good deal, but that point certainly comes into it.'

'Quite. Well, I've read three or four of the books and Meadowes talked to me about others, and they're not so good for all that. Where he scores is in plausibility. As a matter of fact none of his plots would work out in real life. They depend on coincidences. The circumstances are prearranged so that they'll work, but in real life that wouldn't obtain.'

Edgar was looking more interested. 'Can you give me an instance of that?'

'Yes, sir. In one story in which a corpse was got rid of by carrying it off in a car, the leading up had to be done over ground which was normally soft and which would have shown footprints. To get out of the difficulty Meadowes made it a cold night with the ground frozen. In real life he couldn't have arranged that.'

'I follow,' Edgar spoke thoughtfully. 'And you think all his work is of the same calibre?'

'Very distinctly, sir. In every book it was the same. The

weather always suited. Then people knew or remembered just what was required and forgot upsetting details. Without this prearranged setting the plots wouldn't have worked at all.'

Edgar smiled slowly. 'So that's the way it's done, is it? I see. Well, what's your second point, Chief Inspector?'

'Not so tangible, I'm afraid. It's simply my estimate of his character. I don't believe—and this is quite honestly, sir, and without trying to make a case—I don't believe he has the guts to have carried out this murder. It's one thing to imagine these things: it's quite another to do them. Of course, again, I don't know the exact details, but if it meant handling and arranging the corpse of the man he had murdered, I believe his nerve would have cracked up.'

'An opinion of that sort weighs, I agree, but it doesn't weigh very much. You know that yourself, Mr French.'

'I know it well, and I'm not making a great deal of it. I dare say I'm inclined to give it more weight because of that Little Bitton case I was on a little time ago. I expect you remember it: an innocent girl was sentenced to death through the evidence I brought forward. I can tell you, sir, I'm not proud of that case.'

'I heard about it. You weren't to blame.'

'Perhaps not directly. But it gave me a nasty jolt. In that case I had the very same feeling about that girl that I have now about young Meadowes. I agree it's not evidence, but—there it is.'

'Of course that case was put right before it was too late.'

'Yes, sir, but it was a near thing. However, that's past and done with. I'd like to say, though, that it was the remembrance of that case, added to what I've told you, that has brought me here this evening. And I'd like to say again how much I appreciate the way you have met me.'

141

Edgar made a gesture dismissing that side of the question. 'I'm glad you came to me: I think you were quite right. But I don't know that it's going to get us very much further. You know very well that I'm just as anxious as you are to avoid a miscarriage of justice. What do you suggest? Would you like to see the evidence?'

French was genuinely surprised. 'I never for one moment expected that you would let me see that, sir. All I hoped for was that perhaps you would yourself review it.'

'In a way it's out of my hands now. As you will realize, the papers are with the public prosecutor. Of course I could reopen any point if I saw reason to do so.'

'I appreciate that, sir. I'm in your hands. If you will allow me unofficially to read the file, I should, of course, take it as an immense favour. But—' French hesitated, then plunged— 'it's only fair to say that it would be with the hope of assisting the defence. So perhaps you'd prefer to reconsider your permission?'

Edgar hesitated in his turn. 'It's a rather unusual situation, isn't it, Chief Inspector? However, I appreciate the direct way you've spoken, and I certainly won't reconsider anything I've said. Indeed, if you can see anything in the file that we've missed, well, I'll be all the better pleased.'

'Again, it's extraordinarily good of you, sir.'

'But it's not so simple as all that. Where and when can you do it? I don't think I could let you take the file away.'

'Of course not, sir. If I might go down to the station now, I could read it there. If necessary I could spend the night there.'

'Very well, I'll ring up and give the instructions.'

Edgar left the room, and French could hear his muffled voice telephoning. In a few moments he came back.

'Luckily for you, Mr French, Inspector Jackson is at the station, clearing up some work. He's in charge of the case, and I've asked him to give you all the particulars you want.'

French could scarcely believe that the interview was over, and over so satisfactorily. He felt extraordinarily relieved, as if a weight which had been pressing him down had been removed. He had tackled an unpleasant job because he had believed it to be his duty, and now, whatever happened, his conscience would be clear. If the case against Tony were conclusive, he would admit it unhesitatingly to Edgar, whereas if he found a flaw, he knew Edgar would give it every consideration.

At the police station Inspector Jackson met him with official correctness, but with a personal manner frigid and unhelpful to the nth degree. 'Superintendent Edgar has instructed me to show you any of the papers in the Reeve case that you require, sir,' he replied to French's greeting, contriving to put into the words his own surprise and profound disapproval. 'I hadn't myself heard that the Yard was coming into the case, but if you tell me what you want to see, I'll get it for you.'

French, of course, saw what was wrong.

'Thank you, Inspector,' he returned. 'Very good of you, particularly at this late hour. But first I want to explain why I've come quite privately and unofficially. The Yard is not coming into the case, and I'm not acting for the Yard. I'm here by Superintendent Edgar's goodwill, and your own, because I happen to have met young Meadowes and his family, and I have a sort of liking for the fellow. He's a complete young fool in many ways, but as I was saying to the super, I could not see him carrying out a premeditated and deliberate crime of that sort. I called to ask the super if there was no chance of another interpretation of the facts, and he very kindly said I might see the evidence. So don't think I'm here to interfere with your handling of things. If I happen to see any fresh points, I'll simply tell you, but all credit and action will remain yours.'

This was it. Jackson at once thawed.

'I'm sure, sir,' he said with a complete change of manner, 'you know we don't want a conviction unless the chap's guilty. I'll be very pleased to let you have all the details, and very grateful for any hints you may give me.'

'Very good of you. I'd like a chat with you sometime, but I can't, of course, keep you up now. Suppose you let me have the file? I'll read it here, and perhaps tomorrow night we could have our talk?'

'It's nothing, sir, my sitting up a bit. I'll be glad to stay now and go through the case with you. It might be a help to you to hear by word of mouth what we have done.'

French again saw what was in the man's mind. He thought he was going to get free expert advice about his case, and he wanted to make the most of it. Well, so he should. If French could give him any help, he would certainly do it.

It ended in Jackson's stoking up the fire and the two men's settling down to make a night of it. 'Now, Inspector, since you're so good, just go ahead and tell me about it.' French held out his pouch. 'Do you smoke a pipe?'

They made such arrangements as they could for their comfort, and then Jackson took up his tale. He spoke carefully and with thought, as if trying to put his best foot forward before this exalted officer of the Yard. An eye to the main chance, of course, but it suited French.

'It was on Tuesday, the twenty-fifth of September, that the case began. Shortly before four that morning a labourer's wife, who was up attending to her sick child, happened to look out and noticed the glare of a fire in the sky. She called her husband, and he saw that it must be coming from a cottage occupied by a man named Reeve. He ran to a neighbour who had the telephone, and they rang up the brigade. The brigade went out and extinguished the fire, but not before the house was badly damaged. Our patrol went out and had a look round with the brigade officer. Here, sir, is an Ordnance map of the district. Here is Myrtle Cottage, which was burnt, and you'll see that it lies a mile and a half from the town, in an isolated position to the north-west.'

French congratulated himself as he looked at the map. This inspector was evidently an efficient chap and was going to tell his story clearly.

'Both the patrol and the brigade officer were worried about the occupant. The mere fact that the fire had broken out in the middle of the night indicated that someone had been there. By this time the woman who looked after Albert Reeve had come up—she's Mrs Porter, the wife of a local gardener—and she said that Reeve had been there on the evening before and had said nothing about leaving.'

'I suppose it wasn't possible to search the house?'

'Not then, sir. It was a small six-roomed cottage, with a square block of four rooms in front, one on each side of a narrow hall and staircase on ground and first floor respectively, and a two-roomed return at the back. This return held the kitchen, scullery, and so on below and Reeve's study above. When the brigade got there, the front block was alight, but not the return. They were able to save the return, but the front block, including Reeve's bedroom, was partially burnt. They were able to break into and search the return rooms, but the rest of the house was too hot to enter.'

'That's very clear.'

'They thought that Reeve must have lost his life, and as soon as the place was cool enough they searched the wreckage. They found a body, or the remains of one, lying just where the bottom of the stairs must have been in the hall. I happened to be here, and Mr Edgar told me to take over.

'I went out and had a look round. The fire appeared to have started in the centre of the house, for that was all burnt out: the stairs, the upper floors, the ceiling, and part of the roof had all gone down. But only that central area was destroyed, the brigade had saved the rest. The front door was charred on the inside only, and most of the window sashes had escaped. A good deal of the furniture near the outside walls was intact, and as I said, the return containing the kitchen below and Reeve's study above was completely saved. Here's a plan of what the house was like before the fire, showing the furniture according to the charwoman's statement.'

'Excellent,' said French. 'I see you've shown the body on your plan.'

'Yes, sir. As far as we could make out, it was lying on its face in the hall at the bottom of the stairs, with its feet where the lower step had been, and its arms spread out above its head. Of course it might have fallen with the floor from upstairs, because of the wreckage which covered it, but we thought not. "We", sir, is Dr Hawke and myself. It looked to both of us as if the man had fallen downstairs and been knocked unconscious. Here are photographs, both of the remains and of the general wreckage.'

'Very good: very clear indeed. Did the body show injuries?'

Jackson turned over his papers. 'None except those due to the fire, sir. As you can see from the medical report, it was very badly burnt: not entirely consumed, but partly so. It was entirely unrecognisable, and my first job was to obtain formal identification. I had no trouble about that. When I was going through Reeve's papers I found a Staining dentist's bill. I got him out, and he was able to identify from the jaws and teeth.

'Beneath the body, where it had been pressing on them, we found some fragments of cloth which showed that the deceased had been wearing pyjamas and a dressing-gown. There's neither gas nor electric light laid in the cottage, so it seemed likely that he had been going downstairs with a lamp or candle and had fallen and been unable to get up, and the candle had started the fire.'

'Very likely. Did you find a candlestick or lamp?'

'Yes, sir, and Mrs Porter identified it as Reeve's.'

'Almost a confirmation of your theory, wasn't it? Then what caused you to change your mind?'

'The medical evidence. Dr Hawke wasn't too clear as to the cause of death. No bones were broken, and it wasn't possible to say why the deceased had been unable to get up and escape. He refused to give a certificate without a post-mortem.'

'A suggestive point.'

'It turned out valuable, sir. When he made his tests he found out that Reeve had been dead long before the fire.'

'Valuable indeed. Could he estimate how long?'

'No, sir. He thought somewhere about six hours, but he said this was little more than a guess.'

'You don't know what he based his opinion on?'

'It's in his report, sir, but I'm not very well up in it, and I'd rather not say.'

'All right, I'll read it later. Go ahead.'

'As you can see, sir, this was rather an important question. If Dr Hawke was right it upset the theory of the fall down the stairs setting the house on fire. It wasn't so easy then to account for the fire. I began to wonder whether I was right in assuming it was an accident.'

French smiled. 'Gave you something to think about, certainly.'

'Yes, sir, it did. And the more I thought, the more doubtful I became. For a time I wondered whether Reeve could have fallen downstairs and been knocked senseless, then have lain there for a few hours and started the fire when he came round. But Dr Hawke was certain that he had been dead too long before the fire for that. So in the end I concluded that accident wouldn't explain the thing. I reported to Mr Edgar, and we agreed that it looked like a very brainy sort of murder.'

'I think I should have agreed with you too. Just break off a moment, will you, till I read Dr Hawke's report? There'—he passed over his pouch again—'have another fill?'

For some moments there was silence in the room while French buried himself in the report. He wondered whimsically what Cecily Meadowes would have said had she seen him and realized that all this nocturnal activity was the result of her despairing appeal.

As he tried to absorb the doctor's technicalities, he wondered also what would come of his interference.

12

The Story of a Crime

Dr Hawke's report was heavy going for the non-scientific reader, and though French had picked up a smattering of medical lore, he could not follow all the doctor's arguments.

After describing the position of the body, the statement explained that it had been partially consumed by the fire, particularly the extremities and the back. The doctor regretted that he was unable to state with certainty the cause of death, owing partly to the destruction of evidence by the fire, but principally to the time which had elapsed between death and his examination of the remains. The deceased seemed to have been in good health, and apart from the bums, there was no obvious injury to the remains, and no trace of poison. The burns would, of course, have been amply sufficient to cause death, but they had not done so. The single fact which was proven beyond doubt was that death had occurred before the fire. This was shown by the absence of carbon monoxide in the blood and of carbon particles in the lungs, as well as directly by the charring which occurs only in the case of dead flesh.

He gave it as his opinion—though as a tentative opinion only—that the deceased had died from asphyxia. This was suggested by the presence of an excess of carbon dioxide in the blood, as well as from an elimination of other causes. Evidence of asphyxiation was unmistakable immediately after death, but it quickly grew less marked, and in this case it was not conclusive. If he were correct in his opinion, the asphyxiation certainly had not been caused by drowning. It might conceivably have been brought about by poison gas, though no traces of this were obtainable. More probably it might have been due to smothering, either by forcible closing of the air passages of the mouth and nose or by constriction of the chest to prevent inhalation. Admittedly no traces of this remained, but under the special circumstances they could not be expected.

There was, however, definite evidence that death had taken place some considerable time before the fire. Hypostasis and cadaveric rigidity appeared to have developed normally, and if so, these suggested that the period was about six hours, but Dr Hawke pointed out that even under the best conditions such estimates were only approximations, while in this case the appearances had probably been modified by the fire.

The usual scientific expert's statement, thought French: vague enough to enable you to take almost any view! Did it, or did it not, rule out Jackson's original theory of the deceased having fallen downstairs, killed himself, and by dropping his lamp or candle, set the house on fire? Apparently it did. It might be wise to see the doctor on the point, though consideration of that could wait.

'Very good,' he remarked; 'you then assumed that Reeve had died before midnight and that the fire had been started by some delayed-action appliance. Right?'

Jackson shook his head. 'We thought of it, sir, but we didn't come to any final conclusion at that stage.'

'Very wise. Then what did you do?'

'I searched the study. Though there was a sitting-room downstairs, Mrs Porter said it was never used, and that the deceased always sat in the return room, which he called his study. It was a man's bachelor sitting-room, with a big leather-covered armchair in front of the fire, a writing table, whisky and soda and glasses, and some books: all just ordinary furniture and comfortable, but all shabby. The one expensive bit of furniture was a safe. It was a small one, but of the very best kind. I thought that anything of interest would be in the safe, for I could find nothing helpful outside it.'

'A job to open it?'

'There I was lucky, sir. A part of the floor of Reeve's bedroom was still standing, and on it I found his keys, discoloured from the fire, but all right otherwise. I got them out through a window with a hook tied to a stick, for I didn't dare stand on the floor. I opened the safe with some little difficulty, and then I learnt a good deal that no one had suspected before.'

'You were in luck.'

'I think, sir, you'd better see for yourself what I found. The stuff is all here. But in the meantime I'll just give you an idea. There was first a card index of thirty-seven cards, and every card referred to a separate person and gave certain numbers and dates and sums of money. A second index gave what appeared to be "dead" transactions. When I looked further I found what the numbers meant. They referred to folders in a small vertical file, and in each folder were papers about the person on the corresponding card. The papers I was able to divide into two lots. The first showed that Reeve had lent these people money and gave the circumstances and conditions of each loan. The totals of these loans were given on the cards, and the other sums apparently represented repayments: instalments and the amounts still due. The other set of papers were much more interesting. They showed that as well as being a moneylender, Reeve was a professional blackmailer. In it up to the neck.'

'By Jove! That suggests enemies!'

'That's what it suggested to me, sir. There were twelve cases of blackmail and twenty-five of moneylending, and I thought that each separate one of the whole thirty-seven had a motive to murder Reeve.'

'I confess I should have sympathy with twelve of them.'

Jackson gave a crooked smile. 'That's so, sir: a blackmailer's not much use to the world. But I wasn't thinking of that: I was thinking of thirty-seven alibis to be tested and wondering how we were going to manage it.'

'Call in the Yard,' said French, quickly deciding that he might be facetious.

Jackson glanced questioningly at him, then grinned with genuine appreciation. 'We thought it wasn't quite as bad as that, sir,' he returned with a chuckle. 'Well, I found I had some pretty powerful stuff about me. Some of those papers were about as safe as sticks of dynamite. You wouldn't believe the people he'd got hold of people in high positions and well respected and all that. And what's more, you wouldn't believe the things they'd been up to. But there it was, in black and white, as the saying is. I thought if I could start with the old chap's stock in trade, I'd make a darned sight more than I'd ever get out of the police.' Again there came a questioning glance to see how French would take this.

French was very pleased. It showed that the man was

enjoying himself and had developed no grievance. He decided to play up, but not too effusively.

'And get yourself knocked out and burnt, as he did. A good idea.'

Jackson seemed slightly dashed. 'Well, he wasn't very wise there, right enough, sir.' He grinned more doubtfully. 'I thought it was a bit of a responsibility to be handling all those papers, so I locked them up again in the safe, and got the safe in here. It's next door, if you wish to look over it.'

'Yes, I'd like to do that later on.'

'I then made a list of names and addresses from the cards. Here's a copy. As you'll see, most of them were in or near London, but there were some in the country, one as far as Lincoln and another in Devon, and so on. One was actually in Staining—that was young Meadowes, of course—and another some three miles out of the town, a Mrs Marjorie Broad. Her butler, a man named Cullen, was mentioned in the "dead" pack as having sold a letter. Mr Edgar then sent me to the coroner to ask for an adjournment of the inquest. I'm afraid you'll think we weren't working very fast, but by that time it was seven o'clock: I mean on Wednesday evening, the day after the fire.'

'Not at all. Inspector. I think you did very well in the time. You searched the grounds, I suppose?'

'Oh, yes, sir, but we found nothing.'

'No marks of a parked car?'

'No, and if a car had come in we'd have seen it. The brigade vehicles were clearly marked. We wondered if this meant that the murderer was a local?'

'Not necessarily, I'm afraid.'

'I agree, sir, but we thought it was a point to be kept in view. Well, I was preparing to go home for a bite of supper when Mr Edgar rang for me. Young Meadowes had called to make a statement. He said he had been up at the cottage on the previous evening,' and Jackson described the interview. 'He said he had used the hall door knocker and knob—we gathered, with his bare hands—so Mr Edgar got his prints by a trick with a sketch map. Of course at that time we didn't suspect him. His coming to report seemed at first sight to clear him.'

'Also his story fitted in with the medical evidence as to the time of death,' put in French.

'So we thought at the time, sir. I'll come to that in a moment.'

'Right; go ahead in your own way.'

'I drafted out a request for information about the people on the list and kept a constable on duty that night to ring up the police stations involved. Next morning I went out to the cottage again, and got prints on the knob, and these proved to be Meadowes'.'

'Further confirmation of his story?'

'It looked it at the moment. Then I went up to Town to Reeve's office and saw the clerk; we had got the address from Meadowes' statement. The clerk said he didn't know anything about the blackmail, but had always thought Reeve was a moneylender only. That may or may not have been true. He was giving nothing away until I told him he was engaged in a criminal business and his only chance was to come clean. Then he talked.

'He told me first about the business. It had been started years earlier by Reeve's brother. Then the two of them had run it till the brother died. This Reeve, Albert Reeve, had then carried on alone. All that had happened before the clerk was engaged, but he had discovered it from reading old papers. So far as he knew, Albert had never taken another partner, and there was therefore no one to carry on the business. Nor did he believe that Albert had either relatives living or any close friends. He was upset because he thought his job had come to an end.'

'I suppose none of Reeve's papers mentioned a partner or relatives?'

'No, sir, not that I could find.'

'And his charwoman knew nothing?'

'Nothing, sir. He was an ingenious lad, that clerk. He had the notion that the more knowledge he had of his employer's business, the better for himself. Whether he intended to blackmail the blackmailer, he didn't say, but he had bought a second-hand stethoscope and fitted it with a plug the shape of the keyhole, and when this was in place he could hear everything that was said in Reeve's private room. I thought that was smart, sir.'

'Very. The makings of a good criminal there, I imagine.'

'It made me add his name to the list of suspects, at all events. Then I asked him about recent callers, and I got quite a lot of information.' Jackson once again turned over the papers in the file. 'First there was Meadowes, and I saw at once that he hadn't told us all the truth. He had mentioned the debt and that he couldn't pay, but he hadn't said anything about a row he'd had with Reeve. Apparently he had threatened he'd do something desperate if Reeve wouldn't allow him more time, and they'd both been pretty hot. It was then that the first suspicion that Meadowes might be guilty occurred to me, but I merely noted it as a point to be considered.

'Another client that had cut up rough was Thomas Cullen. Cullen was butler to a Mr Howard Broad, of The Limes, Merlock, which is about three miles from here. I had been interested in him from the start, because, as I mentioned, Mrs

Broad's name was also on Reeve's list. It seemed that Cullen had found some letter which involved Mrs Broad and had sold it to Reeve. He wanted £500 for it, but Reeve would only give him £50. Cullen seems to have been pretty badly upset about it. I didn't believe anyone would commit murder from such a motive, but it was another case to be looked into.

'Mrs Broad herself I didn't suspect: it didn't look to me like a woman's job. But the letter was from a lover—I saw it in Reeve's file—and he might have been involved on her behalf. I therefore made a note to find him.'

'Very good, Inspector. I think you handled it admirably.'

'Thank you, sir. Then I asked the clerk where he had been on the night of the crime. He made a statement, but I hadn't time to check it then.

'As you'll guess, I next started on the other alibis. We already had Meadowes' statement; so I went out to The Limes and saw Cullen. At first he took a high hand and denied everything, but when he realized that if he wasn't careful he might be charged with murder, he changed his tune. He then admitted that he wanted money and had taken a mould of Mrs Broad's key and searched her davenport in the hope of finding papers to blackmail her. I told him blackmail was a serious matter and that I wanted him to come in with me to the station so that a formal statement might be taken from him. Just to put the wind up, you know, sir.'

'I know,' said French feelingly. 'Did it work?'

Jackson smiled reminiscently. 'Yes, sir, it worked. I brought him in and questioned him before Mr Edgar, after a very formal caution. We told him that if he gave no trouble and told us everything, we might not press a charge of blackmail, but that any attempt to prevaricate would finish him. He was properly cooled down by the time we'd done with him.

'We got a good deal out of him. First we asked him how he came to suspect that Mrs Broad might have such a letter. He said he had guessed from her manner, first that she had fallen in love, and secondly that by a certain post she had received a letter. He searched and found it. It was from a lover, and it referred to her agreement to go away with him for a weekend. It appears that her husband is a very strict old boy, and to have shown him the letter would have meant a complete bust-up. We had a bit more trouble figuring out who the lover was, but we were pretty sure Cullen knew, and so he did. It was a man named Sinclair Nettlefold, a novelist or playwright, who lives in a small cottage about half a mile from the town. It was clear that Nettlefold had a motive for doing Reeve in, both on his own behalf and on Mrs Broad's; so he went down on the list of suspects.'

'A juicy witness.'

'Wasn't he sir? Next, of course, we asked where he had been on the night of the murder. He hadn't any special alibi, but said that he carried out his duties as usual at The Limes. This, if true, would have cleared him up to about 11.00 p.m., but after that he might, so far as we knew, have slipped out of the house and been at Myrtle Cottage by midnight.'

'Too late to commit the murder, unless you strain the medical evidence.'

'That's true, sir, but only the part that Dr Hawke admitted he was doubtful about. However, there it was: another matter to be gone into.

'Next day I went out and saw Nettlefold. He was terribly upset when he found what I wanted, but I thought, rightly or wrongly, it was more on Mrs Broad's account than his own. I told him I was interested in the murder and not in his friendship with Mrs Broad, nor yet in Cullen's actions, unless any of these should be found to be connected with the murder. Then I asked for his alibi, but he had none, except that he said he had not been out of his rooms all that night. This I could neither confirm nor disprove.

'These two statements, I mean Cullen's and Nettlefold's, with young Meadowes' and possibly Mrs Broad's, if it became necessary to get hers, I decided to investigate later. I'll go into them in detail if you like, but the details are all given in the file, and you may only wish to discuss my conclusions.'

'Thank you, Inspector, I'll think about that. In the meantime carry on as you're doing.'

'By this time answers were beginning to come in about the other suspects on my list. I was anxious to divide them into three classes: those whose alibis were absolutely watertight and who might be crossed off the list; those whose alibis appeared to be sound, but could not be absolutely established; and those who had no real alibi. I can tell you, sir, I was a bit surprised when I got my results.

'Of the thirty-nine people—that is, the thirty-seven on Reeve's cards, his clerk, and Nettlefold—thirty-one were absolutely cleared, either they lived too far away or were seen too near the time to have got to Myrtle Cottage. These alibis I didn't go into myself; I took the reports from the local forces.

'That left six: Meadowes, Cullen, Nettlefold, Mrs Broad, a master plumber called Walters in Hammersmith, and a clerk named Eastman who lived near Godalming. Each had a kind of alibi, but they weren't exactly convincing.

'Well, sir, I went into these six. The details are given in the file, but perhaps for the moment it's enough to say that I was satisfied with five of them, and so was Mr Edgar. But there was one we could get no confirmation for. That was Meadowes'.'

'I begin to see, Sergeant.'

'Well, that was what our investigation led to. Of thirty-nine suspects—all we could find—thirty-eight were innocent. Therefore our suspicion lay on Meadowes.'

'Naturally.'

'I then checked up what I could of his statement. Quite definitely he was with the Farsons at 9.00 p.m., for Mr and Mrs Farson both remember his being there when the time signal sounded. Meadowes then went home, about three minutes' walk, and spoke to their servant Kate. She was engaged in the hall for three or four minutes after that, so that Meadowes couldn't have left the house before about ten minutes past nine. We could find no bicycle there nor any evidence that he had taken out his sister's car; so we assumed he walked to the Cottage as he said. So he could not have got there before about 9.25.

'But there's no real evidence as to when he got back. Miss Meadowes was at Farsons', rehearsing with Miss Farson in connection with the local dramatic society, and states that she got home at 11.00 p.m. This appears to be true, as far as we could check up. She says her brother had then gone to bed, or at least was in his room. He called out some remark about the dramatic society, and this may have been to demonstrate that he was there. If Miss Meadowes' statement is true, he must have left Myrtle Cottage at 10.45 at the latest. But as he couldn't tell to a minute when she would get back, we assumed a slightly earlier hour.'

'Then you doubted Miss Meadowes' statement?'

'Well, we thought that if she had any idea that her brother was guilty of murder, she would naturally lie. But even if she were speaking the truth, he could have had an hour or more there. So I asked myself, could he have done what was done in the time?'

'What was done, Sergeant?'

'That's just the point, sir. I tried to reconstruct. I imagined Meadowes going to the door, knocking, and Reeve coming down from his study and opening the door. Probably their going upstairs and talking. Then Meadowes knocking Reeve out. He might have sandbagged him or hit him on the jaw or perhaps chloroformed him. Reeve was a small, weak specimen, as well as old; no match for Meadowes. At all events I assumed he killed him in some way which left no traces which were not destroyed by the fire. Then I assumed that he stripped the body, clothed it in pyjamas and dressing-gown, got it down-stairs, and placed it to look as if Reeve had fallen down the steps and killed himself. I thought he had then fixed up some delayed-action arrangement to start the fire at a time when he couldn't possibly be there. He would think this made him safe.'

French thought this over. 'Rather imaginative, all that, surely? You can't prove that it took place.'

'Perhaps not, sir, but it fits the circumstances pretty well. Something of the kind must have happened because of the medical evidence. If Reeve was dead some time before the fire, he couldn't have started it by his fall; and if he didn't start it by his fall, either someone must have been there at 3.30 a.m., or there was a delayed-action mechanism. We couldn't find anyone who was there at 3.30, so that it looks like the mechanism.'

'That certainly sounds reasonable.'

'Then there were the two confirmatory points that I think you know. This sort of ingenious murder was just the kind Meadowes described in his books; so he had the ability to think it out, and very few people have that power. The other point is that we found notes about delayed-action appliances in his desk.'

'And you made your arrest on that?'

'There were two more points. One was that Meadowes had called on the morning after the fire at Reeve's office, as if to prove that he knew nothing of the man's death. The second was that when at lunch that day a friend named Richards told him of the affair he again pretended ignorance.'

'Not proof of guilt, you know.'

'No, sir, but it's cumulative evidence.'

'Then that was your case?'

'Yes, sir. First, that he had the motive, good and plenty; second, that he had the opportunity; third, that the plan adopted suited his special type of mind, a very uncommon type; fourth, that he had been considering delayed-action appliances; fifth, that there was no evidence conflicting with this view; and sixth, that we couldn't find anyone else who might be guilty.'

'And you don't think his coming here to report to you an indication of innocence?'

'Well, no, sir. I talked that over with Mr Edgar, and we didn't think so. With anyone else it might have been, but not with him. We thought it was the kind of thing he would do, hoping to mislead us in that very way.'

'But he needn't have admitted he was there.'

'We had his name on the cards and his prints on the knob. He couldn't have denied it.'

French considered. He felt he had ample to think over. 'I admit you've got a case, Sergeant, and again I'm very grateful to you for telling me about it. I suggest that's enough for tonight. You go off home, and I'll have a Shakedown here till the morning. Then I'll think over what you've told me and, if I may, come back on Saturday afternoon, to read those alibis.'

'Fine, sir. I'll have everything ready for you.'

'Thank you. But this time reading will be enough. I don't intend to spoil your afternoon.'

French was tired, and after Jackson left he got a little sleep. But he woke in time to catch the first train to Town, where, after a bath and breakfast, he turned up at his normal time at the Yard, fresh and ready for his day's work.

13

The Fruits of an Analysis

Not till that evening did French have time to think again of the Reeve case, but after supper he sat down in his easy chair before the fire, lit his pipe, and set himself to go over the notes he had made.

Jackson's argument could be stated in four propositions:

1. Reeve had been murdered
2. Meadowes could have committed the murder.
3. No one but Meadowes could have done so.
4. Therefore Meadowes was guilty.

If the first three of these were true, the fourth obviously followed. But were they true? French took them in turn.

No. 1, that Reeve had been murdered.

French began by considering the alternatives, accident and suicide. How, he asked himself, could the death have been accidental? Rack his brains as he would, he could think of no way other than that already suggested by Jackson: that the man had been killed by the fall and had started the fire by dropping his candle. But this on the face of it was most unlikely. French did not believe, for one thing, that such a fall would prove fatal unless some dislocation or fracture had been sustained, and none had. For another, he thought that in at least nine cases out of ten the candle would have gone out on striking the ground.

But the decisive factor was the medical evidence. The accident theory could only be true if the fall and the fire had occurred at or about the same hour, but from Dr Hawkes' report these were separated by a considerable time, probably as much as six hours.

From these facts French found himself forced to rule out accident.

What then of suicide?

The difficulties here seemed even greater. How could Reeve have committed suicide without leaving traces on his body? Why should he stage such an elaborate plant to make his suicide look like an accident, including, as it would, a delayed appliance to start the fire? French felt that suicide was also out of the question.

That left only murder, and he therefore ticked off as correct No. 1 of Jackson's propositions.

No. 2 was that Tony Meadowes could have committed the murder. This seemed so obvious that French spent but little time on it. Tony would have had no difficulty in obtaining admission to the house: Reeve would have let him in. He could easily have knocked the old man out: a blow on the chin would have done it. With Tony's specialized knowledge the delayed-action appliance could have been easily arranged. He could have walked out of the door and by merely pulling it would have latched behind him. Yes, it was certain that Jackson's proposition No. 2 was also true.

But here for a moment French left the direct line of his argument. *Had* Tony committed the crime? He took a sheet of paper and wrote down on the left side the arguments which Jackson had advanced for the young man's guilt, and on the right a criticism as to their validity. When he had finished, the statement read as follows:

Argument	*Criticism*
Tony had an adequate motive.	This was a matter of opinion, and a good counsel could throw doubts on it.
He had the ingenious type of mind which could have thought out the murder.	He excelled in plausibility, not in real ingenuity. His book plots would not have worked in real life.
He had been studying delayed-action fire-raising mechanisms.	This study might have been for a book. (*Note.* Ascertain if this was so.)
He had been at the cottage on the night of the murder.	He had reported his visit to the police. His presence was accounted for by his story, and in any case was no proof of guilt.
His fingerprints on the knob of the hall door suggested that he had been in the cottage and had pulled the door behind him when leaving.	His statement that he had shaken the door to see if he could open it, accounted for this satisfactorily.
According to the medical evidence his visit to the cottage was at the time of the murder.	The medical evidence was doubtful. The time was the only time he could have gone.
He only reported his visit when he realized that it would become known in any case.	His statement that he reported directly he learnt that there might be a suspicion of foul play was equally reasonable.
Since Reeve had definitely refused to grant him relief about the debt, it was unlikely that he had visited the cottage merely to repeat his request.	His character would tend to prevent him from accepting a disagreeable decision and would make him hope that it would be reversed.
He had visited Reeve's office on the day following the murder to make it appear that he did not know that anything had happened to Reeve.	His own explanation of this that he did not want his call at the cottage to come out was satisfactory.
His manner to Richards when told of the fire was equally suspicious.	Again his own explanation was adequate.
The fact that no car marks were found near the cottage increased the probability that the murderer was a local.	No one but a fool would have brought a car onto that soft ground. A car might have been left on the road, or the murderer might have come on a bicycle, by water or by bus or rail.

It was clear from this that not a single one of Jackson's points was conclusive. All could be equally well explained on the ground of Tony's innocence. French found himself considerably impressed by his results.

There were, moreover, two other points. strongly in Tony's favour. The first was the original one that he had mentioned to Edgar: that Tony simply had not the guts to carry out such a crime. French was convinced that he could neither have dealt with the body, nor, were he guilty, have put up such a show of innocence.

The other point was even more convincing. If Tony had wished to establish an alibi by means of the delayed-action apparatus, he had made no attempt to complete it. The whole point of the alleged alibi was to prove that the murderer had not been at the cottage when the fire started. But Tony had offered no proof as to his whereabouts at the time of the fire. His sister could have sworn that he was in his room at eleven, but not that he didn't go out later. Tony's work on his detective stories would have prevented him from making a mistake on so vital a point. Jackson could not have his novelist argument both ways, and it looked as if he were here hoist with his own petard. No, French was sure that one thing which would characterize the murderer would be an absolutely watertight alibi for the critical hour of from 3.00 to 4.00 a.m.

There was then a great deal more to be said for Tony than French had at first realized. What now could be made of Jackson's proposition No. 3, that no one but Tony could be guilty?

Of course, with several hundred million other people in the world, such a statement was logically absurd. But French took it as Jackson had meant it: that he had not been able to find any other possible suspect. But this was not conclusive. Reeve's enemies were not necessarily confined to Jackson's suspects. French thought that not only was this argument intrinsically unsound, but that in court it could quickly be broken down.

In spite of all this, given a good prosecuting counsel or an unsympathetic judge, the verdict might easily go against Tony. There was in fact only one thing that would inevitably save him, and that was to prove the guilt of someone else.

French saw that if he were to do anything with the case, an immense amount of work would be required. For one thing, he would have to check Jackson's conclusions on the thirty-nine alibis. Situated as he was, this alone would be an impossible task. Even if he gave it his full time and with all the resources of the Yard behind him, it would be no joke. As it was, he need not think of attempting it.

He put down his notes, and sitting back in his chair, re-lit his pipe and became buried in thought. Apart from the case itself, what about his own position? Had his interference been merely a bit of gratuitous meddling? Was there any use in trying to carry on? Should he not drop it before he became further involved?

Then he saw that these questions hinged on another, a fundamental one: did he believe Tony to be guilty or innocent? If guilty, they were all solved; but if innocent, where did he stand?

As he pondered over the problem, it was gradually borne in upon him that he really did, in his heart of hearts, believe Tony to be innocent. That had been his view when first he heard the story, and all that he had since learnt had only tended to strengthen his opinion.

At the end of an hour his mind was made up. He could

not leave the young man to his fate without doing everything in his power to establish the truth. How he was going to manage it he did not know, but at least he could see his next step. He would read and ponder all that was in the file. Perhaps he could find enough to induce Superintendent Edgar to reopen the investigation.

That evening and the three following he spent in examining Reeve's cards, checking Jackson's list of suspects, and considering their alibis.

The more he did so, the more impressed he became with the excellence of the work which had been done. The first name was that of a civil engineer in Cheltenham. This gentleman had been interrogated by the local police, who had also checked his statement. On the night of the crime he had been present at a Masonic gathering from 9.00 till 11.30 (vouched for by four members who were also present). He reached home before midnight and went to his room about 12.30 (vouched for by three other members of the family and a Major Hicks, a guest). He was up at 7.30 next morning, fresh and normal in manner (vouched for by the butler), and breakfasted as usual (vouched for by the entire household). His car had not been taken out during the night (vouched for by the chauffeur).

This case was a fair sample of some 70 per cent of those in question. French felt, as Jackson had before him, that in the light of the confirmation obtained by the local police, suspicion of the civil engineer was no longer possible. As Jackson had before him, he crossed his name and those of some two dozen others off the list.

In the cases of the remaining dozen names, there was no actual proof of innocence. But equally there was none of guilt. These people had, according to their own statements, done what was natural and reasonable in their various circumstances, but the nature of these actions was such that no confirmation was obtainable. Here French thought that a consideration of motive would be his most helpful line.

To get them out of the way he took first those who had not been specially mentioned by Jackson. In all of them he reached the same conclusion as the inspector: that there was no reason to assume them anything but innocent. Then he came to the three local suspects, Cullen, Marjorie Broad, and Nettlefold.

A careful study of Cullen's dossier revealed the fact he also had very little motive, if any. His transactions with Reeve were confined to the sale for £50 of a letter stolen from Marjorie Broad. He had been paid his money in full, and his only grievance with Reeve was that the sum was a tenth of what he had hoped for. His motive therefore could only have been the completely inadequate one of revenge for having been worsted in a bargain.

It looked then as if Cullen might be eliminated. What about Marjorie Broad?

Mrs Broad, it appeared, was faced with a demand for £500 or—not ruin: French could not believe the alternative was as bad as that—but an extremely unpleasant experience. What could she do to help herself? She could raise the money by getting copies made of her jewels and selling the originals, and if she didn't like deceiving her husband to this extent, it would at least be a bagatelle compared to murder. Or she could have refused to pay, got her divorce, married Nettlefold, and put up with poverty. Here again, French was satisfied, there was no adequate motive for murder.

But when he came to consider Nettlefold, French saw that he was dealing with a very different proposition. Nettlefold was in love, and Reeve was hurting the woman he loved. A man who would not dream of taking extreme measures to ease his own position might not hesitate if his beloved's happiness was at stake. Here at last was the necessary motive.

As a result, then, of his analysis, French found that of the thirty-nine persons on Jackson's list, Nettlefold was the only one of whom he still remained doubtful. It was true that Jackson had eliminated Nettlefold, but this was only through the absence of actual incriminating evidence. French determined to review the case of Nettlefold for himself. He could do so if he liked, as Edgar had given him a free hand in such matters. But though this was Saturday, he decided that the work must wait till the following day. He had had a heavy week, and he was stale and tired. With a sigh or relief, he spent the afternoon in the garden, and then after supper set off with his Em to the pictures.

When he looked out next morning at low clouds and driving rain, listened to the wind moaning round the chimneys, and thought of the slippered ease which might be his on this otherwise vacant Sunday, he recalled the Reeve case with disgust. But a little further thought evoked a mental picture of Tony Meadowes sitting despairingly in his cell, and with a shrug he pulled on his outdoor shoes and told Mrs French that he would be away for the day. By ten o'clock he had turned off the main road running west from Staining into Lett's Lane, in which was Mrs Simpson's house.

Marazion, as it called itself, was a four-roomed workman's cottage to which a return had been added, probably to provide a bathroom above and a scullery below. Its red bricks and tiles had grown dark and mellow from age, and climbing roses over the porch softened its somewhat uncompromising outlines. It stood in the middle of a tiny but well-kept garden, and its nearest neighbour was three hundred yards away. It was, in short, what a house agent would have called a small but desirable property.

Now ensued a tedious delay. French wished to interview the landlady alone, and that meant waiting till Nettlefold went out. For an hour he took cover, keeping a discreet eye on the cottage. The rain fortunately had passed over, but it was still windy and cold. At long last, when he felt that he just could bear no more, his patience was rewarded. A man whom he recognized from Jackson's photographs as Nettlefold left the house and walked quickly away. Five minutes later French was at the door, which was at the side of the little building.

For a moment there was no reply to his knock, and he strolled to the rear, thinking that perhaps the back door only was used, as sometimes happens in small houses. Behind there was a sort of unenclosed yard with a shed containing a large stock of firewood blocks, an old-fashioned mangle, a bicycle, and the usual household objects which find their way into such a place. French hesitated, and then he heard the click of the side door.

Mrs Simpson was a little old woman with apple cheeks and bright blue eyes, a manner suggesting character, and a steady flow of not uninteresting conversation. French bade her good morning and signified that he wished to discuss I important business.

She invited him into the kitchen, spotless and comfortable, and pointed to an easy chair.

'What a charming little place you have,' he essayed as he sat down.

'It isn't so bad, is it?' she returned. 'My late husband bought it. He was head gardener up at Rylands—that's Sir Montague Swannington's, you know. Then when he passed over I thought

I'd give it up, but I managed by taking a lodger. I have a nice young man at present; so I'm lucky. Not that I make a lot out of him, you know: just enough, with my own money, to keep the place going.'

French interrupted her. 'Well, now, Mrs Simpson, before you say too much I must tell you that I'm a police officer, and I've come to ask you if you can give me a little help in an inquiry I'm making.'

She looked at him shrewdly. 'You're not my idea of a policeman,' she declared. 'You're not loud enough in the voice and hectoring enough in your manner. A police inspector was here not long ago. I wasn't sorry to see the last of him.'

French smiled. 'For my sins I know a good deal about the police, and I know that they're often worried about their work, just like other people. When that's so they're inclined to be short: we all are. But on the whole they're not a bad lot.'

'That may be, and I may have been unlucky. He was asking about Mr Nettlefold; that's my lodger, you know. But I didn't see why he should come to me. "If you want information about Mr Nettlefold, go to him," I said. And don't you think that was right?'

'About Mr Nettlefold?' French returned in a tone of interested surprise. 'Was it about a divorce he asked you?'

'A divorce?' Her eyes goggled. 'You don't mean to say that Mr Nettlefold's married? Well, well! I'd never have suspected it.'

French smiled. 'No, no; it's not his own divorce. It's the possible divorce of a very nice lady he's interested in.'

'That would be the lady—' Mrs Simpson spoke eagerly, then was silent as if ashamed of having said so much.

But she was no match for French. In a couple of minutes

he knew all about Marjorie Broad's call and the note she had left for Nettlefold—all except her name, which Mrs Simpson had not heard.

'But all this is Mr Nettlefold's secret, Mrs Simpson,' French said. 'You mustn't give it away to anyone else.'

'Law, Mr Policeman, as if I would!'

'I'm sure you wouldn't. You say that was not what the other policeman asked you about?'

'No, I couldn't find out what was in his mind, and I didn't care either. If he wants help, you know, he should learn how to ask for it.'

French had given a good deal of thought to the best way in which to handle the interview. He was in a difficult position, not having the weight and majesty of the law behind him. He must not try to obtain information on false pretences, but on the other hand, strategy to enlist the truth was permissible. He had decided that his only hope was to bluff: to assume that Nettlefold had been out on the night in question and see if she could deny it. As to his being interested in a hypothetical divorce, he hadn't said so, and if she chose to leap to conclusions, that was her lookout.

'You're very hard on the poor man,' he smiled. 'Now, I wonder, can you carry your mind back to the night of Tuesday, the twenty-fifth of last month: that's nearly a month ago. Is there any way in which you can fix it?'

'Why, that's the night the inspector asked me about,' she exclaimed. 'It was the night of the terrible fire when that poor old man was burnt.'

'Was that the night? Well, that's fortunate for me, if it helps you to remember it.' French had been chatting in a light, easy style, but now his manner changed, 'I think I should tell you, Mrs Simpson, that I'm on serious business. What I want to

173

know is the hour at which Mr Nettlefold left this house and returned to it on that night.'

French bluffed well, No one could have doubted his certainty of his major premise. Then to his own amazement, he found that his bluff had worked.

Mrs Simpson's jaw dropped, and for once she seemed at a loss for a reply. Then she stammered, 'The hours? But I don't know.'

'Perhaps we may be able to fix them. To start with, how did you know he had been out? Did you hear him?'

'Well,' she said, 'I didn't say anything about it to the inspector, and I wasn't going to tell you either, for Mr Nettlefold's a nice young man and I wouldn't harm him on any account. But since you know all about it, I may tell you. I heard him coming in.'

French could scarcely credit his good luck. 'Quite,' he returned in a matter-of-fact tone. 'Coming in. But not going out?'

'No, I've no idea when he went out.'

'Very well. Now when did you hear him coming in?'

'Just before three. I happened to be awake, and I heard the clock strike just after he came in.'

'I suppose you were pretty curious about his being out at that time in the morning?'

'Oh, no. You see I didn't know then that he was out—not then. I thought he had just gone down to his sitting-room for something.'

French was puzzled, but he must not show it. 'I understand. It wasn't till afterwards that you discovered he had been out. Just how did you learn it?'

Mrs Simpson hesitated and looked as if she was sorry she had spoken. But again she was no match for French, and soon she told him. 'It was the shoe box,' she explained reluctantly. 'I have a box in the kitchen with brushes and so on for the shoes, you know, and I saw that morning that it had been disturbed: not left as I had left it, if you understand. Well, that made me think, because, you know, it could only have been Mr Nettlefold. I wondered why he had been there.'

'He doesn't clean his own shoes?'

'No, no; that's part of the service he pays for. I do them.'

'I follow. You wondered what he had been doing?'

'Yes, because his soiled shoes were here in the kitchen, just as I had brought them down the night before. So I was interested. I shouldn't have been, of course, for it was no business of mine, but there it was: just an old woman's curiosity.'

'Very natural, and no "old" about it either,' French said smoothly. 'And how did you satisfy your curiosity?' He wished she would get on quicker.

'When I was doing his room I looked at the shoes that were there, and one pair that I knew he hadn't worn for three or four days were very wet. But they had been cleaned.'

'My word,' French smiled, 'we'll have to get you into the force to give us a hand. That was very good. Did you find out anything else?'

'Well, I did, but I'm not proud of it. I had a look at the coats hanging in the passage, and one was wet. It was a heavy one that I hadn't seen Mr Nettlefold wear for some days.'

French was profoundly impressed with this news, but he joked with the old lady and made light of it. A few more adroit questions, and he became satisfied that he had learnt all that she could tell him.

'Just one other point,' he concluded. 'Why did you not tell the inspector what you've told me?'

She tossed her head. 'Tell him anything? Not me! He'll have to learn some manners first!'

'But don't you know,' French said mildly—he had got what he wanted—'that it's a serious matter to keep back information from the police?'

'I kept back no information. I didn't know that Mr Nettlefold was out. I took it I should not report my suppositions as facts.'

French stood up to go. 'That's all right,' he smiled. 'Now I want this interview to be a little secret between you and me. I shall have to come back to see Mr Nettlefold in any case, but there's no reason that he should know of your researches into his secrets. He mightn't like it. Better say nothing to him about it, and neither will I.' He could see that now she bitterly regretted her indiscretion, but he felt that she would follow his advice.

Returning to the main road, he walked into Staining, got himself some lunch, and called at Jackson's house.

'Sorry to worry you on a Sunday,' he apologized, 'but I think I'm on to something which will interest you. It seems to me a case for striking while the iron's hot. Any objection to coming on duty for a while?'

'Of course not, sir. What am I to do?'

'Come with me to interview Nettlefold,' and French explained what he had learnt.

French had seldom seen anyone so crestfallen as Jackson. 'And I reported him O.K.,' he kept on saying. 'The super'll have something to say about that. How did you get on to it, sir?'

French told him, adding that he must not assume that their problem had been solved. It was still possible that Nettlefold could explain his action innocently.

But when an hour later they put the question to the man himself, he did not attempt to explain it. Instead he denied it, and that with a fine show of indignation. 'I told you before, Inspector,' he declared, 'that I had not been out on that or any other night, and I tell you so again. If you don't believe me, you don't, and that's all there's to it. I'm not interested in your theories, but I am in your actions, and if you annoy me I shall know where to look for redress.'

Jackson, who had handled the interview, was about to press the man further, but at a sign from French he desisted, and presently they took their leave.

'That's all we want for the present,' French pointed out. 'The matter has been put to him, and he's denied it point-blank. But he doesn't know whether he has satisfied us, and if he has accomplices he'll communicate with them. Now will you arrange a shadow? I'll wait here till your man arrives, and if Nettlefold comes out and I have to follow him, I'll put a note under this stone.'

For nearly an hour French waited; then Jackson reappeared with a constable. 'I thought I'd come along myself with the car,' he explained, 'so as to give you a seat back into Staining. What's our next step, sir?'

'Don't you think we should report to Superintendent Edgar? He'd probably be interested.'

'I expect you're right,' Jackson agreed gloomily; 'in fact, of course you are. I'd have to in any case, and I should be much better pleased if you were there.'

Edgar heard the story impassively. He formally thanked French for his efforts, which, though he had not forgotten the motive, looked as if they were going to bear fruit. He would think over the information and let French know later what action he was taking.

'But we've put a watch on Nettlefold, sir,' put in Jackson anxiously.

'That's all right: an excellent move.'

There was no mistaking Edgar's manner, and French reluctantly took his leave. He wondered whether he had done all that he could, and if the matter was now to be taken out of his hands. If he heard no more or if Edgar's communication was unsympathetic, he did not think he dared interest himself any further in the case.

However, next afternoon he found out that Edgar had done better than he could have hoped. The assistant commissioner, Sir Mortimer Ellison, called him to his room and handed him a letter. It was from Major Goodliffe, the chief constable of the Staining county, officially asking for French's help in the case. 'My superintendent informs me that your chief inspector approached him on the matter,' he wrote, 'unofficially and in a perfectly correct manner, as he happened to know the man who has been arrested for the crime, and from his knowledge of his character, he believed him innocent. As you can imagine, we are as anxious as Mr French to avoid charging the wrong man, and my superintendent arranged for Mr French to see the case file. From this, working during the weekend, Mr French made a discovery which may vitally affect the issue.

'As a result of a suggestion from my superintendent—in which I concur—I now ask whether you could allow Chief Inspector French to complete the work he has begun? If so, please accept this letter as a definite application for help in the case.'

It was in this way that French obtained what he had never hoped for: not only all the time that he wanted to investigate the affair, but also an official standing which would put behind him the entire weight of the county and Yard forces. Slightly overwhelmed by what his action had brought about, he told himself that now at all events he could not afford to fail in the job.

14

The Progress of an Investigation

Next morning French was at Staining early, this time with his 'murder bag' in his hand and Sergeant Carter in attendance: both symbols of Yard authority. In his new position he expected to receive a very different greeting from Jackson, who would now naturally fear the loss of whatever credit the case might have brought him. But Jackson was just as friendly as ever, and French supposed that in view of the new turn in the affair, he was glad to be relieved of responsibility.

'You were right about Nettlefold, sir,' he said when French had reported his arrival to Edgar, who happened that week to be acting chief constable. 'He did just what you said: came into Staining after we left on Sunday, and phoned from a street booth.'

'Yes, sir. Our shadow rang up the exchange when he left the booth and asked them to note the call. Mr Edgar got the number later from the postmaster. It was to Mrs Broad.'

'Then we might get something out of Mrs Broad. You haven't seen her?'

'No, sir. I waited for you.'

'Then I think w'e'd better do it first thing. Can you come, Inspector, or shall I take Carter?'

Jackson hesitated. 'I would be glad if you could excuse me, sir,' he said reluctantly. 'I've got badly behind with my other work.'

French felt for the man, as he recognized Edgar's hand in the decision. For himself, he was pleased. He and Carter knew each other's ways and suited each other.

'As you like, but I shall be sorry not to have you with me.' Lying from kindliness French thought a virtue. 'Very well, if you can't come, we'll get on.'

On general principles French had intended to interrogate Marjorie Broad as one of his first steps, and this news that Nettlefold had rung her up made him even keener to hear her statement. Edgar had put a small car at his disposal, and he and Carter were soon driving out westwards along a road from which, between trees and across fields, occasional views of the Thames could be obtained.

It was a pleasant country, though a little too sophisticated for French. He preferred the heaths of Surrey or the hills and moors of Devon to the 'places' of the well-to-do. The Limes was pre-eminently of the latter class. It was some three miles from Staining, and like most of the neighbouring properties, stretched from the road to the river. It covered an area, French imagined, of five or six acres, all well wooded, and from the front of the house, when presently they drove up, there was a charming view of a long curving reach.

The door was opened by the butler. Mrs Broad, he explained had gone out. He didn't know when she would be in, but he thought shortly.

'I see,' said French. 'You're Cullen, I suppose?'

'I'm the butler,' he replied with veiled insolence in his tones.

French took a sudden decision. He had not intended to interrogate this man until later. Now he saw he would be unlikely to have a better opportunity. Rapidly he sized him up. To be kind and considerate to those with whom he came into contact was a major article of his creed, but he realized that there were cases in which the velvet glove would achieve nothing. This, he thought, was one of them. To obtain Cullen's information would, he felt sure, require something more drastic.

'I see,' he repeated. 'Well, butler, I'm Chief Inspector French of Scotland Yard, and I'd be glad of a word with you.'

The man stiffened as if he scented danger. 'What is it you require?' he asked, still standing at the door.

A little suggestion appeared to be indicated. 'Blackmail is an ugly-sounding word,' French remarked casually. 'Would you prefer to discuss it here, or somewhere more private?'

There was no mistaking the mixture of fear and hate which showed in Cullen's eyes. But he opened the door and motioned them in. 'Come in here,' he invited, not too graciously.

He showed them to a plainly furnished room just inside the door and stood waiting. French and Carter sat down, the latter ostentatiously opening his notebook. Both men had serious expressions.

'Now Cullen—have you yet remembered your name?'

'I never denied my name. I'm not ashamed of it.'

'Naturally. Now, Cullen, as I was saying, blackmail is an ugly crime, and a conviction always means a long stretch. Eh? What did you say?'

'I didn't say anything, but I don't know why you should be talking like this.' His voice was still gruff, but the fear in his eyes was growing.

'You don't? Well, I shall explain. But there's another ugly crime that the judges dislike equally, and that's conspiracy to blackmail: I mean when one party supplies the evidence and the other demands cash.'

Cullen hung his head. 'That other inspector said there'd be nothing about it,' he murmured.

'Ah, but this is worse than mere conspiracy to blackmail, bad as that is. Theft's a very serious matter, Cullen; stealing letters out of a desk is a thing—' French shook his head as if words failed him to do justice to his theme.

The man was ghastly. He attempted a reply, but his voice faltered and died away inconclusively. French believed he would now get what he wanted.

'We don't wish to charge you with that at the moment, but we can do so at any time, and don't you forget it. I'm investigating the murder of Albert Reeve, and I want to ask you a few questions.'

The new subject did not seem more to Cullen's taste. He murmured that he knew nothing of it.

'I think you can help me all the same. What I want is everything you can tell me about the friendship between Mrs Broad and Mr Nettlefold. I wish to explain I'm not concerned with their likes or dislikes, but only with Reeve's murder. So you won't injure either of them by anything you may say— unless of course you can connect them with the murder, which I don't imagine you can.'

A flash of relief passed over Cullen's face. 'I can't connect either of them with that, sir,' and his manner was now more respectful, 'because I'm certain they're both innocent.'

He spoke with such conviction that French was impressed. 'Now that interests me,' he said more pleasantly. 'How are you so sure?'

'Well—er—I feel sure—er—that neither of them would do that sort of thing.'

'I see. You know Mrs Broad well, of course?'

'I've been in her service for over five years.'

'Quite. How well do you know Mr Nettlefold?'

Cullen's face fell.

'You scarcely know him at all,' French broke in. 'How many times in your life have you seen him?'

'He's been here—different times.'

'How many? Remember I can check what you say.' The sweat broke out on Cullen's forehead, but he made no reply.

'I see,' said French. 'You don't know him at all. But you were sure of his innocence. Just why?'

The man hesitated as if in thought. 'I didn't—er—believe that Mrs Broad would have—er—taken up with anyone that was—wasn't—er—all right.'

French frowned angrily. 'Don't talk rubbish, man! You know he's innocent, but you won't say how.' Just one other turn of the screw, he thought, and thrusting forward his face aggressively, he said in a tone of surprise: 'It's not that you were at Myrtle Cottage yourself that night, is it? Can you account for your own time on the night of the murder?'

The question was rhetorical: part of French's technique, but its effects were far-reaching.

'You don't suspect me of the murder?' Cullen gasped with horror-stricken features.

French called into play his immense powers of bluff, which had so often stood him in good stead in the past. 'By your own showing you know something that happened that night and you refuse to say what it was. What else can I suspect?'

For some moments Cullen did not reply, evidently thinking intently. Then he shrugged.

'I don't know why I shouldn't tell you. It won't hurt anyone. I saw them both that night.'

184

'Oh, you saw them? Where was that?'

'In the summer-house.' He gestured vaguely towards the left.

Without further delay the story came out, or at least its greater part. Cullen's belief, from Marjorie's manner, that she had received Reeve's blackmailing letter, and his suspicion that she had been to consult Nettlefold; his seeing her coming downstairs at half-past one next morning and his following her to the summer-house. Then the interview with Nettlefold, and her return to the house, followed eventually by his own. Only his pursuit of Nettlefold did he keep back.

That he had obtained some important information French saw at once, but he put out of his mind its possible implications and devoted himself to checking up its details. He waited till Marjorie came in, taxed her with the affair, and heard her version. Then he and Carter returned to Nettlefold, and this time had no difficulty in obtaining his.

Perhaps the most important part of the statement was its chronology. Here all three witnesses agreed. They had met at 1.30 a.m. and the lovers had talked for an hour, till just half-past two. Under the special circumstances all three had noted the time.

French felt that he might unhesitatingly accept the statements. They were confirmed by no less than five considerations. First, it was obvious that Cullen had kept his eavesdropping secret from the others and they therefore could not have made up an agreed tale. Secondly, the manner of all three was that of persons speaking the truth. Thirdly, French had questioned them on irrelevant details, which, had they invented the story, they never could have covered. Fourthly, from The Limes to Marazion was two miles, and if Nettlefold had walked home, as he said he had, he would have arrived just when Mrs

Simpson heard him coming in. Lastly, there was the matter of the rain, introduced by Mrs Simpson's investigations. Cullen and Marjorie said that no rain fell while they were out; Nettlefold declared it began just after he left The Limes. From a phone to police headquarters French learnt that a heavy shower had come on just after half-past two and had stopped about three.

To complete the chronology a check on Jackson's timetable of the fire would be required. French therefore drove to the fire station and induced the chief to go out with him to Myrtle Cottage.

The house was less damaged than French had expected. The fire had obviously originated in the hall, and the floor, staircase, ceiling, and roof over this area were completely destroyed. But the hall was separated from the rooms on either side by walls of nine-inch brickwork, and these had stood fast. The doors had burnt out and the rooms had got alight, but they were not gutted like the centre of the house. The hall door was of solid oak, and though it was charred three-quarters of the way through, the outside remained unaffected. Circumstances had conspired against Tony. The wind had clearly kept the knob cool, preserving his fingerprints, while a small overhanging roof had prevented the rain from washing them off.

The hour of the outbreak had been fixed fairly accurately. The brigade had reached the place a minute or two after four, and the chief believed that the house had been burning for about half an hour. As near as didn't matter, therefore, the fire had started about half-past three.

Then as to the murder, assuming for the moment it had been committed at the same time and not on the previous evening. How long would it have taken?

Here French was on less solid ground. Probably the

murderer began by ringing at the door and bringing Reeve down from his bed. That surely could not have been done under, say, three minutes. Then some parley must have taken place to induce Reeve to open the door: say another two minutes. The murder itself, including the arranging of the body, would have taken at least another three. Next would come the starting of the fire. Paraffin had doubtless been poured over the floors, and perhaps piles of sticks built at vital points against woodwork. French did not think this would have been possible in less than seven or eight minutes: say, fifteen minutes altogether. Indeed, though he assumed this figure, he really believed it too low. If correct, it would have fixed the murderer's arrival at 3.15 at the very latest.

It looked therefore as if the meeting at the summer-house would prove an alibi for all three participants. Obviously Nettlefold could not have been at Myrtle Cottage, since he reached Marazion just before 3.00. He was therefore definitely out of it. But what about Cullen and Marjorie?

Here the problem required to be restated. Could a person who was at The Limes at 2.30 have reached Myrtle Cottage by 3.15? The distance via Staining—the nearest bridge—was four and a half miles: therefore it could not have been done by walking. But with a car or bicycle it would have been easy.

French considered making a search for these; then he thought it unnecessary. He felt satisfied that neither of these two was guilty: Marjorie because this was not a woman's crime and because after his interview with her he simply could not conceive of her doing such a thing, and Cullen because, as he had already seen, he had no adequate motive.

French feared that it looked bad for Tony. Here was proof of the innocence of the only other possible suspects of whom he knew.

But stay! Was it? Why should not Nettlefold—or Cullen—have committed the murder before the summer-house meeting: before 9.30 indeed, if the medical evidence and Tony's statement were true?

A moment's thought gave French the answer. At 9.30 neither man had a motive. Before the meeting Nettlefold had not known of Reeve's letter to Marjorie. In Cullen's case French's previous argument still stood.

When late that evening he reached home, French felt tired and dispirited. He had set out believing that he had made a brilliant discovery which would confound the local police and set Tony at liberty, and all he had done was to prove them right and himself wrong. It looked as if he were going to let Cecily Meadowes and her brother down. But after that case of Merle Weir at Little Bitton, he could not afford any further damage to his prestige. In the present affair he simply must not fail.

Of course, the line which he must follow was obvious. If all thirty-nine suspects, including Tony, were innocent, and he now believed they were, it followed that the murderer was not among them and that there must therefore be a fortieth suspect. But how, and where, could he find him?

Reeve's card index was the natural mine for such information. But Jackson had worked it out, and with efficiency. And French had checked his results.

French now realized with what justification Edgar had acted in arresting Tony. In his position he could scarcely have done otherwise. But French's own conviction of Tony's innocence was not a whit weakened by what he had learnt.

He thought over the problem for most of the night, but without result. Fortunately, so far as his next day's activities were concerned, a number of routine matters required attention, and these must be worked off before he need consider striking out on new lines.

The first was to interview Tony. The wisdom of this he had considered carefully. As investigating officer he had to be very circumspect as to his dealings with an arrested suspect, and normally he would have avoided Tony as the plague. But under the special circumstances he felt he must have his story at first hand. He therefore rang up East, told him what he proposed, and invited him to be present. To this East agreed, and the interview was arranged.

Though French did not learn a great deal from Tony, the meeting strengthened his belief in the young man's innocence. Tony's hearing was reassuring. He was evidently profoundly ashamed of the cowardly part he had played in not at once reporting what he had seen. This he admitted and made no attempt to justify, and his attitude induced confidence in the remainder of his statement. French was satisfied also that he was genuinely puzzled as to what had happened to Reeve.

Tony insisted that had it become necessary, he could have obtained the money to pay his debt from his mother. He didn't ask her for it, first, because he didn't want her to know what a fool he had been, and secondly, because it might have meant their leaving Riverview. If this statement were true, and French thought it was, it showed that Tony had no real motive for so grave a crime as murder. Tony also explained satisfactorily why he had chosen 9.30 to pay his call. Another useful statement was that he had been reading up delayed-action fire-raisers for the book on which he was then working.

French next went to Riverview and found the typed chapter in question. From there he called on Dr Hawke who was polite, though anything but cordial. The doctor would neither vary nor add to his formal report and expressed a perhaps

189

justifiable annoyance that he should be asked to repeat it in words. French, while realizing the correctness of his attitude, had hoped to get a more definite opinion as to the time which had elapsed between Reeve's death and the fire, but on this, Hawke was not to be drawn.

Returning to the station, French spent some time in writing up his notes. His morning's activities had thrown no light on his next step, and when presently he went out with Carter for lunch, he felt more dispirited than ever. As he gloomily surveyed the problem over his rapidly disappearing steak and kidney pie, it suddenly occurred to him that there was one matter which he had rather taken for granted. This was that the financial statements on Reeve's cards checked up with those in his bank book. He had compared a number of items at random and found that these did so, but he had not followed the details through consistently.

It seemed an unnecessary labour, and yet here was something checkable, though unchecked. Training and experience had taught him that in his work *nothing* should be taken for granted.

On returning to police headquarters, he therefore set to work. He succeeded in matching most, though not all, of the items. In a large number of cases the figures were identical in both entries, but in others they only approximated. Thus a receipt of, say, £50 on the card might be followed a day or two later by a lodgement of £45 in the bank. French took it that these referred to the same transaction, Reeve having retained £5 for his personal expenses. He thought the coincidence of the dates justified the assumption.

Having found that practically all the card items were represented in the bank book, French turned to the converse inquiry: whether Reeve had had dealings with the bank which were not shown on the cards. This was really the point of his investigation, as it was obvious that other channels of income might represent other potential murderers.

At once he found a series. The entries were all for £75 and appeared at the beginning of every quarter, going back as far as the book, which was eight years old. These were the only such items, and it seemed obvious that the payments came from the same source.

French was keenly interested. Here was some unknown individual who had been bled cruelly by the deceased, and who therefore had as strong a motive for murder as any prosecuting counsel could desire. This was progress! He had only to find the victim, and in all probability his problem would be solved.

But why had there been no card covering these transactions? A moment's thought only was needed. Was it not because the murderer had removed it? It would be an obvious way of attempting to divert suspicion. Reeve's keys were in his bedroom, and it would have been easy to open the safe, take out the card, and lock up again.

Though this seemed reasonable, French was not entirely satisfied with it. Would not the murderer have foreseen the inquiry he had just made?

French thought he might have done so, but would have been unable to safeguard himself. Obviously he could not have altered the bank book. To attempt it would have been to call immediate attention to the transactions. Nor could he have replaced his own card with a forged one bearing the financial items under a false name. This also would have simply advertised the matter. No, all he could do would be to remove the card. There was always the chance that its absence would not be discovered and that if it were it would not lead to him.

That Tony was innocent French was now more than ever convinced, and that he would soon have his hands on the real murderer he was equally sure. But when he began to consider how he was to find the man, he quickly grew less sanguine.

Obviously he must apply to the manager of Reeve's bank in Town. But it was probable that Reeve's transactions had been carried out in cash, so that help from that source was unlikely. If so, what remained? There was no hint as to which bank of all the thousands in the country the unknown might have dealt with, and even if this were ascertained, the manager would never allow the general search of his books necessary for identification.

It was a more difficult problem than French had imagined at first sight; indeed he began to wonder if it were soluble. If not, he was no further on than before he had made his discovery. The knowledge that an unknown existed who probably had a motive to murder Reeve would not help Tony Meadowes.

Six o'clock found French still pondering the matter, and it remained in his thoughts as he left the police station with Carter on his way back to Town. But his day in Staining was not yet ended. He had scarcely gone a hundred yards when a small car slid up to the footpath and he heard his name called.

It was Cecily Meadowes. 'Oh, Mr French,' she cried, 'what does this mean? Does it give me hope?'

Carter walked on as French turned towards her. 'Well, I'm looking into the case,' he answered, 'but I'm afraid it's too soon to talk about hope.'

'Thank God that you're looking into it,' she returned earnestly. 'That does give me hope, and I can't say how grateful I am. But how did you manage it? Do tell me! Look, get in

192

and I'll drive you wherever you were going. Or better still, come home and have supper, and tell me about everything.'

French hesitated. After all, why not? He was really there at her request, and it was natural that she should wish to hear his news. 'It's very kind of you,' he said. 'Very well, I'll accept. But first let me tell my sergeant.'

Having arrived at Riverview, Cecily promptly vanished towards the kitchen. Presently reappearing, she told French that her mother was too ill to come down, but that she had invited Grace Farson, Tony's fiancée, to join them in supper. 'She will be so keen to hear what you have to say,' Cecily went on. 'She's one of the best, and she's very fond of Tony.'

'But, my dear young lady,' French protested, 'I'm afraid you're expecting too much. I have very little to tell you, and none of it particularly hopeful.'

'Never mind; she'd be furious with me if she hadn't seen you.'

Grace came over and was quiet and self-contained. They gave French an excellent meal and did not pester him with questions till it was over. Then, having installed him in the easiest chair before the fire, with his pipe going and a liqueur coffee beside him, Cecily suggested that if there was anything about the case which he thought he could properly tell them, they would be thrilled to hear it.

French, having warned them that all police matters were confidential, recounted a good deal of what he had done. He described Reeve's more criminal activities, mentioned the thirty-nine alibis. He portrayed the lovers' midnight meeting and the butler's solicitude in their proceedings, but without giving away identities. Finally, he explained his analysis of the deceased's finances, and his desire to find someone who drew £75 out of his bank on about the beginning of each quarter.

Open-mouthed, they hung on his words. 'Surely,' they said, 'that means that Tony is innocent?'

French shook his head. 'I warned you not to be too hopeful. Unless we can find this unknown man and prove his guilt, and so far I don't see any way of doing it, it won't help Tony. Of course, I shall try to find him, but you mustn't expect too much. I may admit at once that I'm not likely to succeed.'

'But doesn't the mere fact that someone other than Tony has been involved and has carefully hidden his traces suggest that he, not Tony, is guilty?'

French shrugged. 'It suggests it to you, who already believe in Tony's innocence. But it might not suggest it to a jury, and it by no means proves it. No, unless we can find the man who was being bled, I'm afraid we're no further on.'

More than this French would not say. He was particularly anxious not to raise their hopes unduly. He pretended indeed to more despondency than he actually felt: in their interests.

15

The Assistance of an Amateur

When French had left, the two young women sat on over the fire, talking eagerly.

'I just can't believe it!' Cecily declared again and again. 'I went to see Mr French as a council of despair. It never entered my head that he could do anything himself; at best I thought he might suggest something for Mr East to try. And now he's in the case, and working for Tony! It's better than anything I could have hoped.'

Grace nodded. 'I thought it was hopeless too when you said you were going. I've read that these Scotland Yard men can't interfere unless they're called in by the local police.'

'They can't. Mr French said so himself. But look how he's got over the difficulty!'

'Yes; wonderful! And you think he's really good, Cecily?'

'Well,' Cecily leant forward to stir up the fire, 'he's got a great name, you know. And I thought he was marvellous on that ship. So quiet and pleasant and unassuming, and working away all the time. And getting the murderer! So clever! I heard about his photographic experiments; wonderful, I thought them.'

'I know, I've read about some of his cases. But you know, Cecily, I don't want to pour cold water, but he wasn't very hopeful tonight.'

'That's his way. It was exactly the same on board. I knew the girl who was in love with the suspected man—quite like this case, only that he hadn't been arrested as Tony has—and he wouldn't give her any encouragement, even though he must have known the chap wasn't guilty.'

'Extraordinary. I wonder why?'

'Not to raise false hopes, I think. No, I don't think we need worry about his manner. I don't for a moment believe that he would have taken up the case if he hadn't believed Tony innocent.'

'I'm almost afraid to hope. If I hoped and was disappointed I think I'd die.'

'You won't be disappointed: something tells me. I believe in Mr French and I believe that he'll pull it off. You know, I think he's practically proved Tony's innocence already.'

'Oh, Cecily, how do you make that out? I wish I could see it.'

'Well, look at it! Reeve was blackmailing someone else whom they've not yet traced. This person took his card out of the file. Why should he do so? Surely only to avoid being suspected.'

'Reeve might have taken out the card himself. Or there might never have been a card.'

'Oh, rubbish, Grace!' Cecily was impatient. 'With such carefully kept accounts? What nonsense!'

'I expect you're right; I hope so at all events. Of course Mr French did say that unless they got the man it would be no good. I wonder, Cecily, how he'll trace him?'

Cecily shook her head. 'I don't know, but he'll manage somehow.'

'Yes, but—' Grace came to an abrupt halt and sat staring at her companion. Cecily looked back in sudden surprise.

'What is it?' she asked sharply. 'Probably nothing,' Grace returned, obviously controlling her eagerness. 'All the same, let's go through the points he made.'

'What points?'

'About tracing that man. He could only be traced, he said, through his bank account: by finding an account from which £75 was drawn out every quarter. But there were two difficulties in the way; first, to find the particular bank out of all the thousands there are in the country, and secondly, having found it, to search through the books for the client. He indicated that both were pretty insuperable.'

Cecily made a gesture of exasperation. 'Oh, Grace, don't be so depressing! Here for the first time for weeks we've got some hope, and now you're pouring on cold water!'

'Of course I'm not! It's only'—her voice became hesitating, but still more eager—'because I think I've got an idea.'

Cecily stared. 'An idea! Then for Heaven's sake out with it! What has occurred to you?'

'Don't expect too much; there mayn't be anything in it. It's simply that where Mr French can't get his information, you might be able to.'

Cecily stared. 'For the love of Mike, will you explain that?'

'Do you remember it's only a suggestion,' Grace said earnestly. 'Take difficulty No. 1. Now isn't there at least a sporting chance that the account might be in a staining bank?'

'How do you make that out?'

'Simply from what Mr French told you of the case against Tony. Don't you remember that one of the indications was that the murderer might be a local man because no traces of a car were found: don't you remember?'

'Of course.'

'But if he were a local man he might bank locally.'

Cecily shook her head. 'I don't think there's very much in that, you know. It's not proved he's a local man, and even if he was, he might bank in Town.'

'I agree there's nothing in the nature of proof. But there's what I might call a reasonable chance.'

'Oh, yes, I grant you that. What then?'

'Simply that you have an entry to the books of the principal bank in Staining, and Mr French hasn't.'

'I—?' Cecily looked as if her friend had gone mad.

Grace jerked about impatiently. 'Oh, Cecily, don't be so dense! Don't you see? Ronald Barrymore!'

'You mean—' Cecily stammered.

'Yes, *yes*, YES!' retorted Grace with exasperation. 'I mean that Ronald must search the books!'

'Oh, Grace, do you really think—?'

'Of course I do! It's a chance! We daren't miss it!'

Talking over the idea, Cecily passed rapidly from doubt to hope and from hope to enthusiasm. Then she veered round towards doubt again. 'It's an idea certainly, but I wonder if Ronald would do it. I expect it would be against his principles.'

'Principles!' returned Grace scornfully. 'What do you think *you're* for? If you can't make him, you don't deserve to get Tony back. Why, the chap's crazy about you.'

'I think he's fond of me,' Cecily admitted judicially, 'but he's a bit queer in some ways. I don't mean *that*, you mutt,' as Grace giggled; 'I mean he's very law-abiding and all that. And the bank! Why, it's sacred, and its regulations are laws of nature. Besides, he might get sacked if he was found out.'

'What matter if he was? No, that was silly. I mean, it's for

Tony. Even if he did lose his job, it's a small thing against Tony's life.'

'I could try,' Cecily agreed.

'Try? You'll have to do a fat lot more than try.' Suddenly Grace's whole heart was in her words. 'If you don't make him do it, Cecily, you'll have failed Tony.'

Cecily sighed. 'You're a good sort, Grace. You're right. I'll manage him somehow.'

She continued to think over her problem after Grace had gone home. Of Ronald and his history she knew a good deal, partly from his own confidence, and partly through a former schoolfellow who had known the family intimately. He was, so her friend had said, a home bird, longing for domestic bliss rather than adventure. To come home after a day's work, to meet and greet the Woman of Women, to have a meal together at his own table in his own house, then with her to chat and plan and potter about his own garden: that for him would be heaven. Cecily's friend thought this was due to his upbringing, which had not been too happy. His mother, a charming woman, had given him everything possible of understanding and sympathy. But his mother had died while he was still young, and his stepmother, who arrived a year or so later, had a son of her own and had no tenderness left for Ronald. She was not deliberately unkind, but to Ronald it made the difference between heaven and hell. To get back what he had lost became his subconscious aim, and it was through marriage that he hoped to achieve it.

At school he had proved himself, moderate in all things. In his work he was neither brilliant nor dull, and his play was uninspired though steady. He was slow in everything he did, but tenacious once he got going, and he had a vein of solid common sense which stood by him in the hour of need.

When schooldays were over he took to banking, not because he particularly preferred it, but as the line of least resistance, an uncle being a bank inspector and using his good offices to get him a start. In the bank he had been, as at school, slow, plodding, accurate, and conscientious. It was believed that he gave satisfaction to his superiors and was marked out for moderate promotion. So at least said Cecily's friend.

Then came his meeting with Cecily, who quickly realized that he had fallen for her. But they met but seldom, and she had been impressed by his plan of obtaining contacts by joining the Repertory as a stage carpenter. At the time of Tony's arrest she had been expecting a proposal, and she had practically decided that when it came she would accept him.

Next morning she began the campaign by writing him a short note. She was sorry to have seen so little of him lately, though of course he knew the reason. She was now in a difficulty, and she thought that perhaps he could help her, at least by his advice. If so, she simply could not express her gratitude. Would he come round that night to supper and discuss it? She left the note at his rooms, and later he telephoned acceptance.

He was not one to hide his feelings, and when on arrival he discovered that Grace Farson was to make a third at the party, he looked vastly disappointed. Cecily smiled with satisfaction and was more than charming to him. Grace also was tactful. After the meal she remembered a commission at her home and had to go back for half an hour to see it.

When she returned she found Ronald in the same comfortable chair which French had occupied on the previous evening, with coffee at one side and cigarettes at the other. Cecily was sitting on a humpty on the hearth rug. It was all very intimate and domestic.

'Come along, Grace,' said Cecily. 'Pull in that chair, and then we'll all be comfy. Ronald and I were just talking about the case. I was saying that we were up against a terrible difficulty.'

Grace agreed with fervour.

'I don't know when,' Cecily went on plaintively, 'I've been so worried. You know,' she turned brave but pathetic eyes on Ronald, 'things are not going too well with the defence.'

Ronald was overwhelmed to hear it. He had supposed that there was no slightest doubt of an acquittal.

Grace then took up the tale. There was every doubt of it, and poor Cecily was terribly, *terribly* worried. And the worst of it was that there was a possible line of defence, but it was beyond her power to follow it up herself, and she had no one to do it for her.

'Yes,' Cecily confirmed the story. 'Neither of us can do anything, and we feel so—it's hard to describe—helpless, so frustrated, so alone. But there,' she went on with even more pathetic bravery, 'I mustn't grouse like this. Sorry for being such a wet blanket.'

Ronald looked satisfactorily upset. 'Oh, Cecily,' he exclaimed earnestly, 'if I could only do anything! You said you thought I might help. What is it?'

Cecily looked at him gratefully. 'You are good, Ronald. You did offer to help before, and now perhaps you might. I wondered if your offer still stands?'

'Still stands?' he repeated, indignantly. 'How do you mean, still stands? Why, of course it does! To help would be a delight. Surely I made that clear?'

'Oh, yes, it's not that I questioned. But circumstances change, and we can't always do what we'd like.'

'Nothing would change my wanting to help you. You know that, don't you, Cecily?'

'I never doubted it for a moment. All the same I can't say how grateful I am to hear you renewing your promise. It's tremendous ease to our minds, isn't it, Grace?'

Grace entirely agreed. It *was* an ease to their minds, though she herself had never doubted that they could depend on Ronald. They had not called on him before because there had been nothing that he could do, but the knowledge that he had been there, ready to help, had been a tremendous strength and comfort to both of them.

Cecily, afraid she was overdoing it, glanced at her nervously. But Ronald was not in a critical frame of mind. He reacted magnificently, only growing more and more anxious to justify this wonderful trust. She could almost see him thinking that no one but an out-and-out cad could possibly let them down. She breathed more freely.

When he was pledged absolutely up to the hilt they told him what they wanted. In the strictest confidence Cecily described her interview with French and his statement about the unknown who paid Reeve £75 at the beginning of every quarter. 'Mr French thinks this man is the murderer,' she went on, 'and if so, of course it would save Tony, and all this dreadful affair would be over and we could all be normal again. But the difficulty is to find him. Mr French didn't know how it was to be done.'

'But that's frightfully good,' said Ronald, who had not yet seen where all this was leading. 'That's a definite line of defence, and Scotland Yard is working on it.'

'That's absolutely correct,' Cecily admitted, with evident admiration for his perspicacity. 'But the trouble is that Mr French is completely up against it, because of the difficulty of getting the information. He said that no manager would allow his ledgers to be examined by the police.'

With this, Ronald, who was at last experiencing some misgivings, wholeheartedly agreed. 'Utterly impossible,' he declared promptly. 'He's right there. Banks can't give away information about their clients, and the law protects them in that.'

'So he said.' Cecily's voice was sweet as milk. 'Therefore the murderer can only be discovered by someone in the banking service. Oh, Ronald, won't you help us?'

Ronald looked horrified. At last he saw the cavern opening beneath his feet. 'But, good heavens, Cecily,' he exclaimed in a choked voice, 'you don't mean that I—?'

'I honestly believe,' Cecily spoke in a low tone but very earnestly, 'that Tony's life depends on it.'

'But—' Ronald moved about in his chair and wiped little beads off his forehead—'I don't see how I could. It would mean—' He broke off and sat motionless, slowly weighing up what this outrageous demand really involved. Suddenly he brightened up.

'But why do you think this unknown banks with us?' he said with some eagerness. 'You don't, of course, imagine that I could go to any other branch?'

'No, of course not,' and Cecily explained. His face again fell.

'I'm afraid—' he was beginning at last, but she interrupted him.

'For the sake of Tony's life,' she said softly. 'For the sake of my happiness.'

That did it. He said, and could only say, that he would do his best. He thought it would take a good deal of time, but agreed to hurry as much as possible. Finally a report-progress meeting was arranged for two nights later.

When at the prearranged time he turned up, he looked like

a man who has been through trouble. 'It's rather a job you gave me, you know,' he declared. 'It's not been easy, but I have managed something. I suppose you know that if I'm caught I'll be sacked on the spot?'

They were filled with distress at such a hideous and utterly unforeseen possibility, as well as with praise and gratitude for his marvellous courage and resource. Incidentally they would like to know exactly what he had discovered.

'You know, it hasn't been easy,' Ronald went on, imagining from their manner that they would be interested in the details of his effort. 'It has meant looking up the ledgers. Well, I have to do that quite often; we all have to, and we all have access to them. The trouble is the time it takes. This is not a very big branch, but we have four ledgers, each with something like four hundred accounts. So you see it's a terrific job. However, I pretended to make a mistake in some of my work, and got it arranged that I was to work late to find it. I spent practically all night at it, and I've been through the accounts for one quarter, the beginning of last October. I didn't go through every account—I simply couldn't have done it in the time. I eliminated people that I felt sure must be beyond suspicion.'

'Oh, but, Ronald dear, do you think that was wise?'

'But, Cecily, it wasn't possible to do more in the time. Just think: how long would it take you to look up sixteen hundred accounts? It's a terrific number.'

'I do understand. I think you've done marvellously. Do go on. All this is just thrilling.'

'I chose the end of September and the beginning of October because it was likely to include only quarterly payments; January might have had six-monthly and annual, which I didn't want. Then I was lucky because the figure was £75; if it had been a hundred there would have been a lot more. As it was, I got nineteen withdrawals.'

'Nineteen! In one branch alone!'

'Yes, and that isn't many. You see, lots of people pay out a fixed sum every quarter. Lots of men give their wives a hundred a quarter for the house or for dress money, or a dozen other things. It's quite a common thing. That's why the withdrawals could be part of a blackmailing scheme without causing any suspicion.'

'I see. I never would have thought of that. Grace, we are lucky, aren't we, to get such help?'

Grace was overwhelmed with their good fortune. 'And then that nineteen?' she added to her eulogy.

'That was last night,' Ronald resumed. 'But I wasn't satisfied with it. I thought, now I've gone so far, I might go a little further and perhaps get something a bit more helpful. There was a pointer you'd given me which I hadn't used, and that was that the payments had been going on for eight years. If I looked up these nineteen accounts in the books of eight years ago, it might cut the number down a good deal, for our branch has grown so much lately.'

Again there were appreciative murmurs from both girls. 'With a bit of trouble and some faked excuses I managed to work late again. I found only four of the people had been withdrawing those sums at that time.'

'You've got it down to four! How really splendid, Ronald! Oh, just think if you've really saved Tony!' Cecily's eyes were shining, and there was this time nothing forced in her congratulations.

Ronald obviously felt that he had already been well paid for his work. 'You'll be surprised,' he went on, 'at the names. But please don't forget that this is terribly confidential. As I said, if this got out, I'd be sacked on the spot. They are: James Matthews—that's Matthews of Matthews and Grover, the auctioneers; Mrs Folliot-Upson, whom you know; Robert Cornell, whom'—he looked at Grace—'you know even better; and Arnold Ingram, the solicitor.'

As Cecily listened to this recitation, her heart slowly turned to stone, and she felt a disappointment so bitter as almost to deprive her of words. All these people she knew, none intimately, but as acquaintances. Mr Matthews was a nice man, a little loud and boisterous perhaps, but kind and good-hearted and well respected. His wife was a delightful woman, and they seemed to get on splendidly together. He was not the kind of man to have dark secrets or to commit a murder. Mrs Folliot-Upson: well, the idea in her case was ludicrous. She was a simple, quiet little woman, a widow living alone in a cottage near the town. She could have no tragic secrets either. And as for Mr Cornell, he certainly was secretive and retiring and she did not know him well, but he had been with the Farsons for four years and had always been kind and pleasant. She could not believe that he could be mixed up in such a thing. Mr Ingram she knew less well than the others, but he was universally respected as an honest man and a shrewd lawyer. She was sure—he was much too clever to allow himself to get into the clutches of a black-mailer. No, it looked as if this fine work of Ronald's, of which she had hoped for so much, was going to prove a washout.

Grace seemed equally disappointed. 'Mr Cornell's the only possible one there,' she said after some thought, 'and we know that he didn't do it.'

'I'm afraid none of them are possible,' Cecily agreed unhappily. 'But how are you so sure about Mr Cornell?'

'Why, that's the time he was ill. Don't you remember? He was in bed when the murder took place.'

Cecily remembered it. Oh, well! Either the murderer didn't bank at Ronald's branch, or Ronald had missed some figure in the ledgers. And the former was the more likely. Admittedly, the fact that no marks of a car were found was no proof that the man hadn't come from a distance. There were trains and buses, and—she suddenly thought of it—there was the river.

In any case she had got what she had asked for. She had imagined that she, Cecily Meadowes, could do what Chief Inspector French had believed was impossible for him. What could she expect except what had happened to her?

All the same when Grace and Ronald had gone she rang up French, this time having his number. He was non-committal as to the value of her news, but highly complimentary about her thought and initiative. 'I'll go into what you have told me carefully,' he promised, 'and you may trust me not to compromise Mr Barrymore.'

With this she had to be content.

16

The Testing of an Alibi

To say that Cecily's call surprised French would be to understate his reaction to her news. He had recognized that both she and her friend Grace Farson were competent young women, but he had never expected such a demonstration of efficiency. Of course, there might be nothing in their discovery. Clients who withdrew £75 a quarter could probably be found in nine out of every ten banks in the country, and the fact that the tour in question did so was therefore in itself no reason for suspecting them.

But if the murderer were a local man, as Cecily had assumed, the information took on a different complexion. This assumption was founded on Jackson's report of the absence of car traces near Myrtle Cottage on the night of the crime. French, however, was not impressed by Jackson's argument. He also had thought of trains, buses, boats, and, what he considered more likely than any of them, bicycles. While therefore he was not optimistic as to the result, he decided without hesitation to investigate the lives and movements of these four persons.

He began by consulting Jackson. 'They're all strangers to me,' he explained. 'Tell me what's known about them.'

Jackson shook his head. 'I'm afraid, sir, it doesn't sound very promising. Mr Matthews and Mr Ingram are both well known and respected. They bear very high characters, and on the face of it they're not likely to have committed murder.'

'You never know,' French pointed out.

'Of course, sir, anything's possible, but they're about the last men I'd accuse of a crime of the kind.'

'Then the lady?'

'It just isn't thinkable, sir. She wouldn't be fit to do it, for one thing.'

'And this Cornell?'

'There, sir, I can't offer an opinion. We know nothing against him, at all events. He goes to Town each day, but you don't see him about in the evenings. But we'll probably hear more about him from now on, as he's engaged to Mrs Lambert; that's a rich widow living up the river.'

'Well, how are we going to find out about them? Seeing how I received the information, I don't want to give this Barrymore away.'

A short chat revealed the difficulty of the situation. As Jackson pointed out, unless an officer was able to go to the suspects and say, 'We're questioning everyone who withdraws £75 a quarter from this bank,' it would be difficult to account for the inquiry. But such a phrase would mean an irate application to the bank manager and Barrymore's instant dismissal.

In the end French decided on an old trick. 'Got a good looking constable?' he asked. 'Then send him to the auction-eer's and the lawyer's to make inquiries about a hypothetical tramp or anything else you like. Let him get talking to the maids; take 'em to the pictures and all that. He should find out what the households are like and if there's any suggestive trouble. Mrs Folliot-Upson and Cornell I'll deal with myself. That all clear?'

When half an hour later French presented himself at Moyallon Cottage and was shown into Mrs Folliot-Upson's presence, he saw at a glance that Jackson was right. This frail and kindly old lady with her untroubled eyes and restful manner was not the murderer of a blackmailer. French had a little talk about a mythical burglar who had been tramping the country, and a good deal about Mrs Folliot-Upson's chrysanthemums, which were further advanced than his own. He left with his four new suspects very definitely reduced to three.

Before tackling Cornell, he thought he should learn what Grace Farson had to say about him. He therefore filled in his time with a visit to Mrs Lambert. He found her an extraordinary contrast to his last hostess. Tall, masculine, and with an unpleasantly aggressive manner, she didn't see why she had been appealed to about hypothetical tramps. French should have asked the butler, and without listening to his courteously worded apology, she rang the bell and bade him a sharp good morning.

Had he met her apart from her surroundings he would have asked himself why anyone other than a congenital idiot would have wished to marry her. But Holt End supplied a very cogent reason. Holt End exuded money. Its site alone, at least four acres practically in the town and on the bank of the Thames, must have represented a small fortune, and the luxurious house and elaborately laid-out gardens more than as much again. A weak man marrying its owner would probably have seen none of her money, but if Cornell were able to stand up to her, he would doubtless be assured of ease and plenty for the rest of his life.

French's morning investigations, superficial though they had been, had given him a good deal to think over, as after lunch he settled down for a pipe in the corner of the hotel lounge. Was there not the possibility of a motive emerging from what he had learnt? Was it, or was it not, significant that the murder had taken place shortly after—memo, to find out how long after—Cornell's engagement to Mrs Lambert? If the man were guilty, it might be taken for granted that the £75 a quarter which he had been drawing for the last eight years had gone to Reeve as blackmail against the disclosure of some secret. Cornell appeared to be well off, though not wealthy, and £300 a year was a likely amount to have been fixed. But now Cornell was going to be rich. Would Reeve still be satisfied with the old figure? If not, Cornell might well have been driven into murdering him from the fear that if he lived, all advantage from his marriage would be gone: that the more he screwed out of Mrs Lambert, the more Reeve would take.

All this was possible, though of course there was no scintilla of proof for it.

Through the good offices of Cecily Meadowes, French met Grace that evening at Riverview. 'Mr Cornell's name was on your list,' he explained, 'and I'm therefore collecting information about him. I want you to tell me all you can.'

He did not learn a great deal, or rather, little of what he learnt seemed helpful. Grace explained about the hotel her people had kept and about Cornell's proposal to share a house when that venture came to an end. Cornell had then told her father that he was an Englishman who had lived most of his life in the Argentine, coming to this country a number of years earlier as manager of the London office of a large Argentinian produce firm. He had always been quiet and civil when at the hotel, and her parents thought the house idea a good one. It had now been in operation for four years and had worked extremely well. Cornell was reserved and retiring, had few visitors, and gave but little trouble. He took no part in the social activities of the town and at first remained at home in the evenings. He was a skilful carpenter and metalworker and had fitted up a shed in the yard as a workshop. There he spent a good deal of his time. Within the last year, however, his habits had changed, and now he frequently went out in the evening. They had had no idea where he went until one evening Grace saw him leaving Mrs Lambert's. She then heard that he was a frequent visitor, and later the engagement was announced. That was about three months ago. At the same time he had told Mrs Farson that he would shortly be leaving. This was a blow to the Farsons, who without his help would be unable to keep on the house. The date of the wedding was apparently still unsettled.

'Where did Mr Cornell live before you set up the joint establishment?' French asked.

'I don't know. Slough, I think.'

All this was pretty much what French expected to hear, in that, while containing nothing to demolish the theory of Cornell's guilt, it failed equally to support it. It was true that he had learnt that the man was mechanically minded and skilful with his hands, qualities which would have been helpful in arranging the delayed-action firelighter. But this did not prove that he had arranged it. With some bitterness French thought that nine-tenths of the evidence he received in his various cases was of this description; neither adverse nor favourable to the view he was trying to establish, and half of the remaining tenth, he added cynically, could be made to bear contrary interpretations. However, all this indeterminate information had one feature in common: as it left the point at issue undecided, further research was necessary. French sighed as he turned to the evening of the crime.

Grace remembered that very clearly. 'It was the night I was sweating up Elise's part in *Yesterday's Tomorrow*,' she reminded Cecily. 'You were coaching me and Tony came round. You remember?'

Cecily remembered it also, and between them they were able to tell French all that had occurred. Cornell had come home by an early train, saying he was not feeling fit. He had sat in his room till half-past seven, when his dinner was served. It happened that on this evening their daily help was on leave, and Mrs Farson had herself prepared the meal and carried it up. Cornell was lying slumped in his chair, and she thought he looked pale and ill. He said he wasn't feeling hungry, and when she went up for the tray, she found he had eaten nothing. However, he was well enough to listen to the news, for they had heard the wireless being turned on and off. About quarter past ten he had rung for a hot-water bottle, a thing he normally never used, and then they had heard him going to bed. About two o'clock he called for Mrs Farson, and going up, she found him extremely ill. He complained of violent pains and faintness and said that he had been sick several times. She brought him brandy and hot-water bottles and rang up Dr Hewett. He came shortly, staying for some time and returning twice during the day. Later he told Mrs Farson that he had feared he would be unable to save his patient, but that he had now turned the corner and would probably be all right. Though vastly better, Cornell was still not well.

If this story were true, and French did not doubt it, he need think no further of Cornell. At the same time he could not forget a point which had occurred to him when considering Tony's alibi. Whatever else the murderer might fail in, he would have an absolutely watertight alibi for the time of the fire. And here was such an alibi! Whether it told against Cornell or in his favour French could not yet say; like all the previous evidence it demanded further inquiry.

It was not yet ten, not too late to call on the doctor and still get home. Having rung him up, French walked round to his house. The interview might not be easy, as he wanted information which the doctor would probably refuse to give. However, he felt reassured by the man's appearance. Hewett proved to be a young man of the modern school. He quickly cut short French's apologies for his late call, and pointing to a chair by the fire, produced whisky and soda.

'I heard you had come down about the Reeve case, Chief Inspector,' he said. 'Have a drink.'

French said he didn't usually drink while on duty, but as the doctor was so kind, he would break his rule for once.

'What rules are made for,' remarked Hewett pleasantly.

'I should like to think you meant that, sir,' French said with a sigh.

'Why so?' The doctor filled his own glass.

'Because, strictly in the interests of justice, I want to ask you a question which I'm not sure you'll be willing to answer.'

'Professional secrets?'

'You might consider it so.'

'What's the trouble?'

'I shall have to speak confidentially, Dr Hewett. As you know, young Tony Meadowes has been arrested, but you may not know that there are grave doubts as to his guilt. I myself believe he is innocent, and I am trying to find someone to take his place in the dock.'

'Glad to hear that,' said Hewett as he held out his cigarette case. 'Nice people, the Meadowes. Always thought Tony a bit of a fool, but no murderer.'

'I'm delighted you think so, because you may see your way to help me. Certain facts—I needn't trouble you with details—suggest that one of your patients may be guilty. But he was ill at the time, and what I want to know is whether that illness would have incapacitated him.'

Dr Hewett thought this over. 'Who was it?' he asked.

'Mr Robert Cornell.'

'Cornell? Why, he nearly died. Incapacitated! I should just think so.'

'I had no doubt he was incapacitated. But was he at the time of the murder?'

'When exactly was that?'

'We believe about nine in the evening.'

'I heard that was the idea. Delayed-action fire-raising? You've accepted that, have you?'

'Provisionally.'

'About nine in the evening,' Hewett repeated slowly. 'Well, you know, I can't tell you about that.' He got up, took a casebook from a drawer, and turned the pages. 'I wasn't called till a few minutes after two in the morning, and I didn't get to the house till about half-past.'

'That's what I thought, sir,' said French. 'So far I've been speaking,' went on Hewett, 'from my own knowledge. But I was informed that Mr Cornell was ill on the previous evening, that he came home about five because he felt unwell, and that he got progressively worse.'

'Would that be consistent with the symptoms you observed?'

'Perfectly.'

'Could you express an opinion as to the cause of the illness?'

215

'Enteritis? Yes: eating tainted food of some kind.'

'I think I'm correct in saying that the symptoms of enteritis and of arsenical poisoning are almost indistinguishable?'

The doctor raised his eyebrows. 'It's a well-known fact,' he answered dryly.

French was surprised to be getting so much information. 'All this is very helpful to me, sir,' he said politely. 'Just another two or three questions, if you'll be so good. If Mr Cornell arrived home about five, he must have left Town about four, and in order to decide to go home, must have been feeling ill earlier still. Presumably, therefore, this tainted food must have been eaten at lunch?'

'Sounds reasonable.' The doctor had suddenly grown wary.

'You didn't see him, therefore, for nearly twelve hours after he began to feel ill?'

Hewett, looking still more wary, nodded. 'That is so.'

'Now, sir'—French leant forward and put his question gravely—'did the illness take the course which you would naturally have expected under these circumstances?'

Hewett hesitated. 'I don't think you can ask me that, you know, Chief Inspector,' he said at length. 'It's a purely hypothetical question.'

French thought he had received his answer. 'It was an appeal for an expert opinion,' he countered. 'However, I won't press it. But I should like an answer to this, if you can see your way to give it. Could the symptoms which you observed have been brought about by a deliberate dose of some poison such as arsenic?'

The doctor's eyes flashed. 'There I think you can answer your question,' he declared. 'Whether the unwholesome food was taken deliberately or accidentally would not affect its result.'

French smiled. 'You're right, of course, sir. Might a dose of some poison such as arsenic, taken about ten o'clock, have produced the symptoms you observed?'

The doctor shook his head. 'I see what's in your mind, but I can't confirm your suspicions.'

'Of course not, sir: I don't expect it. All I ask is whether such a dose might have done so.'

'Possible, yes: you might know that also for yourself. But I don't for a moment say it did so or that such a dose was taken.'

'My last question, sir. If the tainted food had been eaten at lunch, would you have expected the symptoms to develop earlier?'

Again Dr Hewett hesitated. 'Effects of this nature vary tremendously. Again I see what's in your mind, and again I can't confirm it.'

French felt he had done well. The illness might have been faked, though he thought it unlikely that anyone would deliberately bring on so severe an attack. On the other hand, it was difficult to forecast the effect of poison.

The net result of the doctor's evidence was then similar to what had gone before it: Cornell might be guilty and he might not, and further investigation was required.

Next morning French began by writing up his notes and planning his day's work. With regard to Cornell, three inquiries remained to be made: first, could he have devised a mechanism to turn on and off his wireless? second, could he have left and regained his room without being heard? and third, where did he lunch on the day before the murder, and was there any reason to suspect that tainted food had been served? French believed that the answers to these questions would settle the matter of Cornell.

217

He began his inquiries with the Farsons. He obtained their recollections of the evening of the crime and then asked to see Cornell. 'He's gone out,' George told him. 'Went off in his boat—for the first time since his illness. And I can guess where: Holt End.'

'If he's out, I wonder could I have a look at his room?'

George grinned. 'Who am I to grant or withhold permission? I can't stand up against the entire British constitution.'

Though he had qualms of conscience about making a search which might be deemed irregular, French felt that under the circumstances he was justified. Having posted Sergeant Carter to watch for Cornell's return, he set to work. But from the man's effects he learnt nothing except that he had cashed a check to self for £75 at the end of each quarter. An excellent portrait autographed 'Robert Cornell' stood on a side table; this, French photographed, then turned his attention to the radio set.

It seemed perfectly normal. It was a mains set and was connected to a plug on the skirting behind the table upon which it stood. He opened the case and had a look inside, but nowhere could he find indications of its having been tampered with. Once again, Cornell might have played tricks with it, or he might not.

His first inquiry having proved indeterminate, French turned to his second: whether Cornell could have secretly left and re-entered the house. First he tried to estimate the hours of these movements. Assuming Cornell were guilty and Tony's statement true, the man the latter had seen leaving Myrtle Cottage was almost certainly Cornell. That was about 9.35. If Cornell had walked, the obvious thing for him to do, he would have reached Brown Eaves about 9.50. When must he have left?

This was not so easy. French recalled his previous attempt when considering Nettlefold's alibi, though Cornell would have taken longer than Nettlefold, owing to his having to undress Reeve and to find his card. Say, five minutes to get into the house and knock out Reeve; fifteen to undress the body and arrange it at the bottom of the stairs; ten to set up the delayed-action plant to start the fire, and fifteen to examine the deceased's papers and remove the card: forty-five minutes altogether. If then he left the cottage about 9.35, he must have reached it about 8.50, and this would have involved starting from Brown Eaves about 8.35. Eight thirty-five to 9.50 away from Brown Eaves: was this possible?

Yes, as far as time was concerned. Tony had reached the house about 8.00, and then Mrs Farson was just bringing down Cornell's rejected dinner. Cornell was not seen again until he rang for a hot-water bottle about quarter past ten.

Eight to 10.15! Given the automatic turning on of the set, ample time was left to have committed the murder.

Then as to the actual leaving and re-entering of the house. When mounting, French had noticed that the stairs creaked so loud that he did not believe anyone could pass up and down unheard. For Cornell to use them would in any case have been dangerous, as someone might have come into the hall as he was passing. French rejected the possibility.

What then about the windows? He went from one to another. Ah, this was more promising! Some four feet beneath the bathroom window, the lower sash of which opened wide, was the roof of a shed. It was of a flattish pitch, and French dropped down. He moved round it, looking for a way to the ground, and at one end he found it. A large rainwater barrel, painted a vivid green, stood in the angle between the shed and the house, with a downspout which formed a convenient handrail.

French retreated through the bathroom window, and going downstairs in the orthodox manner, went round to the back of the house. There he made a minute examination of the barrel and pipe, in the hope of finding telltale scrapings or shoe marks. He could see no scratches on the pipe, but on the top edge of the barrel there were faint traces as if some of the paint, which was dry and hard, had been ground off. This might have been done by someone standing on the edge or by resting a watering can on it or in a dozen other ways.

The workshop was in the corner of the yard, and French took it next. It proved an amateurish place, very untidy and with only a few simple tools. Evidently Cornell was not such an expert as the Farsons thought. French's search, now grown hasty, as the owner might be back at any moment, showed that Cornell worked with electrical apparatus as well as in metal and wood. Besides filings and shavings there were boxes of small fittings such as binding screws and simple wireless gadgets. French knew that delayed-action appliances, both for raising fires and for switching on or off a set, could easily be made, but though he felt satisfied that Cornell could have put such together, he could find no evidence that he had. He sighed with exasperation. Here again was the same thing: the possibility of Cornell's guilt, but no proof. In spite of his researches, he was little further on.

He began chatting again to George Farson, aimlessly in a way, yet in the hope that somehow a helpful hint might be forthcoming.

'Did you not discuss with Mr Cornell where he got the food which disagreed with him?' he asked. It was a point which he had supposed Hewett would have ascertained, but the doctor knew nothing about it. He was therefore agreeably surprised when Farson answered: 'Oh! yes. It was at some restaurant in Town; the Holly, I think.'

'Did he take the matter up with the manager?'

'I asked him if he was going to and he said "No". He said that whatever he might suspect, he couldn't prove anything, and that it was not worth while.'

French nodded. But before returning next day he saw the manager of the Holly. He felt that the interview would require careful handling, as the suggestion that the manager had nearly poisoned one of his customers might not be received too favourably. Therefore he made his approaches with guile.

'My business is very confidential,' he explained, having handed over his card, 'and rather serious, as it concerns a man's innocence or guilt of murder. A man whom I will call X had a sharp attack of enteritis. This may have been due to some accidental defect in his food or to an attempt to poison him. Naturally, for all concerned, we should like to find that it was accidental. We are therefore trying to trace all the meals he had at the critical time, and we are informed that one of them was taken here: lunch on Tuesday, the twenty-fifth of September. Now, sir, you mustn't imagine that this question is a reflection on the excellence of your cuisine. You know, I'm sure, better than I do, that defective food often appears absolutely perfect. But if you were able to tell me that there had been other cases of illness after that lunch, it would be a great ease to a lot of minds.'

The very idea that such a thing could be suspected obviously horrified the manager. 'Your suggestion would be a very serious matter for us if it were true, Chief Inspector,' he returned, 'but I am glad to be able to assure you that it is not. There have never been any complaints of the kind you mention; at least, not since I took over, two years ago. You gave me rather a fright at first.'

'I'm sorry, sir,' French smiled. 'It was only in the way of duty. I suppose if anything of the kind had occurred there would have been complaints?'

The manager laughed unmirthfully. 'There would,' he said dryly: 'nothing more certain in this life.'

A pleasurable glow warmed French's being as he left the building. Here at last was something tangible! Cornell had lied. Wherever he had obtained the injurious food, it was not at the Holly. Did this mean that he had himself taken poison to sustain his alibi?

No: there was no proof that he had lunched at the Holly. That might merely have been a tale to satisfy George Farson's curiosity. Of course in that case he had still lied, but it would not necessarily involve anything more serious. As French thought over it, the glow slowly faded.

There was another point. Would a man who had been accepted by these Farsons as an ordinary decent sort of fellow keep silence and let another man be hanged, if he were himself guilty? French doubted it. The glow went out altogether.

The reports which were awaiting him on reaching Staining were equally discouraging. Jackson had made inquiries about both Matthews and Ingram, the auctioneer and solicitor who also drew £75 a quarter from the bank, and had learnt nothing suggestive of an ugly secret in the life of either. On the contrary, both lived as if they had easy minds, and the atmosphere in their houses was happy. Jackson had not sent the young constable to take the maids to the pictures, but had found out other connections enabling him to apply direct to members of the staffs.

As French sat down to consider his next move he felt badly up against it. Cornell seemed the only possible suspect, but that was as far as he could go. And without some definite evidence against him, little would be gained by questioning him. But now he did not see what else he could do. Despondently he began to write up his notes.

17

The Result of an Assault

Cecily was thrilled when, early that afternoon, she heard from George Farson that French had made a search of Cornell's rooms on the previous day.

'Oh, tell me,' she cried eagerly, 'did he find anything?'

'He omitted to mention it if he did,' George grinned. 'Good at keeping his own counsel, that one.'

'Isn't that tantalizing! What did he look: pleased or otherwise?'

'Bored, as if he was glad the job was over and lunchtime had arrived.'

'I'm afraid you're hopeless!'

'So he seemed to think. But he was very friendly and pleasant. Not my idea of a Scotland Yard detective.'

'What was your idea?'

'Oh, I don't know. Stern and sharp enough to cut himself. A man who would throw his weight about and not see a joke.'

'Not much of a joke in this business,' Cecily declared.

'Well, if I had thought of one, I'd have made it, feeling sure it would have been well received. What; you're not off already? Won't you wait for tea?'

The truth was that a daring idea had just leaped into Cecily's mind. She felt she must know how French's researches were progressing, and she thought that she saw a way of finding out.

From remarks he had dropped, she knew that he was living at home, and from having met him on the way to the station she had an idea of the train he left by. She now went to the station an hour before that time, and having taken a return ticket to Town, hid behind the footbridge staircase and watched the entrance to the platform. For ninety minutes she waited, and then she saw French and Carter coming in. Carter turned off to the bookstall, while French strolled in her direction. Immediately she began sauntering on in front of him, and in a few seconds she heard his voice wishing her good evening.

She was suitably surprised. 'Oh, how nice!' she exclaimed. 'I didn't expect to have company up to Town. I thought you went earlier than this?'

'I try to,' he answered, 'but tonight I was detained. You're late yourself, aren't you?'

'Not really: it's only to meet a friend.'

They chatted till the train came in, when Cecily saw to it that they found an empty compartment. Carter discreetly vanished into another carriage.

After some general remarks, Cecily decided it was time to open the action. Turning the conversation to the case, she went on: 'I had simply no idea how dreadful these affairs could be. I sometimes feel that I just can't live through another moment. And if it's bad for me, what must it be for Tony?'

French murmured sympathetically.

'It's the suspense, you know: not knowing how things will go. If one was sure of a good defence it would make it bearable.'

She gave a pathetic little sigh, then after a pause went on: 'I suppose none of those four names that Ronald Barrymore found is any good? Or perhaps you haven't had time to go into them yet?'

She thought he looked distressingly wary.

'Well,' he answered, 'I had a look through Mr Cornell's things. But did you not know that?'

'Oh, yes, Mr Farson told me. But he said you hadn't discovered anything of interest.'

'I wonder how he knew?' French smiled.

Cecily registered an awakening excitement. 'Then did you?' she said. 'Or is that a question I must not ask?'

'Oh, yes, you may ask it.' His voice was dry, but there was an alleviating gleam in his eye. 'In fact, I couldn't prevent you if I tried.'

She grimaced. 'But you're not going to answer it! Oh, well, I suppose I mustn't be inquisitive.' She showed a carefully modulated amount of hurt disappointment.

'I didn't say that,' French pointed out, 'but really I have nothing to tell you. I've made preliminary inquiries in all four cases. Mrs Folliot-Upson I've practically eliminated, and Mr Matthews and Mr Ingram both seem unlikely to be guilty. I haven't got enough information about Mr Cornell to reach a definite conclusion.'

At this she was really disappointed. 'Grace and I were talking about him. We didn't see how he could be guilty.'

'Oh?' French's manner remained kindly, but it was also slightly bored. Cecily persisted in her attack.

'Well, from what you told me the murder took place about nine or half-past. But Mr Cornell was then in his room. They all heard him turn the wireless on and off.'

French hesitated, and with a thrill she felt he was considering taking her into his confidence. Could she sway him at all, or would she do harm by speaking?

'Probably I'm talking through my hat,' she added, 'but then of course I don't know about such things. In any case I feel very grateful to you for discussing it with me.'

'You're certainly not talking through your hat,' French rejoined. Then to her delight he went on: 'It's quite a sound point, which of course I've considered. But while I'm making no charge against Mr Cornell, that in itself is not an alibi.'

'No? I wonder how you make that out?'

'Simply because it's easy to make an apparatus to turn a set on and off at any given time.'

'*Oh!*' She gazed at him in admiration. 'And you think he did?'

He shook his head. 'Ah, that's a horse of another colour, as my esteemed grandfather would have said. I found nothing to suggest it.'

'Then there was the illness. We both supposed that he wasn't well enough to have gone out.'

'That again hasn't been proved. Probably it's as you say, but it's an old trick to pretend to be ill, go out and commit a crime, and then come back and take a small dose of a mild poison to make the illness real. I'm not, of course, insinuating that Mr Cornell did so.'

How she had misjudged this clever, painstaking man! thought Cecily ruefully. So far from showing slackness about the case, he had gone far more deeply into it than she could have imagined.

'All that,' she said earnestly, 'is simply thrilling, and I'll not breathe a word to anyone: except perhaps Grace, if you have no objection. But then, if I'm not boring you too dreadfully, there was the point about the creaking stairs: Mr Farson told

227

me you remarked about them and thought Mr Cornell would not have risked using them.'

'That's equally inconclusive. There's a convenient shed and barrel just below Mr Cornell's bathroom. Anyone could climb up or down, but again there's no evidence.'

'But how,' persisted Cecily, 'could you possibly tell about a thing of that kind? I mean, unless someone saw him? And it's a good while now since the murder.'

'Yes, that does make a difference. If I had been called in at once it would have been easier. But there are several possible indications. If, for instance, I had found marks on the shed or barrel, I should be suspicious.'

'There weren't any?'

'There were marks on the top edge of the barrel: too indefinite to prove anything. But if I had found tar or paint or rust on Mr Cornell's clothes I should be suspicious, whereas if I had seen his footprint on the tarred roof, I should be sure.'

'Again there weren't any?'

'None.'

Cecily sighed. 'It's a problem, isn't it? I do think you're marvellous! If I were in your place I shouldn't have the foggiest idea of what to do next. I'd simply give it up.'

'Oh, no, you wouldn't,' French smiled. 'If it was your job you'd go ahead with it. You'd have to.'

'But I shouldn't know what to do. What more investigating can be done? Haven't you covered everything?'

'Nothing like it.' He seemed to have got over his hesitation and to be enjoying the discussion. 'I can ask Mr Cornell where the £75 a quarter went to. I can show his photograph to Reeve's clerk and find out if he was known in the office. I can make inquiries as to whether he could have obtained arsenic or some similar poison. Or if he made delayed-action

228

appliances for turning on his wireless and starting the fire at Reeve's. And so on. There are all sorts of inquiries still unmade.'

Again she registered admiration. 'And will you do that tomorrow?' she asked.

French did not answer. His expression had grown rapt, and for a moment he sat staring before him, apparently at nothing in particular. Then he pulled himself together, smiled in a friendly way, and drew his notebook from his pocket.

'Sorry,' he apologized, 'I'm afraid you've caught me day-dreaming. I just want to make a note of something while it's fresh in my memory.'

He wrote slowly, evidently thinking over his subject, while Cecily grew more and more impatient and the train approached nearer and nearer Paddington. Then just as they were entering the terminus he closed his book.

'Sorry,' he said again; 'that was too bad of me. I believe you asked me a question which I never answered?'

'It was nothing,' Cecily declared. 'I only asked if you were going to make those inquiries about Mr Cornell tomorrow?'

'Tomorrow?' French shook his head. 'I'm afraid I shall not be able. I have another job to do first.'

'Oh,' she said, '*what* a pity! I mean every day is so important.'

He smiled. 'A lot of people have wanted to be in two places at the same time, but I've never heard of anyone yet managing it.'

'I shouldn't have said that,' Cecily admitted. 'I mustn't be impatient, particularly when I'm so intensely grateful for all you're doing.'

'Aren't we polite, apologizing to one another like little Erics? But you know this is just my job.'

'I know better than that. If you had done no more than your job, you wouldn't have been bothered with it at all.'

229

As a matter of fact an exceedingly intriguing idea had shot into French's mind, filling it to the exclusion of all else. It was a simple idea: so simple and obvious that for the life of him he could not understand why he had not thought of it earlier. Suddenly it had occurred to him that in pursuing this matter of Cornell he was on the wrong track. There was a more direct and satisfactory explanation of the crime. In Cornell's case he had proved opportunity, but neither motive nor threats: in this other there were all three.

French was so excited by the possibilities opening out to him that in spite of Cecily's presence he could not dismiss the matter from his mind. The plea of making notes would cover any discourtesy.

He had always realized that the evidence against Cornell was purely circumstantial and did not amount to proof of guilt. The whole edifice had been built up on the fact that he had been drawing £75 a quarter from his bank. That, however, was a poor foundation. There was no evidence that these sums had been paid to Reeve or indeed that there was any connection between the two men. Further, on the probabilities, it was more likely that Cornell's illness was genuine, in which case he was necessarily innocent. French's difficulty, of course, had been that he could find no other suspect. But now he saw that he had been wrong. There was another suspect: Sinclair Nettlefold!

As a result of what he now realized had been only a very partial and inadequate investigation, he had come to the conclusion that Nettlefold's alibi was watertight. Now he saw that it was nothing of the kind. Nettlefold might well be guilty!

This sudden reversal of all his previous ideas overwhelmed French. He entirely forgot his whereabouts, forgot Cecily and her question and forgot that time was passing, as he followed up his thought.

Suppose Nettlefold, on parting from Marjorie at half-past two on the morning of Wednesday, the twenty-sixth of September, had decided that he would visit Reeve at once and try to obtain the letter. If feasible, this would have important advantages. First, it would prevent the blackmailer from leaving a precautionary note of any proposed meeting. Such a record would be most undesirable from Nettlefold's point of view because of the risk of his accidentally killing Reeve. Then it would save Nettlefold from having to leave his rooms on a second night, a proceeding which would necessarily increase his chances of discovery. Further, there would be the joy of immediately producing the letter and ending Marjorie's distress, a powerful incentive. French felt sure that if Nettlefold could devise a plan of campaign for that same night, he would do so.

These considerations French had noted before, but he had decided that Nettlefold would not have had time to reach the cottage. Now he saw that he was wrong: Nettlefold could have done it.

Suppose the man had hurried from his interview at The Limes. He would reach Marazion a few minutes before 3.00, as he said he had. Suppose he slipped softly in, and holding up the striker of the hall clock, advanced the hands through eleven hours, thus leaving the clock one hour slow.

Suppose he then crept out again and took young Simpson's bicycle out of the woodshed, riding it to Reeve's. It was a ten-minute ride, and he could easily have been there by 3.20.

Suppose now that he roused Reeve and persuaded him to open the door, perhaps by saying that he had the £500 with him and wanted to deliver it in absolute secrecy. Suppose then that the accident happened and that he killed Reeve. Instantly his major preoccupation would be to escape the consequences. The letter would become secondary, not only intrinsically, but because if Reeve were dead he could not try to recover on it. Nettlefold might look for the letter and be unable to find it, or he might even forget about it altogether. The need to cover up his crime would in any case be paramount, and to do this he would arrange the fall downstairs and set the house on fire. He should easily manage this in twenty or twenty-five minutes and be on his bicycle again by 3.45. He would return the machine to the woodshed, slip into the house and up to bed, and in two or three minutes the clock would strike three.

He would then only have to go down again later in the night and put on the clock one hour, and his alibi would be complete. If Mrs Simpson noticed any irregularity in the striking, she would never dream that it had been tampered with, but would assume she had made a mistake.

Of course this alibi would only come into force if Mrs Simpson happened to be awake and heard him come in. But that was all that Nettlefold would require. If she did not know he was out, so much the better.

Consideration of these points kept French occupied till the train reached Paddington, and it was only when Cecily repeated her question about his next day's work that he saw that his new idea was more promising and that he must deal with it first.

They parted with a warm exchange of good nights, and Cecily watched him going towards the tube, while she moved off in another direction. As soon as he was out of sight she retraced her steps and got into the next train for Staining, which by a stroke of luck was just about to start. A little more than an hour later she was closeted with Grace Farson in her room.

'Oh, Grace, I've had the most wonderful time!' she exclaimed. 'I've seen Mr French and heard all he's been doing.'

Grace was suitably impressed and demanded details.

'He's such a kind man,' Cecily remarked when these had been discussed. 'I really can't understand how he ever took up that dreadful work.'

'Nonsense! it's not dreadful. If no one did it, it would be a bad lookout for the rest of us.'

'Of course I know: but I mean getting people arrested and convicted of crimes; it *is* dreadful, even though it has to be done.'

Grace made an impatient gesture. 'Well, we can't do anything about it, so we needn't worry. What a pity Mr French is busy on something else!'

'That's what I said. The days are passing so quickly, and there's still no proper defence. There are questions to be asked Mr Cornell, about the money and so on, and because of this other business nothing can be done.'

'And no doubt it'll take time and it mayn't be done before the trial: don't I know! It's been worrying me dreadfully.'

'I said practically that to Mr French, and he said—What is it, Grace? What have you thought of?'

Grace's expression had changed from depression to eagerness, and she had made a sudden gesture. 'Mr Cornell's clothes!' she now exclaimed. 'It's just occurred to me. Don't you see, Cecily? Don't you see?'

'See what? For Heaven's sake don't ask riddles.'

'Mr French didn't see his clothes; not all of them. He was out when Mr French came. Perhaps there were marks on the clothes he was wearing!'

Cecily gasped. 'Yes, of course! I hadn't thought of that. But Mr French is no fool. He would have thought of it all right.'

233

'But he didn't say anything about it!' Grace grew more enthusiastic. 'When Mr French came yesterday morning Mr Cornell had gone out in his boat. It was the first time he had gone on the river since his illness, I know that, because Mummie was speaking about it at supper. And it's easy to guess where he went—across to Holt End. Now that means he was wearing plus fours and rubber-soled shoes.'

'You don't know that.'

'He usually does. We can find out in any case from Daddy. He's certain to have noticed.'

'All right. Pass that.'

'Well, does plus fours and rubber soles suggest anything to you?'

Cecily moved impatiently. 'Oh, go on, Grace, and say what's in your mind,' she said irritably. 'It's not a game we're playing.'

'What I mean is: if you were going to climb in and out of windows and commit murders and so on, what. kind of clothes would you wear? Would it be your well-cut town suit or a country rig?'

Cecily caught her breath. 'Oh, Grace! I believe you're right! We must suggest it to Mr French first thing when he comes down.'

Grace looked at her strangely. 'Must we? Are you sure we must?'

'What is it now?' Cecily's voice sharpened. 'Have you thought of something else?'

'Why,' asked Grace in an intent tone, 'should we not look ourselves?'

For a moment Cecily felt doubtful; then she found herself carried away by the grandeur of the idea. If only they could find something, *what* a relief it would be to both of them!

With this possibility in her mind, she felt that she really could not wait till French was available.

Besides it would save time, and time was more than money. If they found anything, French would no doubt put someone on his other business and come himself to Brown Eaves.

'Oh, Grace, wouldn't it be wonderful!' she cried. 'Just fancy if we were to find something!'

'And this time we can do it ourselves. I always thought that other was hard lines on poor Ronald.'

'And you were the one who suggested the whole thing!' Cecily retorted indignantly.

'Oh, yes; for the common good. But it was hard lines, and he was very nice about it.'

'He's off tomorrow about the job. I hope the poor lamb will get it, if he wants it.'

'The job?'

Cecily stared. 'Didn't you know? Why, I believe I forgot to tell you! It shows how beastly selfish all this business makes one. I can think of nothing but the case.'

'What about the job?'

'A customer of the bank, the manager of a large textile firm in the north, who was on a visit to Staining, wanted some special financial work done, and Ronald did it. He pleased the man so much that he offered him a job in his firm. Ronald's going to Liverpool tomorrow about it.'

'A good job?'

'I think so.'

'I'm so glad,' Grace said warmly. 'He deserves anything that's going. But I bet,' she grinned, 'he's divided about taking it.'

'I've been telling him he Ought to. If it's a chance he shouldn't miss it.'

235

'You'll have to tell him something more than that if you want to influence him. There, don't get on your hind legs; I didn't mean any harm. Now about this search.'

For another hour they discussed their plans. They were expecting that Cornell would return to work on the following day, and if he did so, Grace would stay at home and they would examine the clothes and shoes. If they found anything Cecily would try to get in touch with French.

Next morning while Cecily was at breakfast Grace rang her up. 'Speaking from the station,' she said. 'He's not going to business today, but he's dining in Town this evening. So we can do it then, and I'll not have to miss the office.'

'This evening then; splendid.' Cecily was thrilled.

'But look here, Cecily, it hasn't been all plain sailing. I felt in my bones the parents wouldn't stand for what we are doing. But I think I've fixed it. You know they were wanting to go to that New Zealand film that's on in the Playhouse, so I said: "Why not go tonight when Mr Cornell will be away, and Cecily's asked me to have dinner with her?" You see then what you have to do.'

'Right, I'll be looking out for you.'

'It's a chance for the parents because Daddy's busy this week in the afternoon, and tonight they can have supper early. So that's settled. Gladys goes home about eight, and then we'll have the house to ourselves.'

For Cecily the day dragged interminably. She spent a good deal of time with her mother, who had one of her attacks. She took a bus four miles up the river and tramped home. She did some sewing and tried to read. But she could not hasten the passing of the hours, and it was with a sigh of relief that she greeted Grace shortly before eight.

She would have been content with a cup of tea and a biscuit, so as to get off quickly to their task. But her guest had to have a proper meal, and they sat down to a normal dinner.

'Great excitement getting the parents off,' said Grace when Kate, having served the soup, left the room. 'They finished supper all right and were just going to start to walk round in their leisurely way when Daddy looked again at the paper and found the film started at 7.30 instead of 7.50 as he had supposed. So there was an almighty fuss, for there wasn't time to walk, and Daddy thought a taxi would be an extravagance.'

'What did they do?'

'Took Mr Cornell's boat: in spite of Mummie's wails. There was a difficulty about how they'd come back in the dark; so I'm to leave a lantern on the slip for them.'

'They'll be all right. When did Mr Cornell go up?'

'Left by the 5.40 apparently. He's dining with a friend and won't be back till about eleven.'

'How do you know?'

'He told Mummie. They seem to have had words about it. She was all het up about his staying up so late when he's not really well yet.'

When they had finished the last course Cecily could stand it no longer. 'What about going and making our search now, and coming back to coffee?' she suggested. 'Then we could sit over it with an easy mind.'

'Yes, let's. I'm terribly keen to know.'

Five minutes later Grace opened the Brown Eaves door. The house was in darkness, and they decided that they would not turn on any lights. 'We're not supposed to be here,' Grace explained, 'and no one must be able to prove otherwise. I have a torch in my bag.'

By the dim pencil of light they went upstairs, and feeling greatly daring, pushed open the door of Cornell's bedroom.

'Drat this torch,' Grace muttered. 'I thought it was all right, but it's nearly done, and Daddy's taken the only other one in the house. I'm afraid we'll never find paint stains with this.'

'I have a new one in the car,' Cecily answered. 'I'll slip home and get it.'

'Too bad, old thing, but I really think we'll be sunk without it. I'll light you down to the hall.'

It was not so dark out. There was a moon, but the sky was heavily overcast. Cecily could see dimly for a hundred yards along the road. Unexpectedly she was experiencing a revulsion of feeling. Somehow a great deal of her keenness for their adventure had evaporated. In the abstract it was thrilling enough, but when it came to opening Cornell's wardrobe and making the actual search of his clothes, the whole thing seemed less attractive. Forebodings also had taken possession of her mind; not exactly the fear of definite disaster, but a general premonition of evil and danger. For a moment she began to wish she had never embarked on the scheme; then she remembered that it was Tony and that success might save him. With such an object, her own feelings must necessarily fade out of the picture.

She got the key of the garage and found the torch. Then relocking the shed, she hurried back the way she had come.

As she stepped out on the road she saw in the distance the figure of a man. He was approaching with long strides from the direction of Staining. Not wishing to be seen, she shrank back among the bushes at the end of the drive until he should pass.

But he did not pass. He turned into the gate of Brown Eaves, and as he did so she recognized him. It was Robert Cornell!

Her heart beat more quickly as she silently slipped after

him. What about Grace? Would she be waiting below stairs for the torch, or looking about in Cornell's room?

As she approached the door she heard it close. She waited till Cornell would have moved on, then silently opened it with the key that was kept hidden in the porch. He had switched on the hall light, and she heard his footsteps going upstairs. Like a shadow she tiptoed after him. The door of his room opened, and there was silence. It continued, growing heavy with foreboding. Then at last came Cornell's voice, strangely harsh.

'Well, Miss Farson, what's going on here?'

There was no answer, and the silence grew more oppressive still. Then Cornell's voice came again, this time sharp with anxiety and menace.

'What have you been doing with this?'

Cecily, her heart pounding, slipped farther up the stairs till she could peep into the room. Grace and Cornell were standing motionless, facing one another. He was holding one of his rubber shoes, staring at its rubber sole. His expression was such as Cecily hoped she would never again see on human countenance. In a flash it told her the truth. Cornell was guilty! And on that shoe was the evidence that would prove it!

But there was more in that hideous expression than fear and guilt. There was also desperation. Sick with horror, she realized that Grace was in appalling danger.

What was to be done? Her brain worked at fever heat. From the point of view of force she was helpless. Cornell could overcome her with one hand. Screams would not be heard. To get into his power would be the end for them both. Her only plan was to summon help. Grace would be expecting her return and would fight desperately to gain time. She could ring up the police from next door and be back inside two or

239

three minutes. Then would be the time to interfere. She could cling to Cornell and hamper him so that he could not hurt Grace before help arrived.

Turning, she fled down the stairs like a phantom, and out through the hall into the night. Not till then, when it was too late, did she realize the mistake she had made. She had not shouted to let Cornell know that he had been seen and that help for Grace was coming. As she sped along a deadly fear that she had failed her friend welled up in her heart.

18

The Genesis of a Crime

It was in a mood of black and bitter despondency that, an hour before he reached Brown Eaves on this tragic evening, Robert Cornell stepped into the 7.45 train at Paddington. He was still feeling the effects of his illness, and it had been much against his will that he had gone to Town. A wealthy Argentinian magnate who had just reached England on a business tour had asked him to dine. This man was in close touch with the heads of Cornell's firm in Buenos Aires and therefore his invitation could not be ignored.

From this particular annoyance Cornell had, however, been miraculously delivered. When he reached the visitor's hotel, he found that the management had been trying to ring him up. The magnate had met with a slight motoring accident and much regretted he would be unable to keep his engagement. Relieved, Cornell had gone out and got himself the sandwich and whisky his internal economy demanded, and he was now looking forward to his armchair and fire, with the prospect of an early bed to follow.

But the dinner had been a pinprick compared to his real

trouble, the weight of which had grown almost more than he could bear. Now that his thoughts were free to roam, they reverted immediately to their familiar channel: the appalling situation in which he found himself. Admittedly he had once made a bad break, but that was half a lifetime ago, and he would have long since lived it down, had it not been for the almost unbelievable ill luck which had since dogged his footsteps. Sinking back into his corner seat and passing his hand wearily over his eyes, he began almost automatically to review the events which had led him to his present ghastly position.

How well he remembered that bright May morning some seven and thirty years earlier when he and his parents had left England for Australia, where his father had been offered a responsible job in a brewery, and how delighted he had been, during his first week in Sydney, with the city's novel sights and sounds. Then his despair on that terrible morning which had shattered his hopes and marked the beginning of his troubles, when the train in which his parents were travelling on a house-hunting expedition was wrecked and they were both killed. So at the age of eighteen he was left to fend for himself in a city which he soon found to be callous and completely uninterested in his fate.

Fortunately he had had a good education, and with his father's ready money he managed to exist till he got a job as junior clerk in the cashier's department of the large produce firm of Porter, Mayberry & Co. Fearful of losing his only means of support, he worked hard, receiving a corresponding reward. He was promoted on different occasions, until eventually he became second in his department. It was then that he made his break and that disaster overtook him.

His was the familiar story of boredom with a humdrum life, leading to a craving for excitement which he had attempted to satisfy by gambling. Needless to say, he lost. Gradually Peters, for that was then his name, got more and more deeply involved, until at last he woke up to find that only the immediate payment of some hundreds of pounds could stave off ruin.

Then a horrible temptation arose. His chief was old and ill and had lost his grip on the business. Until his retirement, which was almost due, Peters had practical control of the books. He saw a chance and netted £4,000 by a clever forgery. This he then himself 'discovered', and for a time it looked as if he was going to get away with it. But a tiny slip aroused suspicion, and he was arrested and got seven years. The principal witness for the prosecution was another member of the department, a clerk named Albert Reeve.

In prison Peters made plans for his future. Realizing that he would be better out of Australia, he taught himself Spanish, and when he was released, he worked his way as a coal trimmer to Buenos Aires. Taking the name of Cornell, he obtained a job in an even larger produce concern. Here his efficiency and willingness to take responsibility earned him rapid promotion, and when after a dozen or more years a new manager was wanted for the London office, he was sent over. That was nine years ago, and he had since carried on successfully. He had lived in a private hotel in Slough and was beginning to think that his troubles were over and that he might settle down to happiness for the remainder of his life.

Then disaster once more descended on him. On his way home one evening he met Reeve. For a moment he did not know him. The man was considerably altered and had grown a goatee. At the ensuing interview Cornell learnt, as had many another before him, that paying the legal price for his crime did not settle the score. Reeve, it appeared, knew a good thing when he saw it. He found he could sell Cornell social security and the tenure of his job, and he proceeded to do so. For £300 a year, paid in single notes at the beginning of each quarter, he would keep secret the fact that Cornell was an old lag.

Cornell knew when he was beaten. Three hundred pounds a year was not to him a large sum, particularly as he was unmarried and living alone. He thought of murdering Reeve, decided the game would not be worth the candle, and agreed to pay. Since then both parties had kept their bargain. With unfailing regularity the notes had gone by post to Reeve, buried in the pages of a book. On his part Reeve had been as silent as the grave.

Five years later had come Cornell's change of residence. His salary had been increased, and his commissions were now on a more generous scale, so that he was able to afford better accommodation. When he heard about the Farsons' giving up their hotel, the idea of sharing a house with them occurred to him, and when he found the house of his dreams which would enable him to indulge his passion for boating, he made the proposal of which we know.

For obvious reasons Cornell avoided publicity. He felt that he ran enough risks in his business without adding to them by unnecessary social contacts. He found that his work gave him, if not all the society he would have liked, at least enough to keep his brain from stagnation. He obtained his exercise on the river or by walking and his relaxation from books and the wireless. So he led a fairly safe, if not a very exhilarating, existence.

Then a freak of Fate introduced a new factor into his life. Sculling one Saturday afternoon near Holt End, he overtook a punt in which were Mrs Lambert and two children. He had then never met Mrs Lambert, but he knew her by sight. Just as he passed them a boat coming in the opposite direction swung suddenly off its course, due to one of its too jovial oarsmen catching a crab, and hit Mrs Lambert's punt a heavy glancing blow. As a result the smaller child, who was leaning over the side, fell into the water. To backwater, ship his oars, throw off his coat, and leap in was for Cornell the work of a moment. In a few seconds he had restored the terrified child to the punt, and swimming back to his own boat, had climbed aboard.

He was about to row off, but Mrs Lambert would not hear it. He must come ashore and have a hot bath and some whisky and rest while his clothes were being dried. In vain he pleaded that he had better row home; the imperious lady would not be denied. In the end a fellow guest lent him some clothes, and he spent a pleasant couple of hours chatting with his hostess.

A week later an invitation to dinner arrived. Cornell accepted and again enjoyed himself. Suddenly he realized what he had been missing in his withdrawal from the social side of life, and he made the most of his new opportunity, calling again and again.

He got on well with Mrs Lambert, who liked to dominate, but apparently liked still better his refusal to be dominated by her. Gradually they grew more intimate, until to his utter amazement, for he was not conceited, he realized that she was growing attached to him.

From this emerged the great question: would she marry him? If he could bring off such a triumph, his financial future would be assured. He could give up slaving at the office, for she would pay him far more for being her husband than the Argentine directors did for managing their London business.

More than this, he would be vastly safer out of commercial London. As the master of Holt End, the chances of recognition as Frank Peters would be infinitesimal compared to those which dogged him in the City.

There was but one snag: Albert Reeve. Yet his marriage should not interest Reeve. The man would still get his £300 a year, and it would make no difference to him whether it originally came from the Argentine or from Mrs Lambert.

Cornell now played his cards with skill. Every time he visited Holt End he was obviously more attracted to its owner, for her own sake. He called more frequently, stayed longer, and was unable to hide his pleasure when he found her alone. Then he began what were clearly proposals, breaking them off in the middle, as if shocked by his own temerity.

At last she gave him a direct opening. He leaped at it, while appearing to hesitate. But he didn't hesitate long enough to miss the opportunity. His emotions obviously overcame him and he plunged, this time proposing beyond all possibility of misunderstanding. But he immediately withdrew what he had said. She must forgive him for allowing his feelings to get the better of him. He knew only too well that a marriage between them could never take place. She was rich, but he was a poor man, comparatively. He could not allow his wife to support him. His pride as well as his love for her would prohibit it.

She reacted even more admirably than he could have hoped. She appreciated, she declared, his lofty and disinterested motives, but his objections did not in point of fact amount to a row of pins. At least that was what he understood her to mean. Here, she said, was a chance of happiness: why should they throw it away because of a stupid convention?

Cornell did not see any reason, but it would not do to say so. Once again he hesitated, but once again not too long. A week later the engagement was announced.

Still another week, and there was a note from Reeve. He would like to meet Cornell to discuss a small matter of business, and what about the private bar of the Three Frogs in Greek Street at twelve next day?

A sense of foreboding weighed on Cornell's spirits as he kept the appointment. Soon his worst fears were realized. With an evil smile Reeve congratulated him on his approaching marriage. 'Wonderful how some people have all the luck,' he went on with a sad lack of originality. 'You certainly have struck it rich. I was hoping that in the excitement of it all you wouldn't forget your old pal?'

'Forget you, Reeve? I wish I could!'

'Now, now, not the way to talk to an old friend, surely. I hoped for better than that.'

'You'll get it. This is not going to make any difference to our little arrangement. I've paid on the tick up to now, haven't I? I'll continue to do so.'

Reeve shook his head. 'You're not right there, I'm afraid. Your marriage is going to make a very big difference to you. And to me too.'

'What do you mean?' Cornell's voice was sharper, though he knew everything of what was coming save the amount.

'Why, you wouldn't propose to keep all that luck to yourself, would you? Would you not think of sharing a bit with your old pal?'

Cornell realized there was no use in fencing. He was in the man's power. 'How much?' he said, and the cold hate in his voice made the other glance at him uneasily.

Reeve was equally laconic. 'Thousand,' he said shortly.

Cornell was startled. This was double what he had anticipated. 'A thousand!' he exclaimed. 'Not if I know it, Reeve.
Why, you dirty swine, I'd see you dead first. A little increase
I would agree to, say, a maximum of five hundred. But a
thousand: not on your life.'

'A thousand. It's a moderate figure, seeing what you're
marrying: far less in proportion than three hundred on your
old screw. And what's more, you don't have to use insulting
language about it; I don't like it.'

Even as he spoke, Cornell knew that his protests were
useless. He was in a trap. Whatever Reeve chose to say, he
would have to do. In the end he agreed that in the future his
£75 quarterly payments should be increased to £250.

But as he thought over the situation he saw that these
payments would just ruin his happiness. He would be able to
meet them, but they would leave him horribly short of cash.
As Bertha Lambert's husband he would have endless expenses,
and that thousand a year would make the difference between
meeting them easily and with cheese-paring. He would have to
pay insufficient tips if they went visiting, being despised by
servants and misunderstood by his wife; to refuse casual loans
to friends; to be careful about playing bridge or going to the
races, and to save in a hundred uncomfortable ways. Life would
be one succession of petty miseries, and he could never explain
what was wrong. He would indeed be better as he was.

And of course all this would only be the least of his troubles. The real difficulty was that he would remain just as much
in Reeve's power as ever. At any time the man might still
further increase his demands. No, as long as Reeve was there,
Cornell would be living on a volcano.

Then it was that his thoughts turned more seriously to
murder.

If Reeve were to die, all this trouble and wretchedness would be over. Why should not Reeve die? He had asked for it when he had increased that £300 so outrageously. Why should he not get it?

Cornell fought against the idea, though all the time his mind was grappling with schemes to carry it out. He had read many detective novels, and from them murder seemed the simplest thing in the world. But now that he wanted to experiment himself, he found that this was the very opposite of the truth. There was the problem of getting rid of the body, with its telltale evidence of the cause of death. There was the difficulty of establishing an alibi for the hour of the crime. With his name in the old man's books there would be the added puzzle of how either to avoid a police interrogation or to meet it if it came.

He soon saw that he could neither hide nor destroy the body, and therefore decided that he must adopt a device more common in books than in real life. His murder must look like an accident, and suspicion to the contrary must not be allowed to arise. The unskilful use of a boat was a fertile source of accident. He had the necessary river and boat, and the accidental drowning of Reeve haunted his mind.

He remembered having read about such a murder. The victim was rendered helpless with chloroform, put into the boat, pushed out at night into midstream, and the boat overturned. To account for the accident the oars were sent downstream separately, one alone, the other with the boat and body, the suggestion being that the victim had lost an oar and upset the boat in his efforts to recover it. The murderer, of course, had to swim ashore, but in Cornell's case there would be no difficulty about this.

He thought his scheme very promising and spent a lot of

time working out the details. The actual murder he considered entirely feasible, but its setting presented difficulties. If he were to use his own boat, attention would be immediately called to himself, whereas stealing one from a neighbour introduced undesirable complications. Nor could he think of a satisfactory reason why Reeve should row himself across the river at night. These objections he found overwhelming, and regretfully he discarded the entire scheme.

His next plan was also suggested by detective novels he had read. A fall downstairs in his cottage would account for Reeve's being stunned, and a subsequent fire would destroy any inconvenient evidence. If the fall took place at night, as of course it must, a lamp or candle would necessarily be dropped, and this would account for the conflagration. Gradually the scheme took shape in his mind, details and safeguards being worked out, until at last he was ready to put it into operation.

He began by preparing his apparatus. First came that for turning on and off his wireless set. At different shops he bought two alarm clocks, an electric light plug and wall socket, and a length of flex. In his workshop he fitted the clocks with electric contacts, one broken, but to make at 8.58, the other made, but to break at 9.37. Then he connected the clocks in a circuit with the plug and socket.

His method of using the apparatus was as follows: The set being switched off, he would first remove its plug from the wall socket. Then he would connect his apparatus, inserting plug A into the wall socket and the set plug into socket B. He would then turn on the set switch, but the circuit being broken in clock C, it would not start. At 8.58, two minutes before the nine o'clock news, clock C would make contact, and the set would operate till 9.37, two minutes after the end of the talk; when clock D would break contact, stopping the set. On reaching his rooms he would only have to turn off the set switch, remove the clocks and their flex, and insert the set plug in the wall socket; and all trace of what had been done would be gone.

Locking away the clocks and their flex in a suitcase, he turned to the delayed-action fire-raiser. This was of the simplest description: a candlestick containing rags soaked in paraffin, arranged so that when the candle burnt down to a certain point, the rags would catch fire. As a precaution he prepared three of these candles, any one of which would do the needful. The candlesticks were made of cardboard, so that they would burn and leave no evidence.

The most difficult item in his plans was the arranging of his own illness, but this he considered an absolute essential. In a tool shed in the Holt End garden he had noticed a tin of arsenical weed-killer, and now he made an opportunity of slipping unseen into the shed and helping himself to some of the powder. His great problem was to know how much to take. He bought a Taylor's *Medical Jurisprudence* and with its help eventually settled the amount, but he was by no means sure that his calculations were correct, and he had to face the risk of an overdose.

Having thus made his preparation he rang up Reeve at his office. 'I think,' he said, 'I've got a better scheme than that we arranged, one which would insure your money and which would come cheaper to me. I propose that I buy you a Post Office annuity, and I'd expect a reduction in the amount against the lifelong security you'd gain. I don't know how the idea appeals to you, but I think we should discuss it.'

Reeve swallowed the bait, as Cornell was sure that he would, for the outstanding point about an income from black-mail is its uncertainty.

'But I'm not going to meet you in any more private bars,' Cornell went on. 'We've agreed that our association must be kept secret, and bars are too dangerous. Where could I see you really in private?'

This was another hurdle in Cornell's scheme. It demanded that the place of meeting should be Reeve's cottage, the time about 8.30, and the night one on which there was a fifteen-minute talk after the news. To make Reeve himself suggest this was what Cornell wanted, as otherwise he feared the man might grow suspicious.

In the end he carried his point, though not exactly as he had wished. Finding Reeve unhelpful, he suggested several meeting places which he was sure the other would refuse, a boat on the river, a deserted piece of heath land, the Embankment at midnight, and others still more inconvenient. 'Or, if you'd like it, your house,' he ended up. 'I'm sorry I can't ask you here, because this house is full of people, but yours would do, as I understand you're alone in the evenings.'

Reeve was obviously dissatisfied with the proposal, but to Cornell's relief he agreed to it. 'Then shall I stroll up after dinner?' Cornell went on. 'I could be with you about half-past eight, and we could fix up our business in a few minutes.'

Reeve again agreed, and the hurdle was taken. All was now set for the murder.

19

The Shadow of a Disaster

On the fateful day Cornell carried out his plans with cool deliberation. And first as to his illness.

He had made an appointment with a client at Elstree for noon, and this enabled him without remark to avoid lunching at his usual restaurant. He did actually lunch in a small place near St Pancras, then buying some sandwiches in the station refreshment room. Returning to his office, he began to simulate illness, leaving for home about four o'clock.

At Brown Eaves he put over a good representation of a gradually increasing indisposition, dining off his sandwiches and leaving the meal provided by Mrs Farson untouched. When she had taken down the tray he knew he was safe from further interference from the household. He dressed in his golfing outfit, putting on shoes with soft crêpe rubber soles. Then having packed his candles in a dispatch case and plugged in his clocks— which remained hidden in another dispatch case beneath the table which bore the set—he silently opened his bathroom window, dropped lightly on the shed roof, and with the help of the downpipe and barrel, lowered himself to the ground.

His shoes made no sound as he crept round the house. Unobserved, he gained the road and set off to Myrtle Cottage.

Luckily for himself, he met no one on the road. He was admitted by Reeve and instantly put his plan into operation. As Reeve was turning towards him after closing the door, he struck him suddenly on the chin. It was not a heavy blow, but it knocked the old man down. Instantly Cornell knelt on his chest, at the same time pressing his handkerchief over his mouth and nose. In five minutes Reeve was dead.

Now to prepare the accident. Adventuring upstairs, he found Reeve's bedroom, rumpled up the bed as if it had been slept in, and hunting out the man's pyjama's, slippers, and dressing-gown, carried them downstairs. It required all his determination to take off Reeve's clothes and put these on in their place. But he did it, disposing the body at the foot of the stairs as if it had fallen from the landing. The clothes he left in likely positions in the bedroom, putting the keys, money, and so forth on a table at the head of the bed. Then he placed his candles in different parts of the hall, arranging the furniture so that it would catch fire when the rags became alight. He found Reeve's candlestick on a table in his study and laid it on the floor near the body, hoping that it would be found and so would suggest the cause of the outbreak. Then he searched till he found a drum of paraffin, and to help on the good work poured out several quarts in likely places.

One other matter required attention. Taking Reeve's keys, he opened the safe and went through the papers, removing everything which referred to himself. There was a card in the index and a folder containing newspaper reports of the trial of Frank Peters in Sydney, with photographs and the reminder that the convicted man's fingerprints were held by the Sydney police. Then he locked the safe, replaced the keys, and stood looking round to see that nothing had been forgotten.

Believing that all was in order, he opened the hall door, drew it to silently, and after a glance through the keyhole, hurried off. In fifteen minutes he was back at Brown Eaves and had climbed silently back into his room.

But his work was not yet complete. First he disconnected his clock apparatus from the set, climbed down again to the garden, and taking out his boat, threw the apparatus into the middle of the river. Next he burnt the card and folder with its contents, carefully stirring up the ash till it disappeared. Lastly, he rang for a hot-water bottle, and then with fear and trembling took the dose of weed-killer he had measured out.

Though genuinely terrified at the risk he was running from the arsenic, he was well satisfied as to his safety in connection with the murder. How absolutely watertight was his scheme! As he lay fearfully waiting for the results of the poison, he reviewed with immense complacency his position.

In the first place he was now safe from blackmail. That drain on his resources which had handicapped him during all these years was at an end, and the threatened further demand would not materialize. Now he could marry with an easy mind and sustain his new position as he should.

Next, no suspicion could arise, for no one knew that he had a motive for wishing Reeve dead. They had rarely met, and then only in places in which the chances of either's being recognized were infinitesimal. All references to him in Reeve's archives had been removed and destroyed. His payments could not possibly be traced. They had been made in single notes and sent through the post. No one could even find out that he had been paying away £75 per quarter: the bank would not give away this information. He had been careful, moreover, at the cottage. He had worn rubber gloves and had left no trace of his presence. On reviewing his every action he was satisfied that no motive could ever be attributed to him, nor could any connection between himself and Reeve be established.

But even if through some incredible accident suspicion were aroused, his alibi remained. It was absolutely complete and overwhelming. He estimated that the fire would break out about three in the morning, and at that time, if the doctor were not actually with him, the medical evidence would prove that he was too ill, with a *genuine* illness, to have been out of bed. Nor could he have visited Myrtle Cottage earlier in the evening and installed a delayed-action apparatus: the Farsons could not have failed to hear him turning on and off his set. And if he were asked what the news contained, he would be too ill to answer.

All this was infinitely reassuring. He had no regrets for what he had done. What had happened was Reeve's own fault. He had only got what he had asked for.

Some half an hour after Cornell had taken his dose he began to feel very uncomfortable. He grew depressed and experienced nausea and faintness.'I'hen an intense burning pain began in his stomach and grew more and more severe; the sickness which intervened did little to ease it. He bore it as well as he could, until at last he felt so ill that his panic about an overdose revived. With a supreme effort he managed to call Mrs Farson and then collapsed.

What followed was a hideous dream of pain and weakness and misery. Then he began slowly to recover. It was, however, many days before he was well enough to think of anything except his own condition.

When he did so he received a nasty shock. The inquest had been adjourned!

This news so much upset him that he narrowly escaped giving himself away. For a moment he forgot that he knew nothing of Reeve's death or the fire. He sweated in horror as he thought how an admission of that knowledge could, for him, have meant one thing only.

A little later there came a further and infinitely more serious blow. It was now believed that Reeve's death had been no accident, and Tony Meadowes had been arrested for the murder!

Cornell railed bitterly at the fate which in this unexpected way had robbed him of all the advantages of his efforts and anxieties and suffering, which indeed had left him immeasurably worse off than when Reeve was alive. For Cornell was not wholly bad. Whatever he might have done to Reeve, he could not allow another man to suffer for it. Somehow, at whatever cost, Meadowes must be saved.

At the same time that did not mean that he was going to allow himself to be hanged. Immediately Cornell set himself to working out a plan to meet these difficult and contradictory requirements.

He had plenty of time to speculate, lying there in bed or on his sofa, and at last by slow stages he evolved what he thought was a workable scheme.

First, he would realize all the money possible and change it into bearer bonds, which he would either carry with him or send to Chile to be reclaimed when, disguised and under an altered name, he should demand them. In the new personality he would buy the necessary tickets for the journey. Next, as it was reasonable that he should have a change after his illness, he would go to the coast. He would choose a secluded place with strong tidal currents and a sandy shore across which a river or stream flowed into the sea.

When the time came he would write a statement of his entire dealings with Reeve and address it to Superintendent Edgar. On it he would imprint his finger-marks, so that these might be checked by those held by the Sydney police. He would add that while he could not see another man executed for his crime, he could not face that end himself and was therefore committing suicide by swimming out to sea and drowning. This document he would post on the selected evening. As a precaution he would leave a copy in the rooms he had engaged.

When it got dark that evening he would take the disguise he had prepared to a stony or grassy point on the bank of the river, as near its mouth as possible, hiding it in some convenient place. Then he would retrace his steps and from the direction of his rooms would walk down across the sand to the sea. He would undress and, leaving his clothes on the beach, would walk along the shore through the water and up the river to the selected point. There he would put on the disguise and proceed to make his escape to Chile. His footprints would remain leading into the sea, and none would appear coming back. The police might be suspicious, but they would be able to prove nothing. His method of reaching his port of embarkation would depend on the location of his holiday resort, but with his disguise this should not be difficult.

The one real difficulty was in connection with his passport, and here he would have to take a risk. With immense care he altered the R in his name to N where it was written in block letters, becoming Robert Connell. His signature required no alteration, the written *r* being already sufficiently like an *n*.

When going on board he would take off the glasses that were part of his disguise and slip the pads from his cheeks, so that he would resemble his photograph. He realized that if suspicion that he was not drowned were aroused, he would not have a dog's chance of getting through. But he was satisfied that suspicion would not be aroused, for the simple reason that he would be on the high seas before his absence was discovered. Then it would be a sharp passport officer indeed who would remember the Robert Connell who had sailed for South America and connect him with the missing man. All the same, he would take with him a dose of poison, lest the worst should befall.

With this scheme he was in general well pleased, but naturally he would not put it into operation until after Tony's trial. In the meantime he had to find a suitable stretch of coast, and he would do so as soon as he was well enough to travel.

This somewhat depressing review of his career passed through Cornell's mind as he sat in the 7.45 train from Paddington on the evening of his abortive dinner engagement. It made him more bitter than ever against the fate which, after allowing him to carry his dreadful expedient to a successful conclusion, had now snatched away all its gains.

He walked home as quickly as he could, thinking with relief of his fire and armchair. He was surprised, on reaching Brown Eaves, to find the house in darkness. The Farsons must be out, which was unusual for them. Then he guessed that it was his own absence which had given them the opportunity, and he felt slightly conscience-stricken as he realized the worry and trouble his illness had given Mrs Farson.

He switched on the light in the hall and went upstairs to his flat. The door of his bedroom was open. Subconsciously

259

he noted this as unusual, but he would have dismissed it without a thought and passed on into his sitting-room, had he not noticed that the open door was swinging slowly shut. As he reached the landing it came to rest, half closed.

He was slightly surprised. There was no draught to move it, and the Farsons kept no animal. The idea of a burglar shot into his mind, only to he instantly rejected. He had nothing of value to burglars.

All the same he slipped his hand inside the door and switched on the light. Then he stepped into the room.

He could scarcely believe his eyes when he saw Grace Farson standing behind the door. Her face was ghastly with terror. Dully he wondered why. Though she had no business in his room, her presence was not a crime and she could easily have said she had heard a noise or made some other excuse. He asked her what she was doing, but she did not answer: she seemed unable. Then his eyes, darting about to find the explanation of these mysteries, dropped to the floor behind her. There, evidently hurriedly laid down by her, was one of his shoes. He asked her what she had been doing with it, but again she did not, or could not, reply.

Swiftly he picked up the shoe and turned it over. On the rubber instep was a mark of green paint!

For a moment he stared uncomprehendingly, and then the knowledge of what had happened struck him like a physical blow. This girl knew!

He had examined the barrel before that fatal evening and had been satisfied that the paint was dry. He had brushed his clothes well when he took them off. But he had forgotten the soles of his shoes. Now when it was too late he realized that he had stepped on the edge of the barrel in his climb.

And now Grace had found the evidence! Moreover, her

face showed beyond possibility of doubt that she was aware of what it involved.

Cornell was stunned. This was the end! Let her say what she knew, and nothing could save him. If Grace hinted what she had found, he, Robert Cornell, would hang! The knowledge burned itself into his brain. He saw himself back in prison, which he had sworn to die rather than re-enter. He saw the two warders sitting with him during those hideous three weeks of waiting. He saw the last ghastly scenes, the procession to the fatal shed, the chalk circle on the floor . . . No, no; he couldn't face it! Anything but that!

With the sudden reaction from complete security to the certainty of arrest and death, something seemed to give way in Cornell's brain. For a time he was not quite sane. Panic clouded his mind, and his thoughts became concentrated on the one question of how to save himself from the immediate peril, irrespective of consequences.

There was, of course, only one possibility: this imbecile girl must be silenced. It would not be his fault: he had no wish to hurt her. Why could she not have minded her own business and let his alone? Well, like Reeve, she had asked for it and she would get it.

But how could he silence her without bringing about the very result from which he was trying to escape? He was scarcely conscious of considering the problem, when like a flash the solution was in his mind. The scheme he had already worked out for Reeve and rejected!

Drowning through upsetting a boat in midstream owing to efforts to recover a lost oar! That was the plan! He had gone into it in the closest detail, and he had been absolutely satisfied with it. It was not because of any inherent defect that he had rejected it, but only because there were difficulties in applying it in Reeve's case. But in the case of this girl these difficulties did not obtain. Grace Farson was in the habit of using his boat to cross the river at night. If her parents had gone to the pictures, as he surmised, it would be natural for her to row across for them.

Then, he thought almost with satisfaction, he could carry out the alibi he had already devised. He would undress, carry the girl to the boat, pull out to midstream, send off one oar, capsize the boat, swim back, dress, and walk to Cherton, which was less than four miles away in a north-easterly direction. He should get there in time to catch the ten o'clock bus to Town, which would enable him to travel back by the 11:15 from Paddington. In case no one whom he knew should be on that train, he would speak to the ticket examiners both in London and at Staining. He would account for his evening in Town by saying that he went to a cinema.

Though it takes time to put all this into words, it flashed almost instantaneously into Cornell's mind, for the reason already mentioned: that it had been thought out with such care. Nothing, he was satisfied, had been overlooked, and he could put it into operation without further consideration. But this very certainty, added to his panic, led him into a ghastly mistake. It never occurred to him that Grace might not be alone. He had found her alone, and his fear drove him on to immediate action.

For a few seconds he stood staring at her, while these thoughts raced through his brain. Then almost automatically he pulled out his handkerchief and, seizing her in his arms, clapped it over her mouth and nose. Before he could silence her she gave one hoarse scream. That he didn't mind: no one would hear. Then he laid her on the floor, and putting his knee on her chest, began to press downwards.

He knew the danger of what he was doing: he had carefully weighed it. He must be gentle. He must not press down the handkerchief hard enough to bruise her face. Nor must he kneel on her heavily enough to mark her chest. Still more important, though he must render her unconscious, he must not kill her. She must be alive when she went into the river, or else she might be found without any water in her lungs. That would indicate murder! It would not be easy, but with care he could manage it.

He was both careful and gentle, and presently he found that she ceased struggling and lay limp on the floor. She was still breathing, and he congratulated himself that his first fence had been taken satisfactorily.

Now he quickly flung off some clothes, and picking up the unconscious girl, wrapped a rug round her and hurried downstairs and into the garden. He carried her across the grass and laid her on the boat-slip, ready to lift into the boat.

So far he had carried out his plan to the letter, but now everything began to go wrong. When he put his hand under the eaves for the key of the boat-house, it was not there. A sharp stab of panic entered his mind, but this was relieved when he found the door unfastened. He pushed it open, and then panic enveloped him again. The boat was gone!

For a moment he clung to the doorpost while his brain reeled in horror. This was absolute disaster! Then he rallied himself. He had gone too far to draw back. What was to be done?

Obviously he must borrow the Meadowes' boat. Without a moment's delay he raced off. He should be back in three or four minutes. Every second was valuable, for there was the danger of Grace's regaining consciousness.

Fortunately the boat was moored at the end of the Riverview

slip and was easy to get at. But the oars were locked in the boat-house! Again Cornell swore luridly. Never mind! A good push off from the slip, plus the current, would carry him back.

He untied the painter and with immense labour swung the boat round till its bow pointed downstream. Then with all his force he pushed off. Gradually losing way, he floated successfully to his own slip. With the painter in his hand he jumped out and turned to pick up Grace. Then he received his third shock. Grace was no longer there.

With his heart pounding so that it sounded like hammer blows in his ears, he stood staring at the place where he had left her. She was gone, but the rug remained. It had become unrolled, and one edge had fallen over the side of the slip and was trailing in the water.

As Cornell stared, his extreme panic subsided. It was bad, but it was not so bad as he had feared. What had taken place was obvious. Grace had regained consciousness, begun to move, and had rolled off the slip into the water. In her weak condition she would be unable to swim; nothing could save her from drowning. The current would carry her down, and it would be assumed that she had gone to the slip, perhaps to meet her parents, and had fallen in.

If this were so, and it *must* be, Cornell's course was clear.

He rushed to the boat-house, got a spare oar, and sculled the boat back to where he had obtained it. Then returning, he replaced the oar and with the rug hurried to the house. There he dressed, had a quick look round to see that all was in order, and taking the paint-marked shoes and switching off the lights, let himself out of the house and hastened away.

Not far along the road was a bridge over a stream. Here he climbed down to the water's edge and pushed the shoes deep into the mud. As he settled down for the three and a half miles' walk to Cherton, he told himself that all would yet be well. Though he had not pulled the affair off as he could have wished, it was done, and done successfully, and there was nothing to connect him with it. And even if suspicion of foul play did arise, it could not settle on him. His alibi would see to that.

Confident that he was safe, he reached Cherton and took the bus to Town.

20

The End of a Felon

On this same evening on which Robert Cornell travelled to Staining by the 7.45 train from Paddington, another member of the Meadowes-Farson circle made a similar journey.

Ronald Barrymore had had a fortunate day. In a not too sanguine mood he had gone that morning to Liverpool to obtain particulars about his proposed job. His reception had delighted him. The manager had been pleasant and sympathetic. The job was better than he could have hoped, and as soon as he had satisfied himself that it was within his capacity, he had accepted it with gratitude. Having been interviewed on arrival, he was able to return to Town on the same day, and he was just in time, after getting some supper at Paddington, to catch the 7.45 home.

As he passed through the barrier he saw Cornell in front of him. But he wished to be alone, and therefore drew back and took another carriage. His mind was too full of his success for trivial conversation. Now he would have enough money to marry. The difficulty which had been blocking his proposal to Cecily Meadowes was a difficulty no longer. He could ask her tonight if he chose, and he believed she would say yes.

Or rather he could have asked her except for this ghastly business about Tony. Under the present circumstances he knew she would not consider marriage. Nor could he expect her to. Till after the trial she would not think of her own future. But after the trial? . . .

If Tony were acquitted, of course, it would be all right. Her anxiety would be over, and things would again go on normally. But suppose the unthinkable happened and he were convicted . . . ?

Then Cecily would never marry: Ronald was sure of it. And what about himself? Would he still want to marry her? There would be a social slur, and he must consider possible children.

Ronald had only to put the question to learn the answer. Slur or no slur, children or no children, he would marry her if she would have him. What more could he wish than to share her trouble? What greater joy than to support and comfort her? The one drawback to his new job was that it would take him away from Staining before the trial. He would have given it up without a thought if by staying he could have been by her side during that ordeal, but until they were engaged he knew that he could not have that privilege. Better, he thought, to be in a position to marry her and take her to fresh surroundings than to hang about Staining, unable to help her as he would like.

All the same she was so unselfish that in spite of her trouble she would be pleased by his success. He would go straight to Riverview and tell her. She would not be expecting him till the following day, and he would give her what he believed would be a pleasant surprise. With what intense eagerness he looked forward to the meeting!

At Staining he held back to let Cornell pass out through the barrier before him. In his impatience he would have overtaken him on the road, but his thoughts were too precious to sacrifice, and he slacked down and kept well behind, Cornell drew out of sight, and presently even the sound of his footsteps faded.

At Riverview, Ronald learnt that Grace had dined with Cecily, but that both young women had just gone out. The Farsons, he thought, might know where they were. He turned back, hurrying in his eagerness.

As he reached the road a figure dashed out of the Brown Eaves gate. Dark though it was, there could be no mistaking that form.

'Cecily!' he called sharply. 'What are you up to?'

She stopped as if shot. 'Ronald!' she cried, and he felt the fear and the urgency in her tone. 'Quick! Grace! Cornell's murdering her! In his room! I'll ring up the police!'

She was gone before Ronald could pull his scattered wits together. Cornell! He thought of his banking investigation. Then Cornell must be guilty, and in some way Grace must have found it out! The girls must have been investigating when he arrived. Well, thank God, at least Cecily was safe!

While these thoughts chased themselves through his mind, Ronald was hurrying to Brown Eaves. The hall door was at the side of the house, and as he rushed up to the gate he saw Cornell leave it. He was carrying something: something silent and motionless. Checking his haste and taking cover behind shrubs, Ronald stealthily followed.

Cornell stepped down the boat-slip and laid his burden on the planks. Then he hurried to the boat-house. Ronald could see him putting his hand up for the key and hear his muttered oaths when he could not find it. However, in a moment he tried the door, found it open, and vanished within.

Ronald had just decided to rush forward and try to get Grace away before Cornell could untie the boat when Cornell reappeared. He was growling out even more furious curses, but he turned and, running lightly for so large a man, vanished in the direction of Riverview.

Ronald could now act. He hurried down the slip and was beginning to lift Grace when he heard Cecily behind him.

'Don't take the rug,' she whispered urgently, 'nor the bandage across her face. Leave them on the slip. And don't take her to the house. Get her behind the hedge into the Dicksons' garden. Then start artificial respiration.'

Ronald quickly obeyed. Presently Cecily rejoined him.

'I left the rug trailing in the water,' she whispered. 'Perhaps he'll think she's rolled in and not search for her. Keep on with that while I watch.'

She glided silently away while Ronald worked over the motionless form. The minutes passed, and he began to grow tired. Then Cecily as silently reappeared.

'He borrowed our boat when he couldn't find his own,' she explained. 'When he saw the rug he looked into the water and downstream. Evidently he thinks she's drowned. Now he's gone back to the house.'

'You got the police?'

'Yes, they'll be round at once.'

'I think one of us had better keep a lookout. I'll go if you'll take over here. Or will you go?'

'No, I'll take a turn at that. But don't be long.'

Ronald crept up to the house and crouched behind some shrubs close to the road. His brain was whirling. He had not yet had time to assess the results of these happenings.

First and most important of all, Grace was safe, or he thought so; he had somehow felt that she was alive. But then what else followed? Was Cornell guilty of the Reeve murder? If so, did it mean the clearing of Tony? Ronald grew even more excited. That would mean, he believed, marriage! It would mean—Suddenly he noticed the light in the hall disappear, leaving the house in complete darkness. Once more he was keenly on the alert. He heard the door close softly. Cornell slipped silently past him to the road and vanished like a shadow into the night.

There being no further need to watch, he ran back to where he had left Cecily. 'She's all right,' came a whisper. 'She's coming round. What has happened?'

Ronald explained.

'Then we'll carry her to the house. Help me, Ronald. You take her shoulders, and I'll take her feet.'

As they reached the door Inspector Jackson and three constables ran up from a car which had just stopped. A couple of minutes put them in possession of the facts. 'He's only just gone, has he?' said Jackson. 'Then we'll follow him. Back to the car, men!'

Half an hour later they returned. In some way Cornell had given them the slip, but they had put all sorts of inquiries into operation and were satisfied his capture would he only a matter of hours. Also they had rung up French, who was on his way down.

Then ensued an orgy of discussion and the taking of statements, varied by a search for the paint-stained shoes, which had disappeared. Grace, Cecily, and Ronald told their stories, first to Jackson, then to George and Mrs Farson, and lastly to French, as these successively arrived.

French immediately took charge, and at once a sense of ordered action replaced the apparently aimless endeavour which had hitherto ruled.

'We can't do much more here tonight,' he decided. 'We'll go back to the station and concentrate on finding Cornell. Then tomorrow I shall want some local inquiries made, Jackson, which I hope you can undertake. We'll say good night, Mr Farson, and again congratulations, Miss Farson, on your escape.'

As they turned towards the door, the telephone rang. George lifted the receiver. 'It's for you, Mr Jackson,' he said.

Jackson listened, then his face changed. 'They're on to Cornell, sir,' he exclaimed. 'He got out of the 11:15 train from Paddington here in Staining. He seemed so normal the constable did not stop him. He left the station, walking at his usual pace in this direction.'

'Then he'll be here in a few minutes. He evidently thinks Miss Farson is drowned and that no one saw him. Well, we'll let him preserve his illusion—for the time being.' French shook his head. 'Poor fool! It's a losing game, is crime. It did for Reeve, and now it's going to do for him.'

He shrugged, stood for a moment in thought, and then went on. 'Now listen to me, everyone, for we've very little time. You, Miss Farson, slip away and keep out of sight. But I'd like you to watch me. Can you do that?'

'If I go into the kitchen and leave the door open I can see you through the crack at the hinge.'

'Admirable! Then when I put my handkerchief to my face, like this, you steal silently to this door and stand motionless. Is that clear?'

'Perfectly.'

'Very good. Miss Meadowes and Mr Barrymore, please go with Miss Farson and keep out of sight. Mr Farson, you and Mrs Farson sit here. You are to be delighted about a statement I've just made. You needn't talk: leave that to me. Jackson, you and I are just about to get on to the real murderer in the Reeve case, and we've called to tell Miss Farson that the charge against Meadowes will be withdrawn. That's your good news,' he glanced at the Farsons. 'You two constables, get into the front room or some place where you'll be ready if you're wanted. And mind, everyone, let me do the talking.'

Ronald was bitterly disappointed at being ordered away, and so, he was sure, was Cecily. But they went with Grace, and as she had foretold, they were able to see through the slot of the kitchen door. The others had scarcely carried out their dispositions when a footstep was heard on the gravel, followed by the sound of a key in the front-door lock. A moment later Cornell stood in the hall. French moved to the sitting-room door.

'Good evening. Mr Cornell. You'll be surprised to see Inspector Jackson and me here, but we've just called with some good news for Mr and Mrs Farson. I hope you're better, sir?'

'Yes, thank you.' Cornell's manner was strained.

'It's about the Reeve affair,' French went on. 'You know they're interested owing to Miss Farson's engagement to young Meadowes. I dare say you'll be interested too. Won't you come in and join us?'

French stepped back, and Cornell had to follow. French, as he sat down, pulled out a chair; and, again at the risk of seeming discourteous, Cornell had to take it. He looked tired and ill. He was evidently on edge, and his eye was wary.

'I'm always glad to hear good news,' he said rather grimly. 'What is it?'

'Just that we believe we're on to the real murderer,' French answered easily, 'and if so, of course it will mean Meadowes' release.'

Cornell controlled himself with an obvious effort. 'Then I congratulate you.' He turned to the Farsons. 'Who is it, if it's not a secret?' He spoke normally, but his face had gone grey.

'He's a clever man,' French went on as if he had not heard the question, 'but he made some mistakes. They all do, you know. Would you be interested to hear his scheme, Mr Cornell? I was just going to tell Mr and Mrs Farson.'

Cornell nodded shortly, as if he could not trust himself to speak.

French had suddenly seen the way to profit by the exceptional situation which had developed. He was not entirely satisfied that it squared with the judges' rules. Perhaps it approximated more closely to third-degree methods than was smiled on in England. At the same time he thought he was justified. Had he been going to arrest Cornell on a charge of murdering Reeve, he would not have risked it, but he was not going to do so. He would arrest him for the attempted murder of Grace, and about that he would not speak. The graver charge could follow when he had obtained his proof.

'It was an ingenious scheme,' he continued conversationally, 'but just not ingenious enough. I don't say that we've got all the details right, but we're sure of the general outline. First as to motive. Reeve was blackmailing the man for years to the tune of £75 a quarter. The man then became engaged to marry money, and we believe Reeve took the opportunity to increase his demands. The man saw that his married life would be ruined, and determined to take action. Many people would say he was justified, but of course that's not our business.'

French glanced round his listeners, his gaze resting equally on all three. Cornell had now evidently realized his danger and braced himself to meet it.

'Then as regards the method. There was first the actual

crime, and second the precautions against discovery. These were so interconnected that I'd better tell you just what he did without trying to separate them out.

'He began by making a most ingenious apparatus to switch his wireless set on and off, so as to suggest that he was in his rooms at the time of the murder. Then on the fatal evening he came home early, simulating illness, and for the same reason he did not eat his dinner. When the meal had been cleared away he climbed down from the window of his room by a convenient roof and barrel, went to Myrtle Cottage, murdered Reeve by smothering, dressed the body in night-clothes, and laid it at the bottom of the stairs. Then he fixed a delayed-action apparatus which he had prepared to set the cottage on fire in about six hours' time. He came home, climbed back to his room, and took a dose of poison. He therefore became really ill, and when Myrtle Cottage went up in flames, he was in bed with the doctor attending him. A clever scheme, don't you think?'

Mrs Farson nodded, while George murmured his agreement. Cornell was now ghastly, and beads of perspiration showed on his forehead. His face was set, grim and rigid. He made no move nor reply.

'In spite of its excellence,' French went on, 'the man gave himself away in various minor directions, but he made one extremely bad bloomer which he won't be able to explain away and which will finally convict him. And that is—' French coughed and put his handkerchief to his mouth. 'Ah, yes here's the evidence.'

Cornell, following the direction of his eyes, swung round. Grace was standing motionless at the open door. Cornell's jaw dropped. He sat rigid like a block of marble, staring at her as if she had come from the grave to condemn him. For a moment there was a deathlike silence, and then French's voice came again. 'It's no use, Mr Cornell. The game's up. You've had your fling, and you've—'

Suddenly, with an inarticulate roar as from a trapped beast, Cornell sprang to his feet and, sweeping Grace aside, rushed out into the hall. French leaped simultaneously, while Jackson, swinging forward, caught Grace before she fell. A terrible din immediately arose in the hall. Cornell had dashed into the arms of the two constables, and French instantly joined in the fray. For some moments there were scufflings and thuds and heavy breathing, with the shattering crash of the table into which the four bodies had cannoned and which splintered into matchwood. Then the snap of handcuffs sounded, followed by a comparative silence. French staggered back into the sitting-room, panting and with a closing eye and a torn collar.

'Miss Farson all right?' he gasped.

'None the worse,' answered Jackson, as he laid her down on the settee.

She quickly recovered, and when the police had removed their prisoner, an excited babel of conversation broke out, which lasted till George read the riot act and cleared the house.

At the police station Cornell was charged with the attempted murder of Grace Farson. French saw only too clearly that he had no real case against him in the matter of Reeve, but he concentrated on this and eventually succeeded in building it up. The second charge was then entered.

In his efforts French had one stroke of luck, but otherwise his achievement was due to his steady, systematic work. In his search of Cornell's effects he found a faded photograph of a pretty young woman, apparently retained by some unexpected sentimental streak in the man's makeup. It was in an old pocket-book, locked away with other personal belongings in a drawer in his private office. The girl's face told French nothing, nor did her clothes, except that they were in the fashion of some thirty years earlier, but the background looked promising. It showed a wide river or narrow lake or arm of the sea. In the middle distance were the houses of a village or town, with some low hills beyond. The vegetation was too indistinct to indicate the climate, but there was a certain suggestion of England about the houses. This background was his stroke of luck. He saw that if he could locate the place, he might get a line on Cornell's past.

The trouble was how to do it. No one at the Yard recognized it, and after many failures French concluded it must be somewhere in the Argentine. He therefore had an enlargement made and wirelessed it to the Buenos Aires police, again without result. Then he happened to lunch with a cousin of Mrs French's, an officer in the P. & O. service. Realizing that this young man must have visited a good many harbours, he produced his photograph.

His guest favoured it with an intent stare. 'Why, yes,' he said, 'I know it well. That's Sydney Harbour, or rather Sydney Harbour a good many years ago. The place has grown out of all recognition since that was taken.'

When he went back to the Yard, French wirelessed the photograph to the Sydney police, explaining the circumstances and including Cornell's fingerprints.

The replies were illuminating. From his prints Cornell was at once identified as Peters, and a reference to the records of the trial soon established Reeve's connection. So here was the first plank in French's case: the establishment of motive.

Supplying a number of copies of Cornell's photograph,

French next had an intensive check made on the sale of alarm clocks in the London shops, beginning with those in the neighbourhood of Paddington and Cornell's office. Thanks to the persistence of the constables employed, he was able to find the shop in which one clock had been bought, the salesman picking out Cornell at a subsequent parade. He could not trace the purchase of the second clock, but he thought that what he had obtained would be sufficient for this part of his case. He also found an electrician who was prepared to go into the box and explain how two alarm clocks with certain other fittings could be made to switch a set on and off automatically.

Another highly significant find in Cornell's workshop was a number of splashes of candle-grease. French collected these and had them analysed, learning that they were from wax candles of a specially high grade. Owing to this peculiarity he found it easy to trace their purchase, and again the salesman recognized Cornell as his customer.

The shoes with the green stain having disappeared, French next set himself to finding them. Cornell, to establish his alibi, had chatted to the ticket examiner at Paddington, and this man was therefore able to swear that he had been in Town at 11.15. He had left Brown Eaves about 9.10, which allowed two hours for him to reach Paddington. How could that have been done? French worked out all the possible ways, bearing in mind the fact that Cornell would, where possible, choose routes on which he was not known. Men were instructed to follow up each of these routes, with the result that the conductor of the ten o'clock Green Line coach from Cherton to London came forward and identified him as a passenger.

The time factor suggested that Cornell had walked from Brown Eaves to Cherton. At first this puzzled French, for the first road to be searched by Jackson was that which the man must have used. Then some further thought gave him what he was looking for. A calculation based on the hours at which Cornell and the pursuing police had left Brown Eaves and their respective estimated speeds gave an approximate point at which the fugitive should have been overtaken. This place French found was close to where the road crossed a small river. It therefore seemed reasonable to suppose that Cornell had been down on the bank when Jackson passed. This was suggestive, and a number of constables were set to work, with the result that they presently found the shoes. The green mark had survived the water, and when the colouring pigment was tested, it was found to be similar to that on the water barrel.

When these facts were added to Grace's testimony about her attempted murder, the police prosecutor was satisfied that he had all the evidence necessary for a conviction, and in due course Robert Cornell paid for his crimes with his life. French was congratulated not only by the A.C. at the Yard, Sir Mortimer Ellison, but also most generously by Superintendent Edgar and Inspector Jackson. 'It's been a knock to our pride,' said the super, 'but that's nothing. I never can be thankful enough that the mistake was discovered in time.'

It was a great day for the houses of Meadowes and Farson when Tony, looking but little the worse for his experiences, arrived home free from the conventional stain on his character. When a decent interval had elapsed, two marriages were solemnized. These were followed by a general reshuffle. Cecily went with Ronald Barrymore to the new job in Lancashire, while Tony and Grace became respectively master and mistress of Riverview. Mrs Meadowes moved to Cornell's old flat, thus enabling the Farsons to remain at Brown Eaves.

The case had proved an immense satisfaction to French. He had taken action in it which might well have proved detrimental to his prospects, because he felt it was the decent thing to do, and it had not only not injured his career, but had brought him increased kudos. Thankfully he felt that his partial failure in the Little Bitton case had at last been triumphantly wiped out.

By the same author

Inspector French
and the Sea Mystery

Off the coast of Burry Port in south Wales, two fishermen
discover a shipping crate and manage to haul it ashore. Inside
is the decomposing body of a brutally murdered man. With
nothing to indicate who he is or where it came from, the
local police decide to call in Scotland Yard. Fortunately
Inspector Joseph French does not believe in insoluble cases—
there are always clues to be found if you know what to look
for. Testing his theories with his accustomed thoroughness,
French's ingenuity sets him off on another investigation . . .

'Inspector French is as near the real thing as any sleuth in
fiction.'   SUNDAY TIMES

By the same author

Inspector French: Found Floating

The Carrington family, victims of a strange poisoning, take an Olympic cruise from Glasgow to help them recover. At Creuta one member goes ashore and does not return. Their body is next day found floating in the Straits of Gibraltar. Joining the ship at Marseilles, can Inspector French solve the mystery before they reach Athens?

Introduced by Tony Medawar, this classic Inspector French novel includes unique interludes by Superintendent Walter Hambrook of Scotland Yard, who provides a real-life detective commentary on the case as the mystery unfolds.

'I doubt whether Inspector French has had a more difficult problem to solve than that of the body 'Found Floating' in the Mediterranean.'   SUNDAY TIMES

By the same author

Inspector French: The End of Andrew Harrison

Becoming the social secretary for millionaire financier Andrew Harrison sounded like the dream job: just writing a few letters and making amiable conversation, with luxurious accommodation thrown in. But Markham Crewe had not reckoned on the unpopularity of his employer, especially within his own household, where animosity bordered on sheer hatred. When Harrison is found dead on his Henley houseboat, Crewe is not the only one to doubt the verdict of suicide. Inspector French is another...

'A really satisfying puzzle ... With every fresh detective story Crofts displays new fields of specialised knowledge.'
DAILY MAIL